JOANNA TROLLOPE

City of Friends

First published 2017 by Mantle
an imprint of Pan Macmillan
20 New Wharf Road, London N1 9RR
Associated companies throughout the world
www.panmacmillan.com

ISBN 978-1-5098-2345-1

1 3 5 7 9 8 6 4 2

A CIP catalogue record for this book is available from the British Library.

Printed and bound by CPI Group (UK) Ltd, Croydon, CR0 4YY

CITY OF FRIENDS

Joanna Trollope is the author of nineteen highly acclaimed and bestselling novels, including *The Rector's Wife*, *Marrying the Mistress* and *Daughters-in-Law*. She has also written a study of women in the British Empire, *Britannia's Daughters*, and ten historical novels under the pseudonym of Caroline Harvey. She was appointed OBE in 1996, and a trustee of the National Literacy Trust in 2012. She has chaired the Whitbread and Orange Awards, as well as being a judge of many other literature prizes; she has been part of two DCMS panels on public libraries and is patron of numerous charities, including Meningitis Now, and Chawton House Library. In 2014, she updated Jane Austen's *Sense and Sensibility* as the opening novel in the Austen Project. *City of Friends* is her twentieth novel.

Also by Joanna Trollope

The Choir

A Village Affair

A Passionate Man

The Rector's Wife

The Men and the Girls

A Spanish Lover

The Best of Friends

Next of Kin

Other People's Children

Marrying the Mistress

Girl From the South

Brother & Sister

Second Honeymoon

Friday Nights

The Other Family

Daughters-in-Law

The Soldier's Wife

Sense & Sensibility

Balancing Act

For Colette

CHAPTER ONE

STACEY

The day Stacey Grant lost her job was a Wednesday. Somehow, having Thursday and Friday still to go, in a working week, only added to the shock of what had happened, the violent sense of injustice.

How could this be? How could it? She was, after all, a forty-seven-year-old woman who had been – usefully, commendably – at the same company for sixteen years. Sixteen years! Jeff Dodds, the senior manager who had sacked her, was two years her junior and had joined the company five years after her. He was not, Stacey had repeatedly insisted to her colleagues, a bad person. Despite his habit of sending demanding weekend emails and ringing late at night with urgent requests for feedback, he was only really testing their commitment to the company. He was, she pointed out, almost avuncular in his desire to mentor his teams, to offer advice and guidance. That he didn't understand the realities of their lives was indeed a blind spot, but not a deliberate cruelty. There were worse managers by far, Stacey had told the rest of the team repeatedly, than Jeff Dodds.

So much, she thought now and savagely, for my loyalty. So much for my sense of stupid fair play. So much for doing the decent sodding thing. The eyes of her colleagues were upon her as she packed the contents of her desk into a cardboard box. A few were mildly gleeful – this was a diversion after all – but most looked stricken and sympathetic. Several had tried to speak to her when she came out of the meeting room with Jeff – 'How,' her husband Steve had said, when the move to an open-plan office had first been mooted, 'do you fire someone in front of everyone else?' – but she had made it plain that if she opened her mouth at all, it would be to scream. Which, after the brief, excited moment of release, would leave her feeling worse than ever. She had shaken her head, and tried to smile, and headed back to her desk as if an imperious purpose awaited her there. So they watched her, covertly, while she collected up the pitiful domesticity of her working life, and dropped it in a box.

By the lifts, a colleague came running to intercept her. He was openly agitated. The top button of his shirt collar was undone, under the loosened knot of his tie.

'Stacey–'

'Too late,' she said, indicating an arriving lift.

He stepped in front of her, barring the way. 'I shouldn't have advised you. I shouldn't have told you to ask him.'

She stared down at the box in her arms. 'It wasn't you.'

'But I advised you . . .'

She didn't look up. She found she couldn't. 'He had other ideas. Other ideas entirely, Tim. All I did, in the end, was give him the chance to implement them.'

'I don't understand. He can't just sack you for asking to work flexibly, he can't – it's against the law.'

Stacey sighed. The box in her arms had suddenly become unbearably heavy.

'He's not a monster, Tim,' she said, sadly. 'He's just a dinosaur. He's got a wife to run his domestic life and his own parents are conveniently dead. He just doesn't have a clue.'

Another lift pinged its arrival.

'Please, Stacey . . .'

'I can't stay. Not another minute. Not after this.'

'Please let us take it to another level. Please don't be so impulsive, whatever he said. *Please*.'

Stacey stepped into the lift. Her handbag was slipping awkwardly off her shoulder. She turned to face the open door. 'Just be warned,' she said.

And then the lift doors slid shut across his unhappy face, and she was borne down to the glass and chrome foyer, where Charlie from Ghana was on reception, absorbed in the football results on his smartphone.

—

At the top of Ludgate Hill, in the new precinct to the left of St Paul's Cathedral, Stacey found an empty litterbin. Extracting the few framed photographs from the box, she tipped the rest of the contents into the bin: new packets of tights, sundry redundant cables, energy bars in battered packets, a toothbrush, paperclips, pens, old birthday and Christmas cards, a rubber spider someone had left on her computer screen on April Fools' Day and a small cascade of other objects which represented, that Wednesday afternoon, happier and more certain times. After the box was emptied, she crammed it down on top of everything it had contained, breaking it in order to fit it into the bin. When she was fourteen, she remembered, and her mother's brother had left the Royal Air Force, she had stood in the yard behind her modest childhood home and watched him burn his uniform in a galvanized metal dustbin.

'We don't do nostalgia,' her mother had said to Steve when he was Stacey's fiancé. 'Not as a family. We don't do regrets. We don't look back.' She'd smiled at him. 'We can't afford to.'

Stacey put the photographs – Steve, the dog, Steve and the dog, her mother and the dog – in her bag, and walked across to a coffee shop. She bought a regular cappuccino without chocolate on top, and took it to a seat in St Paul's Churchyard. There was another woman at the far end of the bench, speaking into her phone in rapid Arabic. Stacey set her coffee down and took her own phone out of her pocket. She had deliberately switched it to mute, in order to avoid having to deal with the aftermath of the afternoon's drama. Sure enough, there were five missed calls and a flurry of texts from her now ex-colleagues. She wouldn't, she decided, even look at Twitter. Instead she sent Steve a brief, laconic text to let him know that the meeting was over – 'I'm out. Tell you later.' – and then scrolled to her Favourites section. She stared at the list. Steve, Mum, Beth, Melissa and Gaby. All of them but Mum knew that she was seeing Jeff Dodds today. Mum didn't know because Mum was the reason the interview was necessary. Mum would be furious, livid was her usual word, that Stacey had asked for the unheard of, had asked for flexible hours, had asked for a specific non-linear period of working, had asked, in short, for a form of employment that contravened the accepted model of the white male competitive system.

'It's an outdated model,' Stacey had said boldly to Jeff Dodds. 'It doesn't work.'

He had been smiling at her, and his smile didn't waver. 'I can't agree, Stacey. I see what you'd like to be the case, but I'm afraid you're whistling in the wind.'

'I have an excellent track record.'

'You do indeed.'

'I've brought more investments to this team than anyone.'

'I wouldn't dispute that,' Jeff said, 'for a single minute.'

'And I'll go on doing it. I'll look after all the companies we've bought; they won't even know I'm not at my office desk all the time. Nothing will suffer workwise. I just need to stagger my hours, work from home more, now that my mother will be there. I bought five businesses with the team, last year, as you know. None of those businesses will suffer; I'll visit every one every time something needs assessing or sorting. All I'm asking is that I don't need to be tied to *this* desk, in *this* office, all the time. I can go through all the portfolios every six months, just as I always have, but from home.'

Jeff Dodds went on looking at her, went on smiling Then he leaned forward, put his elbows on the desk, and spoke with quiet unmistakable emphasis. 'No. Sorry, Stacey, but no.'

She took a breath, to steady herself. 'Why not?'

Jeff let his smile fade. He ran a hand down his tie. 'I need someone dedicated to a lockstep career. I need someone who is physically present in this office ten hours a day minimum. I want someone hungry, someone who is at the point of catching their ambition wave.'

She felt a heady rush of fury. 'So you are prepared to derail someone who is truly valuable to the company for some young guy primarily motivated by money?'

Jeff leaned back again and put the tips of his fingers together. 'I wouldn't put it like that—'

'So the answer's yes.'

'Stacey, I really don't want this to get personal and unpleasant . . .'

'It is already,' she said. 'You can ask a man like you to work a sixty-hour week for years on end because most of them don't have the bottom line of family responsibilities. They don't have to think about gender, or race, much either. It's easier for you, Jeff, isn't it, to replace me with a man who mightn't be half as good as I am, than to even try and get your mind round what I'm asking?'

He had let a beat fall, and then he said, 'I'm not talking about replacement.'

Stacey could hear how unprofessionally urgent her voice had become. She said, trying to rein herself in, trying not to sound triumphant, 'But you can't refuse me, Jeff. Not any longer. You can't refuse my request to work flexibly. It isn't legal any more to refuse a request for flexible working.'

He looked at her levelly. 'I'm not,' he said.

'But–'

He moved towards her, very slightly, as if bending stiffly from the waist in an absurd kind of seated bow. 'I'm afraid, Stacey, that we are overmanned at your level. Seriously so. There is no easy way to say this, but I have to lose you. I have, you see – and your coming to me like this is completely random, of course it is – to make you redundant.'

She had felt very little then. It was as if she had been mildly concussed, and was feeling her way back to some kind of reality. She had even allowed him to say several platitudinous things about her contribution to the company, about her ability to be part of a team, even how much they would miss her. And then he said that long drawn-out departures were very destructive both for the departing employee and for team morale, and she found herself agreeing – agreeing! – in a blaze of fury and despair, almost knocking over her chair as she got to her feet and waving away his suggestion that he should call her a taxi.

'I don't want a taxi.'

It was such a small gesture of defiance, she thought now, that it didn't even count. It had barely registered with Jeff. He had even held his hand out, giving her the chance to stare at it, as if she had never seen a hand before, ignore it, and then walk out past him and back to her desk, while everyone watched her, and those who were on the telephone dropped their voices respectfully, as if they were at a funeral. It had been conspicuous behaviour of a kind she had despised all her life, and taken trouble to avoid at all costs. She was, through and through, a team member, an enabler, an accommodator, a diplomat.

But now, and dramatically, there wasn't a team. There was Steve, and the dog – thank the Lord for the dog – and there was Mum. Stacey looked up at the soaring east front of the cathedral, newly cleaned and almost theatrical in size and splendour. Mum. Mum, who had battled for Stacey all her childhood, urging her into the kind of education she had never known herself, confronting teachers and social workers and forceful relations of her dead father's, to keep Stacey focused on learning to stand on her own two feet, fight her own corner, never even to consider being the kind of person who is dependent upon – and thus vulnerable to – others. When Stacey brought Steve home, Mum's first reaction was that he was a lovely boy, but not enough of a personality, not ambitious enough, not sizeable enough for Stacey. But as time went on, she had come to see what Stacey had seen from the start, that there couldn't be two hungry people in a close relationship without there being a dangerous competitiveness, too. Steve was, from the beginning, on Stacey's side. Even when he disagreed with her, he'd acknowledge she had a point. Mum had taken Steve in, not as a rival she would tame over time, but as part of Stacey's life. You couldn't fault Mum for giving Stacey confidence, the confidence that had ended in her becoming a senior partner in a FTSE top-250-listed private equity company, well before she was fifty.

A senior partner who was now sitting on a bench in St Paul's Churchyard holding a phone and a cooling takeaway cup of coffee and facing being unemployed. Unemployed! Without a job. Nearly thirty years of always – effortlessly, it seemed – having a job, and now there abruptly wasn't one. She had gone to Jeff Dodds to suggest a different work schedule because of Mum's situation, and he, as senior manager of three teams in the company, had told her, in so many words, that he was grateful to her for giving him the opportunity he needed to make her redundant. He wouldn't replace her, he would simply turn her team into a more junior malleable collection of people whom he could mould in his own image.

She took a mouthful of coffee. It was lukewarm now, and thin tasting. She set the cup down under the bench she was sitting on. Pure habit, anyway, buying coffee. A kind of knee-jerk reflex. A displacement activity. Jeff Dodds was where he was because he had pulled off a huge coup within two years of joining the company, buying an ailing farm machinery firm and selling it, for five times what the company had paid for it, only three years later. For a while, he'd been admiringly nicknamed Tractor Dodds. He would, Stacey thought bitterly, rest on those old laurels all his career. He'd been promoted, up and up, whizzing past people who had, in fact, made more for the company over the years than he had made in one hit. But it was a spectacular hit, showy. And the result was that he was still in a top job in the company which she had given a third of her whole life to, and she was instead sitting unemployed on a public bench in her work suit and heels which were now, suddenly, as sartorially irrelevant as fancy dress.

Because of Mum. Mum, said the specialist they had seen together at University College Hospital, had subcortical vascular dementia. It was bad luck, he said, as she was not diabetic and had never had high blood pressure and was not a smoker. She was probably, he thought, at about stage three, four possibly, so it wasn't acute yet, but it might become so. The damage to the tiny blood vessels deep in the brain was irreversible and progressive and unfortunately the cholinesterase inhibitors that were often effective for people with Alzheimer's disease were no use for this type of dementia.

'We might try donepezil hydrochloride,' he said, as if suggesting an analgesic for a headache. 'But the trouble is, vascular dementia isn't a single disease. It's a syndrome or group of syndromes, related to cerebrovascular disease in itself.' He'd glanced at Mum. 'It isn't,' he said, and there was no way of knowing if this was good or bad, 'a *mixed* dementia.'

Mum had been very quiet on the way home. Stacey had held her hand, even though she made initial attempts to pull it away, and stared straight ahead, at the glass partition that divided the taxi driver from his passengers.

'At least it's got a name,' Stacey said. 'At least we know what's been the matter the last couple of years.'

Mum said nothing. Her expression was wooden. She said nothing all the way back to the flat in Holloway where she had lived ever since Stacey and Steve were married, and only when the cab stopped outside her block did she speak.

'What if I'm a nuisance?'

—

'Typical,' Stacey said to Steve that night. 'Typical. It's all she could think about. Here we are, reeling from having the diagnosis confirmed, and all she can say is will she be a nuisance? After she'd made a fuss about taking a taxi rather than the bus.'

Steve was polishing the wine glasses they'd used. Usually, they only had wine at weekends but this evening, after the visit to the specialist, had not been usual in any way, and Steve had opened a bottle without asking. And now, characteristically meticulous about such things, he was polishing the glasses they had used with an Irish linen tea towel. 'I know what you want to do, Stace.'

She looked down at the dog. He lay at her feet, on the newish limestone flags, but although he was lying down, he was alert to her mood as he always was.

'Bruno,' she said affectionately.

His ears cocked at once, but he didn't move. He was such an odd dog, a rescued mixture of umpteen breeds, black and shaggy with a nature as compliant as his exterior was unorthodox. They had found him at a dogs' home, seven months old and sitting patiently on his bottom, staring, and straining to be noticed. It was painful, Stacey often thought, to love an animal so much.

'Do you know what I want?' she said to Bruno. 'Do you know what I feel I should do?'

'He does,' Steve said. He put the polished glasses down and flipped the tea towel over his shoulder. 'And so do I.'

She looked across at him. 'It'll change everything,' she said. 'It'll alter everything about our lives if she comes here.'

'There isn't an alternative.'

'No.'

'We've got the space.'

'Yes.'

'Bruno'll love it. Having someone here all the time.'

'Oh, Steve . . .'

'Babe–'

'I've got to do it. I've got to.'

'I know.' He paused. Then he said, 'What about work?'

She put a foot out and prodded Bruno. He rolled over onto his back, displaying a greyish belly covered in wayward tufts of black fur.

'Work!' Stacey said. She'd given a short laugh. And then she said, rubbing Bruno's belly with her stockinged feet, 'Don't worry about work. I'll sort that. In my mind, I already have. I'm going to ask for flexible hours. They'll never refuse me. They can't. They're not allowed to any more.'

—

The girls had assured her that work wouldn't refuse her either. The girls. Well, they were none of them remotely girls any more, they were women: capable, high-earning, professional women. But they had known each other since university, since that first term of being the only girls in a lecture room of men, reading economics. Only Melissa had actually intended to read economics. The others, Stacey included, had started out with ideas of history, and Spanish, and political theory, and had been drawn to economics because it was a new department, and the senior lecturer was possessed of an infectious enthusiasm and eloquence, and the idea of economics had had a heady dash of rule-breaking in it, as a subject for girls.

So they had been a conspicuous minority, the four of them, Melissa and Stacey, Gaby and Beth, and that minority had slowly segued into a companionship which became a friendship, and then a firm friendship which was, Stacey sometimes thought, better than the relationship she might have had with some non-existent sister. They saw each other through their annual exams, then their final exams (only Melissa got a first-class degree) and then through boyfriends and a few fiancés, and a couple of marriages, Gaby's time in New York, Beth telling them, as if they hadn't known already, that she was gay. And the relationships produced some children, and running alongside and behind it all was the steady, strong, highly coloured landscape of their careers, all on a constant upward trajectory, Gaby out-earning her husband, Melissa starting her own company, Beth a professor in a field she had almost invented, the psychology of business.

Even when they couldn't meet, they rang each other, or texted, or tweeted. The inevitable crossed wires of their twenties and thirties had mellowed into a much less judgemental support system in their forties. They knew about Stacey's mum. They discussed and advised on Stacey's solution to her work dilemma. They knew, all three of them, that on Wednesday afternoon, Stacey would be working out some pattern for her future with Jeff Dodds. What they did not know – and anxious messages and texts on her phone indicated that they wanted to – was that she was sitting on a bench like any old unemployed person, having, she was now queasily realizing, simply lost her temper.

Had she, in fact, got nobody to blame but herself? Had she, for once – possibly for the first time in her life – let her temper get the better of her? If she had worked through a definite, timetabled schedule, even of a gradual and dignified departure, and parked it under Jeff Dodds' unimaginative nose, might she still be in that office, and not on a public bench in a public space with a chaotic-looking man digging through a nearby litterbin and stuffing discarded sandwich crusts into his mouth? Had she, in fact, managed to engineer her own downfall, after decades of rescuing other people, in a business sense, from theirs?

She glanced at her phone again. There were appeals from the girls, from her ex-colleagues, a text from Steve saying with uncharacteristic imperiousness, 'Call me.' She couldn't. She couldn't call anyone. She couldn't communicate with anybody right then, having somehow succeeded in separating herself from everyone and everything she knew by what had happened, by what she had done. Or not done. She wondered if she should stand up. She wondered if she *could* stand up. Was this a panic attack? Was this what panic attacks felt like? Was this what Mum felt when she tried to reach for a word that wasn't there any more, or remember whether she had had breakfast, let alone what she'd eaten, if she had? She leaned forward, gripping the edge of the bench, and stared at the ground. God, she thought, am I losing my mind? Is this what happens when you lose your job?

It occurred to her, suddenly, that she had almost stopped breathing. She must breathe. She knew that if you clenched your teeth and held your breath, nothing worked, not your body, not your mind. You couldn't think, if you weren't breathing. But she couldn't seem to breathe, she couldn't let go of the grip of her muscles. She closed her eyes. Pant, she thought, like Bruno. Little breaths, short breaths. Just through the nose to start with. Then deeper, just a little deeper, pushing into those lungs, just a little way—

'You OK?' someone said.

She nodded. Her eyes were still shut. There was no breath to speak with.

'You want to throw up?' the voice said. It was female, and foreign.

Stacey shook her head.

'I got water,' the woman said. 'You want water?'

Her breath was coming easier now, not all the way down to her lungs but easier. She opened her eyes a little. The woman who had been speaking in Arabic at the other end of the bench was holding out a plastic bottle of water towards her.

Stacey smiled and gestured a no thank you.

'You had a shock on your phone?' the woman asked. She was wearing a headscarf decorated around its edge with tiny silver discs. 'These phones bring more bad news than good. That's for sure.'

Stacey made a huge effort. 'Just – not a good day.'

The woman stowed her water bottle away in an immense old cloth bag on the bench beside her.

'I have those every day.'

'I'm sorry,' Stacey said, automatically.

The woman regarded her. 'Nice bag. Nice shoes.'

'Well, I–'

'Troubles don't care about nice things.'

To her abrupt relief, Stacey found that she could stand up. She seemed to be breathing again, too. She said, 'Thank you for asking. And for offering the water. Thank you.'

The woman looked straight ahead of her. 'I didn't get that job.'

'Oh?'

'They said . . .' She flapped an arm. 'No. They didn't say. But I knew. Wrong person. Wrong clothes.' She glanced at Stacey's handbag. 'Wrong bag. Place filled, they said. Already taken. But I knew.'

'I'm so sorry.'

'Only filling shelves. Evening job. Filling shelves.'

Stacey shifted a little on her heels. 'It isn't easy, is it?'

'Not for me,' the woman said, staring ahead again.

'Nor me, actually.'

The woman glanced at her again. 'You got a home to go to?'

'Well, yes . . .'

The woman raised a hand and shook her forefinger at Stacey. 'You go there, then.'

'But will you–'

The woman made a silencing gesture and indicated the phone lying in the capacious folds of her lap. 'I going to ring my daughter. Tell her. I tell my sons and my husband. Now I tell my daughter.'

'You'll be OK?'

The woman picked up her phone. 'I get by,' she said. 'You do the same. You go home and get by.'

—

Every morning and evening, since they had moved to Islington ten years before, Stacey had caught the number 4 bus down to work. It had been an especial pleasure, somehow, to be on public transport dressed for a City office, tidy brown bob smoothly in place, among people of the same kind altogether. The bus ride had been, even in the rain, a brief breath of another air, a piquant alternative to the intense preoccupations of a working day, and a pause before she arrived home to Steve and Bruno, and Steve's beloved jazz playing more often than not, and a feeling, kicking off her shoes in the hall, that she had, in every sense, earned this downtime.

Approaching the house now, from the alley through from Almeida Street, she found herself anticipating, almost imagining, an entirely other homecoming. She would have to recount what had happened, of course she would, but then she would move on, almost briskly. She would start planning, both her own future and Mum's, she would not allow Steve to be sorry for her, or rant about Jeff Dodds, or offer to be some kind of knight in shining armour. The past, she told herself on the bus journey among tired people reading free copies of the evening paper, was the past now, and that was where it was staying. Beth lived with a head-hunter for goodness' sake, so where better to start the next chapter than with Claire? 'You get by,' the woman on the bench had said to her, making it sound like an instruction. 'You go home and get by.' Well, she would do just that, and more. Steve would only be permitted a very brief expression of outraged sympathy, and then the subject would be firmly closed.

As she crossed the square towards the terrace of houses in which she lived, it struck her that her own house did not look like a house in mourning. It was late September, and far from dark, but lights were on, on all floors, and it looked very much as if Steve had even lit the candles in the huge glass storm lanterns that stood in the sitting-room windows. She was very touched. How lovely of him, to read her like this, to understand that for her, if one door in her life slammed shut, it would only mean that another - and probably better - one would shortly open. He was, she thought gratefully and with a surge of optimism, treating this whole episode as worthy of celebration.

She put her key into the door and let herself in. Bruno, waiting for her three feet inside the hall as he always was, went into his usual ecstatic ritual of welcome, forbidden to jump up, so squirming rapturously on the floor round her feet, his tail pounding the flagstones.

She stooped to caress him. 'Hello, Bruno, hello, lovely boy, ooh I've missed you, aren't you good, aren't you gorgeous, who is my own—'

'Hi!' Steve shouted from the basement.

'Hi.'

'Come on down!' he shouted. 'Come down here!'

'Goodness,' Stacey said to Bruno, 'what a day of surprises. What's going on?'

Bruno sprang to his feet and raced towards the basement stairs, then tore back again to herd her down in front of him. There were candles on the basement stairs and a blaze of them on the kitchen table, clustered round an ice bucket and two champagne glasses on the silver tray Stacey had been given by a cattle ear-tag company whom she had rescued from oblivion and sold, at considerable profit, to Argentina.

She looked at Steve, smiling, and put her hand out. 'You're amazing,' she said. 'Are we – are we *celebrating*?'

He came across the room and seized her in his arms. It occurred to her, randomly and perhaps unfairly, that he'd been drinking already. He had on a smile so broad that it almost split his face.

'We sure are, sweetheart,' he said. 'I've been promoted!'

CHAPTER TWO

MELISSA

Melissa's son, Tom, was standing in front of the fridge in their basement kitchen. It was an impressive American-style fridge of brushed stainless steel, with double doors, both of which were open, while Tom ate salami and potato salad and blueberries straight from their plastic containers with his fingers.

He was a handsome boy, with thick hair and bad skin. Melissa spent a lot of time and money on Tom's skin, which had begun to erupt a year before, when he was fourteen, to the point where she frequently wondered if it troubled her far more than it did him. He was wearing his games socks, tartan boxer shorts and his school pink football shirt, and there were some streaks of mud on his bare legs. His striped school tie and dark uniform trousers were slung over the back of an Italian-designed kitchen chair.

She dropped her handbag emphatically onto the table. 'Darling.'

'Hi.' He didn't turn round. He had a gobbet of potato salad balanced on his forefinger.

'A spoon, perhaps? Or even a plate?'

Tom put the potato salad in his mouth and sucked his

finger. Then he peeled off three more slices of salami, dropped the rest of the packet on top of the punnet of blueberries, and slammed the fridge doors shut. 'Don't need one.'

Melissa tried not to notice the smears left by Tom's fingers on the doors of the fridge.

'But I would like you to try and be a bit more civilized, darling. Aren't you even going to say hello?'

He grinned and rubbed the back of his hand across his mouth. Then he padded across the room and planted a garlic-scented kiss on her cheek. 'Hi, Ma.'

She looked at his shirt. 'Football this afternoon?'

'Hockey,' he said. 'At which I am total rubbish.'

'Why do you play, then? Did you sign up for it?'

He shrugged. 'Dunno,' he said. 'Can't remember.'

'I'm sure you're not total rubbish.'

'The Indians are amazing. Three in my year. They are – wow.'

Melissa took off her jacket and hung it neatly on the back of a second chair. She had asked Tom that morning if he liked her dress, and he had peered at her, headphones on, from the planet of heavy metal music that he currently inhabited, and said, 'I dunno. They're all black.'

'But different. Different black.'

He'd turned up the volume by way of reply, smiling at her to ward off further engagement. His teeth were perfect, she'd seen to that, at a stage in Tom's life when he was definitely more biddable than he seemed to be now. She only – and only ever had – wanted the best for him. It was increasingly hard, however, to get him to want it to any meaningful degree, for himself.

He lunged forward now, unexpectedly, and dropped a

second clumsy kiss somewhere near her right cheekbone. 'Can I have some money?'

'No.'

'Ma . . .'

'You've had your allowance for this week. It's only Wednesday. Anyway–'

'What?'

'I would like us to have supper together tonight.'

'Why?'

She looked at him. 'Because I want the company.'

He put a finger into his mouth to dislodge some salami from his teeth. 'Why?'

'I need to be distracted from being worried about Stacey. I don't think Stacey has had a very good day.'

'Well,' Tom said, inspecting his finger, 'ring her.'

'She's not picking up. I've left umpteen messages. So have Gaby and Beth. I've spoken to both of them. None of us can get hold of her.'

'Tell you what,' Tom said, suddenly galvanized by an idea. 'Let's drive over there and find her.'

Melissa sat down on the chair where she had hung her jacket. 'I thought of that.'

'Well, come on then!'

'You've got homework.'

'Stuff that. I've *always* got homework.'

'And anyway . . .'

'Anyway what?'

'I can never decide what I should or shouldn't tell you.' She looked up at him. 'Even after all these years together.'

He said, helpfully, 'I should tell me. I can always blank you if I don't want to know.'

She laughed. 'Too right!'

Tom gestured at the fridge. 'Glass of wine?'

'No, thank you.'

He perched on the table next to her. The mud on his thigh was flaking off as it dried, brownish grey and matte.

'Tom . . .'

'Yup?'

'I think Stacey may have lost her job today.'

'Wow,' Tom said respectfully. And then, almost at once, 'But she'll get another one.'

'It doesn't quite work like that. It's a most terrible blow to your morale if the end of a job is someone else's decision, not yours. Stacey has worked in that company since before you were born. In fact, she got the job almost the same time that I found I was pregnant.'

'Didn't you mean to be?'

'What?'

'Pregnant. You said "found".'

'Yes. Yes, I did. I definitely wanted to be pregnant.'

'Sure?'

'Very sure.'

'But,' Tom said, 'Stacey didn't.'

'I don't think Stacey has ever wanted to be pregnant.'

Tom got off the table with sudden energy. 'I know!'

'What?'

'Ring Steve. Steve'll know.'

Melissa spread her hands out on the table and looked at her rings. A signet ring on the little finger of her left hand and a slender band of diamonds on the third finger of her right. No wedding ring. There had never been a wedding ring. That's what happened when the only person you had ever really wanted to ask you had married someone else.

She said slowly, 'I don't think I can ring Steve.'

'Why not?'

'Because, darling, this has turned out to be a very complicated day. It might – actually, I think it *is* – the day that Stacey lost her job, but it's also the day, quite by chance, that Steve got a promotion.'

'So?'

Melissa gave a little sigh. 'I knew about Steve's promotion.'

'I don't get it,' Tom said. He was pulling off his socks.

'Please don't, darling, not in here.'

'Why wouldn't that cheer Stacey up?'

'It's complicated,' Melissa said, again. 'You see, I knew about Steve's promotion because I recommended it. His company was one of my clients.'

Tom straightened up, holding a sock. His bare foot was a wonderful thing, Melissa thought; if only the nails had been clean.

'Oh my God. So you didn't tell Stacey?'

'No. It was going to be a surprise. If she didn't get what she had asked for at work, Steve thought the blow would be softened if there was at least some good news from him. It was what he wanted.'

'But, Stacey is *your* friend.'

'Yes.'

'Ma,' Tom said seriously. 'That is not good.'

'No.'

'What were you thinking?'

'I don't know,' Melissa said. 'I feel awful. I suppose I went along with what Steve wanted. I can't – I can't have been thinking straight.'

'You helped Steve?'

'I recommended him. I recommended him to the board while I was reconfiguring them. I wasn't wrong. He'll be good.'

Tom dropped his sock. 'But you should have told him you'd have to tell Stacey.'

She looked up at him. 'Sometimes I think I've done an OK job in bringing you up, after all.'

He glanced at the fridge again. 'Hadn't you better have that wine?'

—

Melissa had been named for her father's mother, a girl from Athens her grandfather had met in Cairo, in 1943, during the Second World War. She'd had a job with the exiled Greek government, and Melissa Hathaway's grandfather persuaded her to follow him to England in 1945, after the war was over. Family lore insisted that the original Melissa had never come to terms with living in England, especially bleak, hungry, exhausted post-war England, and she had made several thwarted attempts to take her two little boys back to Athens, encouraged by her own family who had found her choice of husband incomprehensible. But, apart from a month each summer, she was doomed to England, and to a life in the North West whose beauty she was unable to admire through the constant sheets of rain. Her outrage at finding chilblains on her toes in winter became the stuff of family legend. She lived long enough to see her eldest son married – to a young doctor, from Hull – and to know that his first baby, a daughter, would be named for her: a second, and English, Melissa.

Melissa's father was reticent about his Greek mother. He was as dark as she had been, but displayed no sign of her temperament in his own. He was an excellent mathematician, hugely supportive of his daughters' cleverness, and, having married a professional himself, keen that they should exploit that cleverness to the full.

'You've only failed,' he'd say to his two daughters, 'if you haven't had a go.'

Melissa and her sister both went to the local grammar school and then on to London University, her sister to read classics and Melissa, at a different college, economics. And there, in a lecture room full of men, she saw three other girls, not sitting together, but not in any way appearing defensive, and approached the nearest one to ask if she might sit next to her.

The girl was small and blonde, with enormous horn-rimmed spectacles, which she was later to explain were only for show.

'Course,' the girl said, and then added, as if the information might be crucial in such a male-dominated environment, 'I'm Gaby.' She moved slightly to her right, making a polite but unnecessary space.

'Thank you.' Melissa sat down and then held out her hand. 'Melissa.'

'Hey. Pretty—'

'It means honey bee. In Greek.'

'Mine – I mean Gabrielle – means Woman of God, in French. I mean, honestly!' Gaby gave a little snort. 'What were they thinking? We are so completely not French.' She regarded Melissa. Her eyes were magnified by her spectacles to the size of soup plates, round and blue. She said conspiratorially, 'Did you mean to be here?'

'Well, yes, I'm reading economics, I applied to–'

'I should be in a *Spanish* lecture,' Gaby said. 'But I couldn't stand the sight of them. All women students and not a lecturer under a hundred. But look at this room. Just *look* at it.'

'Are – are you here for the boys, then?'

'I'm here,' Gaby said, 'for the *fun*. They said I've got a brain but I won't let that hold me back for a second.' She glanced at Melissa again and winked. 'Has anyone ever called you Melissa the Kisser?'

Gaby turned out to be almost everything her appearance and demeanour indicated that she was not. She was quick and sharp and ambitious, and was, she said, as their friendship developed over shared meals and cups of coffee, the first of her family to go to university.

'They despise cleverness, really. My mother'd live in a gypsy caravan with bells on her toes if she could. They're all very sorry for me, being here – they think it's really sad. My sister's at circus school and that they really get. What about you?'

'Behind me all the way. My mother's always worked.'

'Lucky you.'

'Yes. Lucky me.'

'Hold on to the luck,' Gaby said. 'Hold on to it, until you've got your first job. You won't need it so much after that. Shall I tell you something?' She leaned forward, across the cafe table where they were sitting, and breathed into Melissa's ear. 'I want to make money. Lots and lots of money. I don't want to marry it, I want to *make* it.' She pulled back. 'What about you?'

Melissa glanced across the room and then she looked back at Gaby. 'I just want to do something – a job – really, really well.'

Gaby stared at her. 'You *are* lucky, aren't you?' she said. 'You seriously are.'

The luck held through eight terms of university, and even, academically speaking, through nine. When she sat the final exams, for which she would get her first-class degree, Melissa believed, briefly as it turned out, that Jack Mallory was as smitten with her as she was with him. He was a post-graduate student, with a sports car, a vintage MG, and enough private income to behave as if money was no preoccupation whatsoever. He was funny and clever and well-connected and careless. He was also, Melissa discovered, random and unprincipled. But, with all his profound drawbacks, he could still light up a room for her like no one else, and it took years of her new London life to persuade her that any other man could electrify the moment the way Jack Mallory had done.

So when she met a mercurial theatre producer during a stint working for the BBC, she was looking for someone else who knew how to illuminate the mundane. Connor Corbett was ten years her senior, miraculously unmarried, childless, compelling and energetic. He had a house in Hampstead, full of books and wine bottles, and wore long mufflers and loose linen shirts with the cuffs undone, and was as good at being alone with her as he was in the centre of a party. He gave her books, he gave her flowers, he gave her an antique ring with a cabochon emerald, which he slid onto the third finger of her right hand, he took her to Italy and New York and the street in Athens where her grandmother had grown up. She went with him to endless first nights, to late dinners with famous actors and actresses, to weekends in astonishing houses, and she waited, as her upbringing had trained her to wait, for him to propose.

It was perfectly reasonable, after all, to expect it. He wanted children – he said so, frequently. He loved her – he said that too, even more often. He was proud of her, he said; he urged her to leave the BBC for a better job at Time Warner and then a better job still as the media consultant in the Corporate Finance Department of a renowned City merchant bank. When she was thirty and he took her to Paris, she bought almost an entire new wardrobe in anticipation of returning as Connor's fiancée, and only just managed to prevent herself buying a man's watch in order to have something to give him, when he gave her the ring.

But he didn't. Instead, he took her to Chez Georges, which he had always faintly ridiculed, and plied her with food and wine, and told her, holding her hands and looking directly into her eyes, that they were, as a couple, over.

'You're too good for me, Melissa. I mean that literally. I can't be me while I'm with you. I can't live in your shadow and I can't hold you back while your shadow gets magnificently longer and longer. Do you see? Do you?'

She had gone back to London, alone, first thing the next morning. She left all her hopeful new clothes in Paris and went home in what she stood up in, carrying just her handbag. She returned to her proudly acquired Kensington cottage, and closed the door and all the blinds and curtains, and at last let herself go. Only after three days did she telephone Gaby and Beth and Stacey to tell them what had happened.

Stacey said that she had feared as much and the only way was forward. Beth was extremely sympathetic but said that she, too, wasn't much surprised. Gaby said, 'D'you want me to hunt him down and kill him?' which made her, for the first time in almost a week, laugh.

Two months later, on the grapevine of human gossip that ensures that the bliss of ignorance is seldom permitted to anyone, Melissa heard that Connor Corbett was married. He had married a friend of his much younger sister's, a sweet-faced, domesticated friend whom Connor had known since her childhood, and whom he had described to Melissa as being like a fondly tolerated family pet: constantly in the household and mostly only mildly in the way. The top floor of the bookish Hampstead house was apparently being turned into a nursery with sensible bars on the windows and cloud scenes painted on the ceilings.

Melissa waited for the news to devastate her. Gaby came round with champagne – 'Shock medicine. The only thing.' – and was amazed when Melissa, dry eyed, declined it.

'I'm – I'm fine. I don't know how or why. But I'm fine.'

'She's free,' Beth said. 'She's liberated. She doesn't need to be validated by anyone but herself.'

It was to Beth that she then took the idea she'd had for her own business, a business that would take a long, hard discerning look at company boards and tell them where their strengths and their weaknesses lay, and who of the constituent members needed to be changed. It was a business that required, in essence, nobody but herself and an assistant, a business that would make no money in the early years, which she intended to finance from her lucrative time in the City. Beth and Stacey and Gaby would all provide her with initial contacts, as well as those already known to her. She would call the company Hathaway, after herself, to keep the kind of consultation it represented as discreet as possible. She was fired by an astonishing energy, as if the closing of one set of floodgates had released a perfect storm of water elsewhere. Hathaway was born in Melissa's spare bedroom in the cottage she lived in then, its front garden a beguiling tangle of jasmine and clematis, in Gordon Place, behind Kensington High Street.

Not much more than a year later, there was Tom. Tom was entirely unplanned, unintended, the result of a lavish French holiday courtesy of the chairman of one of Melissa's first clients, who invited her to his house near Aix-en-Provence. There were couples and there were people on their own, and among the latter was a newly divorced barrister who reminded Melissa of Jack Mallory and was quietly delightful company. When the week in the chairman's house was over, the two of them repaired together to a hotel in Aix itself for three nights, a period Melissa remembered for its extraordinary absence of anxiety. It was the first time in her emotional life that she had ever felt no desire or need, whatsoever, to plan.

Pregnancy, of course, demanded some planning. Just because it was unexpected didn't mean it was unwanted. Before she was pregnant, Melissa had fantasized about a brood of clever children in the Hampstead house with Connor. But it had, most definitely, been fantasy, a dreamy picturing of something that her rational self told her would never work out like that. Now, actually pregnant by a man she liked but did not love, who said that keeping the baby was entirely her decision and that he would be an interested but not hands-on father, was the stuff of reality rather than dreams, and this had to be confronted and planned for. There was room for a baby in Gordon Place. There was – just – enough money for a nanny. The two significant clients she had started with had grown to five, with three more applications for her services. She invited Beth and Stacey and Gaby round to Gordon Place, produced the champagne that Gaby had brought after the episode with Connor, and explained, as if announcing that she had just won the lottery, why she would not be drinking it herself.

It was then, in the hubbub of their joint reaction, that Stacey had raised her own glass.

'And I can tell you, I can tell you now—'

'What, Stace? You're not pregnant too?'

'No,' she said. Her face was shining. 'Absolutely no. I'd only want puppies anyway, not a baby, me. But I just heard, I just heard yesterday. I got the job!'

—

Tom was not supposed – rather than forbidden – to have screens in his bedroom. It was no longer the bedroom of his babyhood in Gordon Place, but the whole of the low-ceilinged but luxuriously separate attic floor of the house he and Melissa had moved a few yards to, in Holland Street, when he was six and Hathaway was firmly and lucratively established. It was the end of a flat-fronted white stucco Kensington terrace, with only a patio behind it, but Kensington Gardens was five minutes away and round the corner was a charming alley of eccentric small shops.

When they initially moved to Holland Street, Tom slept

on the first floor, next to his mother's room. But when he was twelve, the whole top floor was made into an adolescent dream space, with navy blue walls at Tom's request, and a walk-in shower. His bedroom, at the back of the house, contained the size of bed that had accommodated Melissa's parents together, all their married lives. Tom was propped up on one elbow in it, with his iPad open, elaborately unperturbed. He had prepared an argument to counter his mother's inevitable objection, which reasoned that a rule imposed when he was eleven could not rationally be supposed to apply to someone four years older, at fifteen.

But Melissa didn't object. She came in, still in her black work dress but with stockinged feet, and sat down on the edge of his bed. He affected not to notice that she was there even though it was impossible not to be acutely aware of her gaze, a gratifying if sometimes overwhelming look of adoration slightly sharpened with exasperation. He strove not to look up, but silence was impossible.

'What, Ma?'

'Your teeth, perhaps? Your hair, certainly.'

'What is the point,' Tom said, swiping his finger rapidly across his iPad, 'of brushing your hair just before it gets all bed-hairy anyway?'

'OK,' Melissa said. 'Compromise. Teeth, then.'

'In a sec.'

'Thank you for this evening.'

He sighed. 'Nothing to thank me for.'

'You listened. You were *there*.'

Tom yawned. 'You got a bit rattled. That's all.' He abruptly flipped the cover of the iPad down and said, apropos of nothing they had talked about all evening, 'Oh, I saw Dad today.'

Melissa was startled. 'Your *father*?'

'Yup.' Tom sat up a little. 'At the hockey. He came to watch the hockey.'

'What?'

'He started coming a year ago when Marnie went into year twelve at school.'

'Marnie? *Your* school?'

Tom looked up at her briefly. 'Yes,' he said. '*You* know. The daughter he had when he was married before me. She started in the sixth form at school. She's year thirteen now. She's quite cool.'

Melissa strove not to sound agitated. 'Tom, darling. Why didn't you say? Why didn't you tell me that he'd been coming to school for a year?'

Tom looked at the ceiling, then at the far wall, and then at his knees, under the duvet. Then he said, 'Dunno.'

'Do – do you talk to him?'

Tom shrugged. 'Not really. Yes. He's OK. He – we talk about Arsenal and stuff. Sometimes the kids come.'

'Kids?'

'The kids he had after me. Boys. They're at school somewhere else. They're just little kids. Well, quite little. They're good fun.'

'Are they?'

'Yeah.'

Melissa straightened up again. 'Marnie was only a baby when – when I met Dad. I know he's always remembered birthdays and things, but I thought he – he was rather wonderfully leaving me alone to bring you up the way I wanted to.'

Tom examined a torn cuticle with tremendous attention. 'He kind of said that, too.'

'Did he?'

'He said – um – he said he did think that for ages, and now he thinks he was wrong.'

'Wrong? Does he think I've done such a bad—'

'No!' Tom said. 'No. He thinks it's him who's been bad. He says he thinks he's neglected me. Well, he has. I didn't contradict him.'

'Goodness,' Melissa said faintly. 'Will Gibbs turns up again after all these years of doing nothing but sending round the odd present and money here and there for tennis coaching and tells you, without telling me, that he thinks he hasn't been much of a father. And you let him know you agree.'

'He said you wanted to pay for stuff yourself.'

'He's right,' Melissa said. 'I did. I do. I'm just – gobsmacked that you've been seeing him for over a year and never saw fit to tell me.'

'I *am* telling you,' Tom said patiently. 'I was always going to. I—'

'Why tonight?'

Tom sighed again. 'I didn't mean to. After all the Stacey stuff.'

Melissa reached out and put a hand on his arm. 'Darling, you always come before Stacey. You come before everyone as far as I'm concerned. You know that.'

'That's why . . .'

'That's why what?'

Tom took a deep breath and slid down in the bed. 'That's why I'd like to try what Dad suggested.'

'What did Dad suggest?'

'He said – well, he and Marnie said, why didn't I go to

theirs one night a week, and have supper with everyone and stay over.'

He slid down a little further, pulling the duvet up to his chin, and then he added, in a lower voice, 'Like a family. They said. They said one night a week I could have a family. At theirs.'

CHAPTER THREE

GABY

When Gaby was twenty-one, not long after she had obtained her solid but unremarkable second-class degree in economics, she abandoned London, apparently on impulse, for New York. It seemed as if one week she was there, complaining noisily about the dreary calibre of jobs on offer in London for women economics graduates, and the next she was ringing round to say that she was packing her bags for America.

Melissa was immediately anxious about the practicalities. 'But, Gaby, what will you live on? I mean, have you got a job? And where will you stay? What about a green card?'

Stacey, newly in a relationship with Steve and doing her trainee accountancy at a firm in the City that prided itself on both encouraging and mentoring the women on its qualifications programmes, thought she was mad. 'But what for? Why not be part of pioneering here? Why go where you won't know anybody and where they put dessert jelly in chicken salads?'

It was Beth who said to the others, 'I think it's because of her family.'

It was, Gaby said later, almost entirely because of her family. At the time, she was consumed, quite simply, with a desire to flee and it was only looking back that she could pinpoint the reason for her almost frantic sense of self-preserving urgency. Gaby's family, in their ramshackle farmhouse in the Black Mountains above Abergavenny, were not unkind, or unloving or even unsupportive in any way that might be traditionally considered destructive, but they had their own immovable, unshakeable creed of unconventionality that was utterly unable to embrace other choices. In their view, after three years of sterile conformity at London University, Gaby was free at last to come home and surrender to the wild. Wild, carefree days and wilder nights. Woodsmoke and mystery and bonfires in the dark offering matchless opportunities to dance round the flames, in the rain, with bare feet and flying hair. Gaby would at last return to the magic of her childhood which had, like all elemental things, been merely sleeping until she came home.

The only thing to do, Gaby explained, when the others visited her in New York, was to get the hell out of it. It wasn't that her family didn't understand so much as that they couldn't hear her in the first place. The only solution was to pack and *go*. And of course she had a job to go to. She would never have embarked on such an adventure without a plan; that was something her childhood had taught her, if only by contrast. She had followed up a lead from one of the American companies that had toured their university department in the final year, looking for high-calibre recruits, and she was going to be a trainee analyst at an old-fashioned New York securities house. They gave her a six-month trial, and initial accommodation in a company apartment in Midtown, which was not sleek or up-to-date glamorous, but old-style New

York, with grimy net curtains and cockroaches scuttling across the kitchen and bathroom floors after dark.

'But I'm free,' Gaby reported, 'I'm *free*. And the Americans seem to like me. They like me being high energy and they don't seem to mind that I have the attention span of a midge. In fact, they seem to think I'm worth investing in. They want me to do an MBA.'

In January of 1992, when she was twenty-five, Gaby embarked on a full-time, sixteen-month course at Columbia University, paid for by her employers. During that year and a half, the others went out, together or separately, to see her, coming back with varying degrees of restlessness, envy, incomprehension and brown bags of shopping from Bloomingdale's. Gaby loved New York. She had even begun to sound faintly New York. She acquired a studio apartment in the Village, a fellow business student boyfriend and a job to go back to at the end of her course. There was nothing, really, for her to return to London for, so they all had to get their heads round factoring in that Gaby was on the road to becoming, with all the zeal of a convert, an American.

But then she came home. She came back as suddenly as she had left. She gave her original company two years of her post-MBA skills, and then she accepted a big job back in London, a banking job. The studio apartment, the boyfriend, the desirable New York lifestyle were, in a matter of weeks, it seemed, behind her. She was focused on the world of banking, the world of big business, she said. She loved the speed of it; she loved how collegiate it was.

'You like the glamour,' Beth said, 'don't you?'

Gaby beamed at her. 'Of course I do.'

In 1997, the year that Melissa failed to be proposed to by Connor Corbett, Gaby met Quin. Quin, named Quintin for his grandfather, had grown up in the Scottish Borders and lived for his childhood years above his father's draper's shop in Elgin, which sold Scottish country clothing and plaid blankets with heavy fringes. Like Gaby, Quin had run away from his childhood, but he had run, more traditionally for a Scot, only to London. He started a version of his father's shop – an edgier, cooler, younger version – first on a stall and then in proper premises, in west London, on the Portobello Road. He sold Gaby a turquoise faux tartan scarf on a Saturday morning, and then ran after her, through the crowds, to ask her slightly breathlessly to have coffee with him. She'd been wearing the scarf already, and he'd been rendered almost speechless by the effect the turquoise plaid had had on her eyes.

She used to tease him later about his incoherence as he tried to ask her out. 'Wha'?' she said he'd said, imitating him, afterwards. 'Wha'?'

He'd sounded Scottish then. He hardly did now, only when he was very tired or drunk, or exasperated with the children. He'd inherited his father's shop, as well as enlarging his own, and changed both of their names to the Elgin Emporium, displaying the stock spilling out of wicker hampers or piled on white painted shelves held up with decoratively knotted ropes. The stock itself had been enlarged to encompass modern tastes in living – picnic rugs rolled up in leather harnesses, dog baskets lined with tartan padding, thornproof jackets with accessible pockets to hold a BlackBerry.

The shops did well, but it was not their profits that had

bought the huge Italianate villa on Ladbroke Road, just down the hill from St John's Church. It was the most substantial house either Gaby or Quin had ever lived in: double fronted with a garage to the side, brown brick above and white stucco below, with arched windows, a pillared porch and a sweep of intricately patterned black and white tiles leading up to the front door. Behind the house was a huge and romantic communal garden, with mature trees and locked iron gates at the sides. When Liam, with his penchant for running and climbing, was small, the fact that he could be released into this giant outdoor playpen was a godsend.

Gaby had found the house six years ago. She wasn't a managing director then, but had every reason to believe that she would be, and had gambled on the promotion. Taylor had then been nine, Claudia seven and Liam a ferociously active and determined two. The girls were still at a private primary school, and they were, as a family, exploding out of the house Gaby and Quin had bought together, in Kensal Rise. A move to Ladbroke Road would mean an enormous mortgage (part tracker, part fixed rate, Gaby decided) but it would also mean the children could all go to Holland School, Quin could walk to work and she, Gaby, could take the Central line from Holland Park tube station – no distance away at all – change to the Jubilee line at Bond Street, and end up in the improbable world of Canary Wharf, where her latest employer occupied two immense glass buildings and employed six thousand people. She didn't travel by public transport as a point of elaborately democratic principle: she travelled that way because she liked it. She put trainers on her feet, and trotted off to the tube station at seven thirty every morning, leaving Quin to try and dissuade Liam from eating leftover pizza for breakfast and to persuade his daughters to eat anything at all.

When the children were younger, there'd been au pair girls and, for one blissful and expensive year, a small, quiet, competent woman from the Philippines, who graded the ironed laundry according to size and gender and effortlessly managed to make Liam stay on his chair at mealtimes. When Gloria left to nurse her old parents in Manila, Gaby and Quin went back to the au pair system, a roller-coaster ride of different temperaments and abilities to cook, smoking and drinking habits, random boyfriends, hazardous approaches to discipline and homework, and an almost universal prevalence of chipped blue and green nail polish. The children wove their way through the irregularity of this aspect of their lives, learning to manipulate and elude where necessary, and aware that the fixed poles in their world were their schools, their friends, their parents occasionally and the immovable and unquestionable fact that their small, energetic mother made work an absolute priority in her life. After Taylor was born, Gaby took five weeks' maternity leave, after Claudia, six. With Liam, she was persuaded to stay at home for eight, but was straining to be back at work for the whole of the second month.

'My husband and children,' Gaby told an important business magazine in an interview, 'would all say that work comes first with me. I'll freely admit, before you ask me, that I'm quite bored by domestic life. I'd love it if my daughters wanted what I'd like for them. Working women should be as commonplace and unremarkable as working men. Work is how I identify myself, as well as being a mother and a wife. It's who I am. I'll stop working when the phone stops ringing.

OK? Now, if you'll excuse me, I'm going to hear my youngest playing the waltz from *Sleeping Beauty* at his school concert. He's chosen to learn the trumpet, for some reason. Can't think why. I can't even toot a tin whistle.'

—

Gaby had risen to be managing director of the investment banking division of a huge global bank. Its London offices looked across a carefully, impersonally manicured square of green, symmetrically dotted with neatly clipped shrubs and trees, to the immense glass facades of two similar institutions. From the square outside her building, all the way to the underground station on the far side of Canary Wharf, Gaby could walk a gleaming underground arcade of cafes, bars and shops which served the area's young and visibly aspirational population. Some of the kids Gaby passed, on her purposeful way between station and office, were not very much older than Taylor, by the looks of them. And what they were being offered, in the shop windows, was certainly not what her Scottish mother-in-law would have approved of as being necessary for keeping body and soul together. Whenever Gaby got back from a business trip in the old days, Quin's mother, who often came to help look after the children and household in general, would look her up and down and say, with grim satisfaction, 'Well, it'll be back to old clothes and porridge for you now. And not before time, in my view.'

It had never been fair, in Gaby's opinion, to treat her as if she was an improperly successful airhead. She had never been a shoes and bags woman, never gone in for discreetly expensive watches or rewarding herself for an outstanding deal with a diamond. Even when Taylor, at fifteen, was at her most indignant and resentful, she could not say that Gaby at work was in any way different from Gaby in the kitchen, boredly trying to remember the sequence of buttons that needed pressing to get the dishwasher going. She loved her children, loved Quin, loved her friends, but she adored work. It gave her immense satisfaction to hear Liam play his trumpet, or have Taylor take the lead in the school production of *Guys and Dolls*, or to see Claudia quietly coming top of her class in most subjects, term after term, but she would candidly admit that she felt the same pride in raising the capital to turn a promising TV cable company into a global phenomenon or buying a despondent business and bringing it back to profitability with the right injection of the right amount of money.

'Nobody should work to the exclusion of all else,' Gaby declared at the seminars she was always being asked to give. 'It is career-enhancing to feed your brain with as many other interests as you can. My aim is to show my team how to wrap life around work, rather than the other way about. It's a work structure thing, not an hours thing. Work and life aren't in opposition to each other, they enrich each other.'

Often, she was asked about the percentage of women in top jobs like her own. She would thump the lectern she was speaking from.

'I try, all the time, to crack the code of not enough women. I am still too rare, but at least I'm no longer The Token. We still lose women at around thirty-five, at associate to vice president level, because of the demands of family life. A gear change in a career hits at exactly the same time as family pressures mount. I want the girls on my team' – here she would look around the room, as if collecting up her juniors –

'to say to me, "I love what I do and please help me to make it work round my family commitments".' Gaby would lean forward. 'I don't care *where* people work. Agile working could be from home, on a bus, in a coffee shop. I want young mothers to feel free to ask for help in making their work lives work. All I ask of them is that they don't hide the fact they're struggling and they don't quit.'

She would then pause, and take off the huge horn-rimmed spectacles that she had worn a version of since she was a teenager. Then she'd say, almost conversationally, 'Women tend to be risk averse. Of course they do. But there's more than a tiny advantage to forcing yourself out of your comfort zone and just *trying*.'

To Taylor she'd say, 'You'll thank me, one day. You will. You think you'd like a cupcake mother right now, but I'll be more use to you over time. You'll see.'

Taylor, sighing and slamming her way round the kitchen cupboards, would affect to be too exasperated to reply.

'You want her to notice you, don't you?' Claudia would say to her sister, pushing her own spectacles up her nose. 'You only claim you don't care because you hope nobody'll notice that you care so much.'

Claudia was small and pretty, like her mother, her looks only enhanced by her glasses. Taylor and Liam were gingery, like their father, and before she was twelve, Taylor was the tallest in her class, even taller than the boys. Her feet earned her the name of Bigfoot. Only when she was on stage, or behind a microphone, and could subsume herself into being someone else, did she feel reconciled to inhabiting her own skin. Then, and on the odd occasions when amidst the ceaseless activity of life in Ladbroke Road, she found herself alone with her mother for a while, and basking in the full wattage of her mother's attention, did she feel almost happy.

She had, with elaborate nonchalance, been tracking Gaby the Thursday evening after Stacey had been fired. The ostensible reason was a thorny novel by George Eliot, part of Taylor's GCSE English syllabus and incomprehensible to her in terms of the density of its language and imagery, but the underlying and more primitive reason was a misunderstanding with a school friend which had preoccupied Taylor for a week. At last, after unsuccessful attempts in the kitchen and television room, Taylor ran her mother to earth in her bathroom. Gaby was sitting on the closed lid of the toilet, her bare feet propped on the side of the bath, clipping her toenails. They were, like her fingernails, unpainted, and Gaby looked as if she might actually stay put for five minutes. The drawback was that Quin was there, too, leaning against the run of opaque glass cabinets that housed their twin basins.

Taylor stopped on the threshold. 'Oh.'

Her father, whom she tolerated as an inevitability, made a face. 'One day, I'll get more than half a minute alone with your mother.'

Taylor flapped her George Eliot paperback. 'I don't get this.'

'I don't understand,' Gaby said, 'why they have to give you such a dreary George Eliot. Why not *The Mill on the Floss*, or *Middlemarch*?'

'I have to, Mum.'

'I know you do. That's not my point.'

'Mum and I,' Quin said, turning round to examine his teeth in the mirror above the basins, 'were actually talking.'

'Sorry,' Taylor said, unapologetically.

Gaby said, 'Can't we go on?'

'With Taylor here?'

'Yes.'

Quin turned back. He said to Taylor, 'We were talking about Stacey,' and then, to Gaby, 'I'm not sure we should–'

'Oh, come on,' Gaby said, clipping carefully round the curve of her big toenail. 'It's an interesting dilemma. It's a modern problem because of work and an ancient one because of morality.'

Taylor put her George Eliot down without noticing she had done so. She dropped to the floor beside the bath. 'What is?'

'You see?' Quin said to Gaby.

'She's fifteen,' Gaby said. 'Not five. She knows about friendship.'

'What friendship?' Taylor said.

'We were just discussing Stacey,' Gaby said.

'What about Stacey?'

'I think Stacey lost her job. Only yesterday. I've tried and tried to get through to her, but she won't answer the phone and she won't reply to emails, and Steve's as bad.'

Taylor sat up a little. 'Oh my God, poor her.'

'Yes,' Quin said. 'Poor her.'

Gaby finished clipping and began to sand off the cut edges with an emery board. Taylor watched her deftness as she did it, flicking and swooping round her toenails as if the emery board was as flexible as rubber.

Taylor said, 'Have you talked to Melissa? Have you talked to Beth?'

Gaby threw the emery board accurately into a clear plastic box of varnishes and manicure implements. 'I have.'

'What did they say?'

Gaby reached under the towel rail and retrieved a pair of suede slippers. 'That's what I was just telling Dad,' she replied, pushing her bare feet into them. 'What they said. And what they both said was that Stacey's experience with private equity made her an ideal person to join my team. Surely, they said, in an organization as big as mine, I could find space somewhere for someone as useful and valuable as Stacey. Beth said that if I were a man I wouldn't think twice about it.'

Taylor shifted on the floor. 'Well, can't you? Can't you find a job for Stacey?'

'Always supposing,' Quin said, 'that she wanted it. That she wanted a favour from a friend.'

'I'd want it,' Taylor said with feeling. 'I'd want a friend to do something kind for me.'

Gaby looked at her sharply. 'What's happened?'

'Nothing.'

'Then why–'

'It's just Flossie,' Taylor muttered. 'It's nothing.'

Gaby crouched on the floor next to Taylor. 'What has Flossie done?'

'Just kind of . . .'

'Kind of what?'

'Just kind of separated people who have boyfriends from people who – don't want boyfriends.'

'Presumably,' Quin said, 'Flossie has a boyfriend?'

'Uh-huh.'

'Well,' Gaby said, 'she didn't two weeks ago, when she was here for the weekend.'

'He's new. He's in year twelve.'

Gaby lowered herself to sit next to Taylor. 'How sad,' she

said, 'to dump your best girlfriend for some boy you've only known for a week.'

Taylor sighed. She said, 'Would you do that?'

'I'd try very hard not to.'

'I mean, if Stacey came on to Dad or something.'

'I'd hit them both with a bucket,' Gaby said. 'You just laugh Flossie off. I bet it'll be over in another week.'

'She won't play netball now,' Taylor said gloomily. 'Because of her make-up.'

Gaby and Quin gave a joint yelp of laughter. 'Pathetic!' they said in unison.

Taylor lifted her head. Her hair was tied back in a high ponytail, but there was a frizz of disobedient reddish curls around her hairline. 'Are you going to offer Stacey a job?'

There was a pause. Gaby ran a finger round the inside of one slipper, against her foot, as if smoothing something out. Then she said, 'Trouble is, I can't.'

'Oh?'

Gaby lifted her head and looked across the bathroom at Quin. She said, clearly,

'Because of Sarah.'

'Oh Lord,' Quin said. 'I'd forgotten about Sarah.'

'Who's Sarah?' Taylor asked.

Gaby got to her feet and perched on the edge of the bath. 'Sarah is Will Gibbs' partner.'

'Who's Will Gibbs?'

'He's Tom Hathaway's father. He and Melissa had a holiday fling years ago and Tom was the result. Will and Sarah met after that, and now they live together and have two little boys. Sarah came to work for me almost eighteen months ago, and she's great.'

'Goodness,' Taylor said. 'Does Tom know?'

'Does Tom know what?'

'Does Tom know,' Taylor repeated patiently, 'that his father's got two more boys and this Sarah person?'

Gaby glanced at Quin. 'Yes. Yes, he does, I talked to Melissa.'

'But why,' Taylor said, 'does that stop you offering a job to Stacey?'

'Because neither Stacey nor Melissa know that I gave a job to Sarah Parker, even though I found out after the event that she lived with Will Gibbs. And, if I'm honest, Sarah does the kind of thing that Stacey might do, if I had room for her. Which I don't. So I can't offer her a job, and I can't tell her why I can't offer her a job. Which puts me in a very awkward position because Melissa has already emailed Stacey, cc'ing me, suggesting that we talk about it.'

'Yikes,' Taylor said.

Quin looked at her. 'What would you do?'

Taylor put her hands behind her head and pulled her ponytail tighter. 'I'd tell everyone everything.'

'No, you wouldn't,' Gaby said. 'That's the problem with you. You don't tell anyone anything and then we're supposed to guess what's the matter from the atmosphere you're creating. I wish you *would* tell everyone everything.'

'I can't,' Taylor said melodramatically. 'I – I *can't*.'

'Well,' Gaby said, 'in this case, nor can I. So I will just have to put up with all of them thinking I'm a selfish, hard-hearted cow.'

Taylor got to her feet.

Gaby said, 'Where are you going?'

Taylor sighed again. 'To Facebook Flossie.'

'But I thought . . .'

Taylor slouched towards the door. 'Maybe I'll text her.'

'I don't get it,' Quin said.

Taylor gave him a brief glance. 'No,' she said.

When she had gone, there was a brief and complicated silence. Then Gaby said, 'Is she miserable?'

'I don't think so,' Quin replied. 'Sometimes, if no one's looking, she even seems quite happy.'

'What am I going to do about Stacey?'

'Nothing.'

'I can't do nothing. I'm in a position of hiring power and I will be expected to help Stacey.'

'Well, help her then. Tell her about Sarah Parker and Melissa and all that.'

'Sarah's good.'

'I'm sure she is.'

'I don't really have space for Stacey.'

'Well, that sorts it then.'

'And,' Gaby said, 'there's something else.'

Quin was standing too, studying the phone which he had taken from his pocket. 'Is there?' he said, absently.

'There's Claire.'

'Claire?'

'Beth's Claire,' Gaby said. 'It was Claire who found me Sarah Parker. Claire has known about the Will Gibbs situation all along. I thought she must have told Beth. I thought she *must* have. Are you listening?'

Quin lifted his head. 'Of course.'

'But from what Beth said earlier, and the suggestions she was making, it seems that she doesn't know.' She gave a little stamp, in her suede slipper. 'Quin,' she said, 'I *loathe* this. I feel awful for Stacey and bad for Melissa and cross with Claire, but what I feel most of all, what I cannot stand most of all, is having work compromised. I tell you, Quin, I won't have it. I won't have work touched, sullied, by any of this. I won't. I tell you. I *won't.*'

Quin put down his phone again and folded his arms. Years of living with Gaby had taught him when to engage and when to allow her as much rope as she needed. He cleared his throat. 'Then don't,' he said.

CHAPTER FOUR

BETH

The house Beth shared with Claire had been bought just before Tower Hamlets became a modish destination for young entrepreneurs of the new technology. When they were first together – a junior academic and a trainee lawyer dissatisfied with the law – they had a flat above the old market in Spitalfields, a series of small dingy rooms whose only advantage was the view from the sitting-room window of Christ Church, Spitalfields, in all its Hawksmoor – although as yet unrestored – glory. The bedroom windows looked down into the shabby ordinariness of Brushfield Street, and the smell of perpetually cooking curry permeated the whole area like fog.

Living in unfashionable east London in the heart of the established Bangladeshi community had been a deliberate choice. Beth had grown up in an Aberdeen suburb with her adoptive parents, and Claire on a farm in the West Country, and both had learned an instinctive avoidance of the expectations of small communities. London offered the first escape, and east London a refinement of it. In the flimsy plywood cupboard that served as their only hanging space in the market flat, Beth hung her claret silk doctoral robe, the wide sleeves held back by claret-coloured cords. The robe was a symbol to both of them of what was to come, rather than representing the disjoint that currently existed between what they were and how they lived.

Beth's father came down from Aberdeen for the ceremony which awarded her a doctorate in psychology. Neither he, nor her late mother, had travelled south for her first degree ceremony, but then her mother, though punctilious in all the duties attached to motherhood, had never been able to refer to Claire as anything other than Beth's friend. After her death, from cancer, Beth's father, an engineer who specialized in the particular deep-sea pumps required by the oil industry, and who had taken a job in Aberdeen accordingly, came down to London on a regular basis, sleeping on a sofa bed in the sitting room of the market flat and marvelling at the way all the streets round about had their names enamelled in Bengali, underneath the English.

He was, Beth knew, very proud of her. In the Aberdeen flat where he had moved after his wife's death, on a highly varnished occasional table prominently positioned in the sitting room, was a framed photograph of Beth, sturdy and serious, but, as an interviewer was later to describe her, 'darkly handsome', taken when she was awarded her PhD. When he wrote to her after the ceremony – and he wrote conscientiously, on paper, every few weeks, even after he had discovered email – he always addressed the envelope with her academic qualifications, carefully specified. When she became an assistant professor, in her early thirties, she knew that he, in his quiet way, had almost nothing left to wish for. And when, later, he offered money to help restore the decayed house in Wilkes Street, it would have broken his heart for her to have done anything other than accept it.

By the time they took the decision to restore the Wilkes Street house, they were both more established, in any case. The rented market flat had given way to a freehold flat in Shoreditch with a scrap of garden and a kitchen big enough to accommodate a dining table. They had acquired two cats, a present from Gaby, whose children had named them Banker and Bonus, and Claire had given up the law to start a small and increasingly successful head-hunting agency, which specialized in finding opportunities for women, especially those who were returning to work after children. When Beth was promoted to associate professor, at the new and architecturally dramatic University of East London, the time had come, they agreed, to graduate from being a couple with cats in a ground-floor flat, to being serious house owners and citizens.

As a house, Wilkes Street offered a very serious proposition indeed. It was properly Georgian, with two bays either side of the front door, three storeys, and a cluster of terracotta chimney pots on the roof. Its neighbour on one side was a similar house, possibly even more decrepit, and on the other, an old textile factory which had been crudely converted into flats, with irregular metal-framed windows and redundant cables looped haphazardly across the facade. The house itself was built of dark brick, the windows outlined in paler brick, with peeling pilasters either side of the sagging front door, concrete infills here and there and sheets of plywood nailed across the windows in place of curtains. The yard behind the house was a vision of dereliction; broken detritus from numerous kitchens and bathrooms lay abandoned among jagged lengths of corrugated iron and rusting coils of wire. If it had not been for the staircase, and the panelling, and the proportions of the rooms, all of which had miraculously survived the aggressive neglect and abuse of decades, they would never, they assured their friends, have even contemplated such a project.

It took them three years. A skip in the street outside became such a permanent fixture that the neighbourhood took to using it for all the rubbish that would not fit conveniently into a standard bin bag. Broken furniture and no longer functioning fridges from other people's lives took up as much space as their own rotten floorboards and historic, if now useless, lumps of lath and plaster. Weekends were spent labouring in the house, week nights poring over plans and estimates. The salvation of Wilkes Street became as all-consuming as if the house had been a human hostage in need of rescue. It made them mildly obsessive, too committed to dare to think about much else, and too tired to be teased. From the relative order of their own houses, the others watched the progress of Wilkes Street with the occasionally exasperated anxiety of those monitoring the haphazard recovery of an addict.

When it was finally done, and the builder had topped out his labours with a bush in a chimney pot as he said his father and grandfather would have done, Beth and Claire threw a party. Most of the rooms were unfurnished still, but there was something glamorous about the resulting empty spaces, with clusters of candles on the cider-coloured floorboards, against the shining dark window glass. There were trestle tables draped in sheets and covered with food and drink, and the newly installed central music system piped Joni Mitchell – Beth's all-time favourite – hauntingly throughout the house. The party went on until four o'clock the next morning, and when Beth went to check on the cats, shut into the new linen cupboard for safety on the top floor, she found them asleep on a couple of guests who had nested among the spare duvets and pillows and were sweetly unconscious themselves.

'I think we've done it,' Beth said to Claire, standing at their bedroom window and looking down into the street where dawn was already making the street lamps redundant. There was no reply. She turned round and saw that Claire was already asleep, neatly on her side as was her habit, her dark, curly head in the exact centre of the pillow and her lashes thick on her cheeks. Beth stood and gazed at her, golden in the glow of the lights that had been ingeniously inserted into the headboard of their lavish and certainly statement bed. It was one of those moments, she told herself, that needed nailing into the memory, as representing the proof that joy, however elusive and occasional, was something that both existed and could be known.

—

That party had been three years ago. They had followed it the subsequent year with a party at Gaby's house to celebrate all four of them turning forty-five. Claire gave Beth a Virginia Overton weathervane, which she had bought from the White Cube gallery, and which featured a metal girl sitting nonchalantly above the indicators of the four poles. Beth had it installed on the brick chimney stack at Wilkes Street, and almost at once, pigeons and seagulls began to colonize it. Then the two of them went to Venice, for the Biennale, to celebrate, and on their return hired a garden designer to make something usable out of the yard behind the house.

This coincided with Beth being made a full professor, in the same month that she was offered a lucrative part-time consultancy as a business psychologist to a major airline, as well as becoming a spokeswoman for the subject across the media. She was suddenly, and alluringly, in demand.

'Professor Mundy,' Claire would say, laughing, 'isn't exactly who I signed up to live with.'

And there was, every time she said it, just the slightest tension in the air; nothing menacing, nothing that needed to be drawn down into a discussion, but there, like the smallest twig in the world tapping on the window. Just once or twice. Lightly.

—

Claire was twelve years younger than Beth. She had been a student of a legal colleague of Beth's during Beth's first academic job, and an introduction hadn't been hard to manage. It was Claire's first major love affair, and the first time that Beth had known that this was in a different league from anything she had been involved in before.

'I think you should leave right now, as a penniless academic can't offer you more than three dreary rooms in east London.' She had said this to Claire, after their first heady full weekend together, and they had both known that she didn't mean a word of it. When Claire was twenty-two, and Beth was thirty-four, Claire moved into the flat above Old Spitalfields Market, revealing a considerable aptitude on the sewing machine. They painted the walls, and built bookshelves out of planks and columns of bricks, and at weekends helped out in the back room of the local gay and lesbian bookshop, unpacking stock and facilitating meetings and making coffee. It was a period when everything seemed to be unrolling in front of them, and the future, being only hinted at, at best, shone with possibilities.

Claire passed all Beth's secret tests. Claire loved Beth's closest friends. She was interested in food, and art-house movies, and Third World music, and radical cultural movements and interior decor. At Beth's suggestion, she took a sauce-making course at their local catering college, cut her exuberant hair shorter and took to painting her nails. Also at Beth's suggestion, she took the plunge of abandoning the law to set up her own business with a friend, Beth nobly guaranteeing the loan taken out for the start-up costs against the value of the Shoreditch flat, which was in both their names even though Beth had paid the lion's share of the deposit. Claire was very grateful for Beth's generosity. She said so often, and demonstrated her gratitude too, in ways that made Beth very slightly uncomfortable because of their servitude. Claire wanted, she often said in the first eight or ten years together, to get married. She wanted Beth to marry her. She wanted Beth to take her father's mother's old brilliant-cut diamond ring out of the jewellery box where she knew it was kept, and slide it onto Claire's wedding finger in front of a registrar in a register office. But Beth, conditioned by who knew what ghosts and circumstances from her past, did not believe in marriage as an institution. She said, frequently, that she gave evidence of her commitment to Claire, and Claire alone, a hundred times a day. There was no moving her. And after the dust had literally settled in Wilkes Street, Claire discovered that the diamond ring was missing from Beth's jewellery box, and when she confronted Beth about it, Beth didn't even look up from her iPad.

'Oh, that,' she said, 'that went towards doing up our bathroom. I asked Dad and he said good use for it, so I sold it. They were good stones, but the cut was so old-fashioned that they weren't worth all that much. I think they paid for the shower. Next time you're having a shower you can say thank you, Granny, for the diamonds.'

Claire took to having showers in the guest bathroom. Unless Beth's father was staying, the guest bathroom was almost unused and, having been made out of a second-floor bedroom, had a window looking east towards Brick Lane and the tall, silvery minaret of the mosque on the corner of Fournier Street. If you were at the back of the house up there, at certain times of day, you could hear the call to prayer. The mosque, Beth said, had been a Methodist chapel and a Jewish synagogue and a Huguenot church, in its time. The minaret had caused a lot of controversy, being so tall and perforated that it resembled – said some locals – a series of drums from a washing machine. Claire, whose upbringing outside Tiverton had suggested that almost all innovation was by its very nature suspect, was secretly charmed by it.

But then, life in Wilkes Street was generally very charming. The graceful proportions of the house, as well as the extravagance of space it afforded, were a joy to come home to. Claire's business was flourishing and the calibre of clients she was attracting was not only impressive, but international. And Beth – well, Beth was becoming something of a superstar for her thinking, and now her hugely successful books, on the way companies and business life were going to change over the coming decade. Her buzzwords were 'innovation' and 'energy'. Her theories about the inescapable march of organizations towards putting the needs of their employees at the centre of their business – in her words, making work fit for humans, not the other way about as was traditionally the case – were becoming increasingly heard and acted upon. In the first interview she gave after she was made consultant to the airline, she declared that the company would have to change its priorities to continue to excel, putting its workforce before its fleet of planes. She wrote three books in three years – *Energy Means Excellence*, *Teamwork – Why We Are Better Together* and *Power to the People* – and all of them won prizes. Two years after Wilkes Street was finished, Beth flew to New York to collect a substantial award as one of the top twenty published strategic business thinkers in the world that year. Claire did not accompany her – they had discussed the idea, and agreed on her staying behind – but organized, through the Internet, for a sheaf of long-stemmed white roses to be waiting in her hotel room. When Beth got back, she went straight to her study and downloaded her publisher's offer for her fourth book, on the topic of how to attract and – even more crucially – keep the best employees. It was to be called *Hand in Glove: The Right People in the Right Places*, and would be launched with a series of articles in the financial press, the first of which was to be entitled 'Mad About the Mission'. Claire wondered if Beth would even take her coat off before she started writing. Her cabin bag from the journey, still bearing its fluorescent priority tags, stood unpacked in the hallway where the taxi driver had left it. Claire walked past it, swiping her jacket off the hook as she went by, and let herself out through the front door, pulling it quietly closed behind her and hearing the lock click into place, smooth and definite.

—

Their habit, on Friday evenings, was to go out to a favourite basement bar on Commercial Road for a couple of cocktails. Beth always drank vodka martinis; Claire liked to experiment. Afterwards, they would go back to their own kitchen and together cook supper from whatever remained in the fridge at the end of the week. It was understood that Saturday was reserved for food shopping, for a leisurely and serious trawl through the markets with which they were now surrounded – Brick Lane, Spitalfields, even as far afield as Borough Market – coming home with food for whoever was coming to dinner, or Sunday lunch, never forgetting particular chocolate truffles from the tiny but magnificent chocolate specialist on Brick Lane. It was a ritual, but an important and soothing one, and it was only disrupted when Beth was travelling.

That Friday, the Friday two days after Stacey had lost her job, was only different from preceding Fridays because Beth was home in Wilkes Street before Claire. She had time to feed the cats, throw out last week's flowers, check her emails for anything that might have come in since she'd left work, and change from her teaching clothes – a trouser suit – to the jeans and sweatshirt uniform of a weekend. She put new lilies in the black glass vase in the hall, explained to the cats that if they had whimsically gone off the flavour of cat food that had been their absolute favourite only the night before, then they could go hungry, tried Stacey's phone yet one more time, and riffled through the evening paper with the lack of concentration characteristic of somebody waiting. When she heard Claire's key in the lock, she had time to drop into a chair and turn to the editorial before Claire entered the kitchen.

Claire was carrying more lilies, and her briefcase. 'Oh, sorry . . .'

Beth held her face up for a kiss. 'Nothing to be sorry for.'

'A last-minute interview. It went on a bit. Wonderful woman, an Indian accountant, but she wouldn't stop talking, she wouldn't–'

'I said,' Beth replied equably, 'that there's nothing to be sorry for.' She nodded at the lilies. 'I got some. Actually.'

'Oh.'

'Doesn't matter. Nice to have lots.'

Claire put the lilies on the table. 'Are you panting for a drink? I won't be a sec–'

'Not panting at all. Take your time.'

Claire looked at her. 'You're being very – *courteous.*'

'Am I?'

'Yes,' Claire said. 'It makes me nervous.'

Beth smiled at her. 'No need.'

Claire took her shoes off and picked them up in one hand. She ran the other hand through her hair. Then she said, 'What's the matter?'

Beth regarded her. 'I don't know.'

Claire groaned. 'Jesus. Here we go again.'

'Go where?'

'Playing games,' Claire said. Her tone was suddenly slightly rattled. 'Unsettling me with insinuations.'

'Insinuations?'

Claire dropped her shoes and turned her back on Beth. She was wearing a skirt suit with a sharply nipped-in jacket, and Beth couldn't help admiring the contrast in width between her shoulders and her waist. She had her head in her hands.

'Come on, honey,' Beth said, in a different tone. 'Turn round and talk to me.'

'What do you want me to say?'

'I want you to explain something.'

'Oh my God,' Claire said, as if to a third invisible person. 'What have I done now?'

'Something I don't understand.'

'You mean something you don't *like*.'

'I just mean,' Beth spoke in the level voice that Claire thought of as professorial, 'that I prefer to understand before I decide what I do and don't like.'

Claire turned round slowly. 'You are so difficult to live with. You've got so bloody *grand*.'

'I think,' Beth said, 'that that is a whole other topic.'

Claire moved suddenly and took a chair opposite Beth, across the table. 'Well?'

'Stacey,' Beth said.

Claire looked at her nails. They were painted deep red, as glossy as cherries. 'Poor Stacey,' she said, in a gentler voice. 'Have you got through to her?'

'Not yet. I think I'm just going to have to go round and *find* her. But I spoke to Gaby today. We were going to have coffee, but then that didn't work, so we spoke on the phone.'

'Has she got any ideas?'

'Well,' Beth said, pushing the newspaper aside and linking her fingers together loosely in front of her. 'She was more interested in responding to Melissa's idea of the next move.'

Claire looked straight at Beth, across the table. 'Which was?'

'You know what it was, honey. I told you. I told you the night we heard, on Wednesday.'

'And?'

'Claire, please don't play the wide-eyed innocent with me. You know what Melissa, and then I, suggested to Gaby, you know about the email we sent. You saw it.'

Claire's gaze never left Beth's face. She said, 'And doesn't Gaby like the idea?'

'All right,' Beth said. 'Play it your way. Pretend you have no idea what I'm getting at. No, Gaby does not like the idea of offering Stacey a job. Not because she doesn't think Stacey would be good both on and for the team. Not because she doesn't want to help one of her best and oldest friends. But because she hasn't space on the team just now for anyone of Stacey's experience and qualifications. Gaby's team is complete right now. It's complete because over a year ago, she took on someone who came via you, honey, in a deal that you brokered. Gaby took on a client of yours called Sarah Parker.'

Claire's gaze still didn't waver. 'So?' she said, steadily.

'Sarah Parker has lived for eight years with Will Gibbs, who is the father of Melissa's Tom.'

'I know,' Claire said.

'And what I don't understand,' Beth said, 'what I am trying to understand in order to make up my mind about what to do next to help Stacey in all this mess, is why you never told me. Why, Claire, didn't you tell me that you had fixed up a job with one of my dearest friends for a woman who happens to live with – another important fact unknown to me – the man who fathered the only child of another of my dearest friends? Why did you not tell me something as huge as that?'

'You'd only have told me not to give her an interview, let alone a job offer,' Claire said, too quickly.

Beth sighed. 'Please don't demean the whole situation by making it about your commission.'

'It wasn't that.'

'No. Perhaps not. I'm glad to hear it.'

Claire leaned back, out of the circle of light cast by the fashionably industrial metal lampshade. 'It was when you went to America, for the prize.'

'Yes.'

'There was so much going on.'

'Possibly. But we talked about you coming. I wanted you to come. I seem to remember you saying you had too much work on.'

'I did,' Claire said.

'Including finding a job with Gaby for Sarah Parker.'

'Gaby knew,' Claire said defensively.

'Gaby didn't know until Sarah had been working there for over six months, and had proved herself excellent.'

'She *is* excellent.'

'That's not the point,' Beth said. 'The point is, why didn't *you* tell *me*.'

'I was afraid to.'

'To be kind,' Beth said, 'I'll pretend I didn't hear that.'

'I don't have to tell you everything!' Claire shouted.

Beth bent her head. Then she raised it a little. 'Of course you don't. But I think you do have to tell me things that affect my relationship with my closest friends.' She paused. 'Were you – are you – trying to punish me?'

Claire gaped exaggeratedly. 'For what?'

Beth shrugged. 'For working. For being absorbed in work. For being older than you, for not wanting to be married . . .' She paused again and then she said, in a lower voice, 'Is there someone else?'

Claire looked at the shadowy ceiling, above the lamplight. 'Not yet.'

'What's that supposed to mean?'

'Exactly what I said. It means I haven't been seeing anyone else, I haven't even met anyone else, but I might. One day.'

'Ah.'

'Someone,' Claire said, 'who isn't obsessed with their media profile. Who wouldn't rather spend time saying the same thing endlessly in their books than spend time with me discovering new stuff. Someone, even, who wants a baby.'

'A *baby*!' Beth was truly startled.

'Why not?' Claire said. 'Why not a baby? Have you ever thought how sterile your perfect life in your perfect house is?'

'Goodness,' Beth said faintly. 'Wow. Here it all comes. Now I know.' She got up unsteadily from the table, held on to the edge for a moment, and then began to move away.

'I'm sorry,' Claire said.

Beth halted. 'What for?'

'For – for not telling you about Sarah. And about Sarah living with Will Gibbs. For all this. Really. Can we . . .'

'Can we what?'

'Maybe we can put all this behind us, now it's out in the open, now that you know.'

Beth was standing, as Claire had earlier, with her back almost turned. 'But it hasn't cleared the air,' she said.

'But – but I've *told* you!'

'And,' Beth said, turning, 'what you've told me has certainly made me understand, but that understanding has led to a terrible knowledge.'

'What d'you mean? Can't we go back? Can't we go on?'

Beth moved slowly towards the door. The cats were flanking it, sitting there, tails furled, as if ready to escort her from the room. She stopped just before she reached them. 'It's time, perhaps, honey, for *you* to understand something. What you did was one thing, but the reason you did it was quite another. And I'm afraid that reason is the kind of thing, the size of thing, that you just can't row back from. Not even you. Not even us.'

CHAPTER FIVE

STACEY

It became apparent within a matter of weeks that the original plan wasn't going to work. They had both thought that Stacey's mum could have the top floor of the house, where there were two bedrooms – one of which could become a sitting room – and a bathroom, plus a cupboard where they had originally kept suitcases but which could quite easily be turned into enough of a kitchen to house a kettle and a small sink and a microwave. Tentatively – he was suggesting a lot of things tentatively these days, after Stacey's disconcerting reaction to his promotion that night – Steve put forward the idea of installing a safety gate at the top of the stairs.

'I don't want to be patronizing or anything, but if she's getting a bit disorientated . . . and suppose she can't remember where she is, in the night . . .'

Stacey had winced. Acknowledging Mum's condition had been one thing; facing its consequences and the alarming evidence of its acceleration was proving quite another. It was made worse, of course, by the fact that Steve left the house on his own shortly after seven each morning, leaving Stacey in the kitchen and still in her dressing gown with a day ahead overseeing the workmen who were adapting the top floor for its new occupant.

'I want it to look like home for her,' Stacey said. She was in pyjama bottoms and a T-shirt, and her hair, whose sleek precision had been a constant in her life previously, was still tousled from being slept on.

Steve was hovering by the doorway in his work suit, his BlackBerry in his hand.

'But it has to be *safe*, Stace. We have to make sure she's safe.'

The security gate, sturdy and painted to match the woodwork of the staircase, went in. So did a plastic seat bolted to the tiled wall of the shower, and taps with levers that could be operated by someone who had lost their manual dexterity. Discreet bars were screwed across the window frames and light switches with large illuminated buttons were installed inside every doorway. Stacey took old curtains from storage in the Holloway flat and had them altered to fit the windows, familiar curtains from her childhood home. When the move actually happened, the furniture that Stacey and Steve had collected in their marriage would be replaced by the things Mum knew from the Holloway flat, and long before: the leatherette sofa with velvet seat cushions, her TV chair, the bedside cabinet with photographs of Stacey trapped under its glass top. Mum would find herself, Stacey determined, in a world where the important elements would all be known to her – her daughter, her son-in-law, the dog, her familiar possessions. She would even drink early-morning tea out of the cup patterned with pussy willow catkins that she had inherited from her own mother.

But it didn't work out like that. First, Mum wouldn't leave the Holloway flat. She sat in the carver chair of her dining-room suite of furniture, gripping the arms and staring ahead fixedly as if she would drown should she let go. When Stacey finally wheedled her into leaving, promising that Bruno was waiting for her, longing to see her, she sat in the taxi on the edge of the seat, tense with anxiety and apprehension. She looked at Stacey's house, when they reached it, with absolute dismay.

'We're home!' Stacey said, trying to inject the moment with a small sense of jubilation. 'Your home too, now, Mum!'

Mum shook her head. 'I don't live here,' she said hoarsely.

'You do now!'

Mum turned to look at her. 'What if I'm a nuisance?'

Nothing on the top floor, so carefully arranged to simulate what was known and comforting, appeared in the least satisfactory. Mum went quickly from bedroom to sitting room and back again with little shuffling steps, as if looking for something that wasn't there. It was a terrible first hour, the pacing and the agitation, never mind Stacey's rising sense of furious and guilty frustration. When she finally, exhaustedly, turned on the new and enormous television, and Mum subsided, abruptly mesmerized, into her customary chair in front of an afternoon quiz show, Stacey went downstairs, bolting the safety gate behind her, and sat on the kitchen floor with her arms round Bruno's neck and wept and wept into his wayward fur.

It became obvious, almost at once, that living on the top floor while life went on below was never going to work. Mum did not call out if she found herself alone up there, but she battled endlessly to open the security gate, and Stacey could hear it, rattle-rattle, rattle-rattle, even in her dreams. Mum could not, it transpired, be left even for an hour. Dreams of a cheerful household in which there was always the harmony of Mum and Bruno to come home to, were dashed within days. Mum was completely disorientated and, perhaps because of that, perhaps anyway, unsteady on her feet. Expecting her to live up two flights of stairs was out of the question. When she was downstairs, and especially with Bruno, she was calmer and less distressingly unhappy. She could even hold a small conversation and perform simple domestic tasks, drying spoons or washing apples.

'I daren't let her near knives or hot water,' Stacey told Steve. 'I've taken the kettle out of her kitchen and unplugged the microwave. I – I think I'm going to have to help shower her.'

Steve stared. '*Shower* her?' He shook his head, helplessly. 'Oh, Stace.'

She was leaning against the sink. She wore jeans and an old sweater of his with the stretched cuffs pushed up above her elbows as if she had been scrubbing something. 'A month ago—'

'Don't.'

'A month ago, I was in a business suit advising a company with a multi-million-pound potential turnover.'

'Stace. Sweetheart. I'm so sorry.'

'I don't want you to be sorry. It isn't your fault.'

'No, but . . .'

'You being successful is the one thing that keeps me going.'

'It doesn't,' Steve said, 'feel like that.'

'Poor her. Poor Mum. It's so sudden.'

'Is she – unhappy?'

'Yes.'

'Are you sure? How can you know?'

'I know,' said Stacey, 'that she's wondering where her mind has gone. Can you imagine anything more frightening than that? Can you imagine anything that would make you *less* happy?'

Steve said awkwardly, 'Stace . . .'

'What?'

'Have you thought about your mother's flat?'

She said sharply, 'What about it?'

'Well, it's standing empty. A flat in Holloway . . .'

'What are you suggesting?'

He put his hands in his trouser pockets. 'I'm suggesting – tentatively, Stace – that we sell it.'

She glared at him. 'Sell it?'

'She can't live there alone again–'

'Steve,' Stacey said, interrupting, 'that flat was Mum's home. For nearly twenty years. I can't just flog it, without her knowing, I can't be that callous. I can't . . .' She stopped and put her hands briefly up to her face. Then she said, more calmly, 'Please don't ask me to again. Please just – don't.'

Steve bent to pull Bruno's ears. 'Have you seen anyone?' he said.

'What d'you mean? Doctors?'

'I mean the girls. Melissa and Gaby and Beth. Have you seen them?'

'There's no point seeing them,' Stacey said, sadly rather than shortly. 'What can they do? Anyway, they're busy.'

'What happened to the suggestion that Gaby might offer you–'

'Nothing,' Stacey said. She turned towards the sink and began washing a saucepan that stood soaking in it.

'But, Stace . . .'

'She wouldn't talk about it. I don't know what was going on, but it was a no-no as far as Gaby was concerned. And Melissa's in a state about something of her own, and I think Beth and Claire are splitting up. All these years together, the house and everything. I don't know what it's about and, quite honestly, I'm too bothered and exhausted to involve myself. So, in answer to your question, I haven't really told them, I haven't really talked to them, and even if they could help, or wanted to, they can't, because of their own stuff.' She banged the washed pan down on the draining board. 'We're all on our own in the end, Steve. That's what it comes down to.'

Steve's heart smote him. His Stacey. His adored Stacey with her modest face and manner reduced to this angry travesty who needed a haircut and a reason to respect herself again. He said, unhappily, 'Sweetheart, please . . .'

He came up behind her and put his arms around her, holding her against his chest. She looked down at his ironed blue cotton shirtsleeves with their double cuffs and cufflinks, across the folds of her ratty old sweater. And then, yet again, and despising herself for doing it, she began to cry.

—

They gave up the idea of Mum living on the top floor. She had taken, not just to rattling the bolt on the safety gate, but to moaning, in a low steady monotone, like an afflicted cow, which she could keep up for hours. So Stacey summoned the removal company who had shifted Mum's furniture from the Holloway flat, and they carried all the furniture down to the ground floor, and took the contents of Stacey and Steve's sitting room up to the top of the house.

It made a small improvement in Mum's mood. She would at least sit for periods of time in front of the television, with Bruno beside her, his head heavy on her feet. The nights were now less disturbed with the addition of sleeping pills to the regime, and, at Steve's insistence, a carer from a local agency came in most days to cajole Mum into the shower. Stacey was persistently reluctant.

'I should be doing it, I should – it's the least I can do after all she's done for me.'

'And ruin whatever dignity is left in your relationship? Would *she* want that? If she was still in her right mind, would she want you to see her like that?'

'But–'

'Would you want me to shower *you*? Would you?'

'No, but I–'

'Think of her pride, Stacey. Think of *her*.'

'Suppose I want to?'

He regarded her for a moment and then he said, bravely, 'But you don't.'

She didn't. She felt terrible about it, but she didn't. She didn't want Mum sleeping in her sitting room, or to have her whole house overtaken by this dreadful adversity, so that nobody visited and she was trapped in there despite it having become, almost overnight it seemed, somewhere alien. Sometimes, tiredly washing something or disinfecting something yet again, she wondered what she would have done if Jeff Dodds had readily agreed to her flexible working plan, or if she had not reacted so impulsively, and tried not to think that it would have made the whole Mum tragedy so much more bearable and manageable, because she would have *had* to leave the house now and then, and she would have *had* to have professional help from outside. If Jeff Dodds had agreed, she would not, all of a sudden, have become the prisoner of a role and a routine that was, she couldn't help thinking, seldom required by society of a man.

It was hard, too, not to now see Steve as a man before she considered him as a human. He had said to her, after the first few shocking days of Mum being with them, that he saw his task as being to support Stacey in every way he could. He was fond of his mother-in-law, and saddened by her condition, but it wasn't right that he should do more for her than was consistent with their past relationship, and their genders. It was Stacey who concerned him, he said, Stacey who needed not to worry about money, or household administration, or the general maintenance of their lives. He would earn, pay bills, clear the gutters, take out the rubbish, worm the dog. He would sit with Mum so that Stacey could take a shower in peace. He would order takeaways when she was too tired or frazzled to cook. He would collect the dry cleaning and phone the council to say that a rat had been spotted near the empty house next door. But he wouldn't do a single intimate thing for Mum, and nor should Stacey. She might be shocked by the violent upheaval in her life the last month, but she was not to divert the magnificent energies that had built her career into a wholly mistaken notion of duty and obligation. He was quite clear about it.

But he could still physically leave. Every morning, showered and wearing a crisply laundered shirt and a suit, he could open the front door and slam it behind him. He was free to stride down Liverpool Road to the bus that would take him to the City, and to an office block with an atrium foyer, a respectful receptionist, silent banks of lifts, and the unutterable luxury of business preoccupations. Once a month, in addition, he could also now enter the boardroom, and sit round a huge blond wood table with eleven other people, to be called upon, now and then, by the chairman, to give his views or express his priorities. When he got home from those meetings, he told Stacey all about them. He asked if she approved of what he had said. He made it plain that he thought her present predicament was only temporary. He was as kind and supportive and encouraging as anyone could reasonably be expected to be, but from where Stacey currently stood, endlessly knocked over by the random waves of Mum's dementia, she could only battle against her resentment, fight against feelings of injustice and anger, and, most days, worn down by the strain and the shame and the misery, lose.

—

It was just an impulse to ring Beth. It wasn't the result of thinking that Beth's academic training might be insightful, or that Beth's reported relationship problems might make her a fellow traveller in emotional wretchedness, but just an impulse. It had been a bad afternoon, in which the visiting carer had had to give up trying to give Mum a shower, and Bruno had been inexplicably sick, on a rug rather than on a stone floor, and Steve had rung to say he was going to have to take a client out for dinner that evening, and Stacey just found herself, mobile in hand, dialling Beth's number. The ringtone went straight to voicemail, and as Stacey took a breath to leave some kind of confused message, Beth's voice cut in.

'Stacey?'

'Oh hi, oh hello, I didn't mean–'

'Stacey,' Beth said, in quite a different tone, 'are you OK? No. Scrub that. You are plainly not OK.'

'I am, I am, I'm fine.'

'You sound awful.'

'So do you. Actually.'

'Well, I'm better. Marginally better. On the scale of awfulness, I've crept from ten to about eight. Seven on a good day.'

'I'm so glad to hear you,' Stacey said, almost in a whisper.

'Me too.'

'Beth?'

'Yes?'

'I'm going mad. I think I'm going mad.'

'Are you alone?'

'No. No, I'm not. In fact, that's part of the trouble.'

'I heard about your trouble. I'm so sorry.'

'Can you come?' Stacey said suddenly.

'Now?'

'When you can. Later. But today.'

'I'm not very good company.'

Stacey gave a little yelp of laughter. 'Join the club!'

'I'd love to see you. I really would. I wanted – I wanted to see all of you. But I just somehow couldn't, not after . . .'

'No. Of course not. But can you come? Can you come later? Can you?' She could hear Beth thinking. She squeezed her eyes shut. If I don't breathe till she speaks, she'll say yes.

'Yes,' Beth said at last. 'Of course. I'll see you later.'

—

Beth brought a bottle of wine and a bag of plums from the tree they had discovered gallantly continuing to fruit under all the rubbish in the yard behind Wilkes Street. She looked gaunt, Stacey thought, and all of her forty-seven years, with her famously dark hair brushed back severely and wearing a black trouser suit only marginally enlivened by the black and grey striped shirt underneath it. She stepped into the hall, put down the wine and the plums, and took Stacey in her arms for a long embrace. It was only after several moments of this that Stacey realized she was crying.

'I'm sorry I look so awful,' Stacey said, pulling away just slightly.

'You don't.'

'I do, Bethie. I look just as beaten up as I feel.'

Beth put the backs of her hands against her eyes and sniffed. She said, slightly muffled, 'Where's your mother?'

Stacey indicated the closed sitting-room door. 'In there. With the dog. He'll be busting to greet you. But he's on Mum-sitting duty, which luckily he takes very seriously.'

Beth gave a wan smile. 'A useful male, for once, then.'

'The males in my life,' Stacey said as if needing to assert something, '*are* wonderful.'

'Actually,' Beth said, finding a tissue in her pocket and blowing her nose, 'my recent experiences indicate to me that good and bad conduct is more a matter of humanity and genetics than gender.'

There was a scrabbling at the far side of the sitting-room door. 'Bruno,' Stacey said, in explanation.

She opened the door wide enough for Bruno to squirm through and begin his ecstatic welcome ritual on the floor. Beth bent to greet him, and then straightened to glance beyond him into the room. Mum was hunched in a chair, slightly collapsed sideways, asleep, with the television blaring.

'Oh, Stacey . . .'

'I know. She looks a hundred.'

'But I remember such a different, energetic–'

'I know,' Stacey repeated. 'It's been three months since the diagnosis. Three months from that person to this.' She was still holding the door. 'Back you go,' she said to Bruno. 'Guard duty, remember?'

Beth touched Stacey's arm. 'You poor thing. You poor, poor thing.'

Stacey closed the door again behind Bruno and headed for the basement stairs. 'Let's open your bottle. I never used to drink except at weekends, then I drank far too much when all this first blew up, then I stopped again in case it was making everything worse. Now, I don't know what I'm doing. I don't know what I'm doing about anything.'

Beth followed her down the stairs to the basement kitchen, with its glass doors at the far end giving on to a patio and steps up to the lawn above. Stacey indicated a sofa in front of a wall-mounted television screen flanked by bookshelves.

'Sit, you. We live down here now that Mum's got the ground floor. It's insane, really, isn't it?'

'I don't know what is or isn't insane any more,' Beth said sadly. 'I think one knows what is convenient for oneself, but never what works for other people.'

Stacey came across the room and handed Beth a couple of wine glasses. 'Hold those while I pull the cork. Steve would congratulate you on bringing wine with a cork. He's worried about all the cork-tree farmers if we all buy wine with screw tops. Beth, do you want to talk about it?'

'Not really. But thank you.'

'What I meant was, do talk about it if you feel you'd like to. I'm not prying, but I'd love to be distracted.'

Beth looked at the glasses she held. She said, 'I don't think it's very distracting. It's too much of a cliché. It all boiled down to my being too old for her, too wrapped up in my work, too materialistic apparently, insufficiently spontaneous and pretty dull. You could have written the script.'

Stacey wound a corkscrew carefully down into the neck of the bottle, holding it between her knees. 'Did you see it coming?'

'Not really. I could make a pattern now, of course, with hindsight, but at the time it blew up, all I was trying to do was to get her to tell me why she had withheld something I needed to know.'

'Had she?'

'Yes,' Beth said. She held out the glasses so Stacey could pour wine into them. 'For quite a long time.' She paused, and then she said, 'The trust thing. You know?'

'That is why,' Stacey said, setting the bottle down and moving to take a glass from Beth and to sit beside her, 'I have Mum here. I can't fault her for being trustworthy. Never could. My greatest champion.'

'Lucky you.'

'Yes.'

Beth looked down into her wine. 'It gives you confidence, being trusted.'

Stacey leaned back and groaned. 'Oh God, Bethie. Confidence . . .'

Beth turned to look at her. 'Go on.'

'I might blub. I blub all the time at the moment. I never used to.'

'Nor me.'

'Is it hormones? The menopause and stuff? It's awful, whatever it is. It seems to take nothing to set me off. I have never, ever, felt this – *helpless*.'

'Because you can't help your mother?'

'No,' Stacey said uncertainly, 'not really. I mean, I can't help her. And that's terrible in a way, as is watching her distort and disappear as a person, but if I'm honest, if I'm completely, utterly, soul-baringly honest . . .'

'Yes?'

'It's work,' Stacey said. She turned slowly to look at Beth. 'I hate, hate, *hate* not going to work.'

Beth said quietly, 'Yes.'

'I took it for granted, Beth. I don't think it ever crossed my mind, from the day I graduated, that I wouldn't have a job, that I wouldn't be paid to do something that I was good at, that interested me, that gave me a visibility and an incentive to go on trying. It never occurred to me that I wouldn't get what I'd asked for, a month ago; it never struck me, for a single second, that all those years of work, all the self-belief that my career had given me, could just drop away, *vanish*, in no time at all. If you'd told me I'd be sitting here with you on a Tuesday evening wearing mum jeans and an old rugby shirt of Steve's, unemployed, I'd have stared at you as if you'd lost your mind.'

Beth took a swallow of wine. Then she reached out and briefly squeezed Stacey's nearest hand. 'If it's any consolation, Stace, I don't feel much more positive than you, and my professional life has probably never been better. It's a huge salvation, still having work to go to, but it doesn't stop me feeling old and unattractive and boring and unadventurous and all the things Claire said I was.'

'But if there wasn't work? If there was just the house, and no Professor Mundy?'

'I'd be desperate. Suicidal, probably.'

'Well,' Stacey said, 'I'm not Professor Mundy, but I *was* Stacey Grant, the reputable, even renowned in some circles, senior partner in private equity.'

Beth looked directly at her. 'Of course.'

'For the first couple of weeks, people from work got in touch all the time, texts, emails, calls, everything. Some of them even wanted to get up some kind of protest campaign and involve the board, but I couldn't let them. I don't know if it was pride, I don't know if I didn't want to risk being pilloried as another woman making a shrill fuss, I don't know if I was just too shocked and confused to think straight, but I made them all promise not to do anything, to leave me alone, and so they have, bless them, and of course I hate that, too.'

Beth gestured towards the ceiling, at the still-audible noise of the TV from the room above them, turned up for Mum's need, these days, to deafening volume. 'While all this was going on.'

'Yes,' Stacey said. '*Yes*. And another thing: you and I have never had children, so we've never known what it's like not to feel free. Whatever we've done, even if we dressed it up by saying, "I have to do this and that", has really been the result of choice. Of course choice has consequences that one can't always control, but we were always able to choose the job or the post, and then were free to devote ourselves to it, to let our work lives dictate our – our, well, our sort of *being*, if you like. And now I'm suddenly not free. Two and a half years off fifty and I'm as stuck as a kid with a new baby and no one to help. It's probably very good for me, if suffering really does any of us any real good. Whatever good is.'

Beth stretched forward to put her wine glass down on the edge of the nearest bookshelf. 'This is rather difficult to ask, but might this situation not last all that long?'

Stacey looked at her. 'Mum is seventy-one. And her heart is very strong and all her other organs are functioning like those of someone a decade younger at least. So, no, is the short answer.'

Beth said, 'I think you should consider part-time work.'

Stacey closed her eyes. 'I wouldn't know where to start.'

'Yes, you would. None of us have worked this long not to have contacts to call on at times like these.'

'Gaby turned me down,' Stacey said, almost in a whisper.

'Well, I don't think it was quite like that.'

Stacey sat suddenly upright. 'What do you mean? What do you know about it?'

'Stace, I don't know any more than that,' Beth said steadily, spreading out her hands as if to smooth things down physically. 'But I don't think she turned you down. I think she couldn't entertain the idea because her team is complete right now, so she couldn't–'

'She wouldn't even *see* me!'

Beth looked at her. 'Did you ask her?'

'What, directly?'

'Yes. Did you ring her and ask her?'

Stacey looked away. 'I was – so hoping she would ring me.

But she didn't. So I rang her and it was really difficult. I shouldn't have had to. She should have rung *me*.'

'We all tried to,' Beth said, 'that dreadful Wednesday. We all tried to get hold of you.'

'I couldn't speak to anyone. I could barely speak to Steve, especially when he kind of let slip that his promotion to the board wasn't completely unexpected. I mean, I know about company confidentiality, and I'm really proud of him, but I couldn't – can't – help feeling left right out of the loop. I know it isn't right or logical, but I just keep thinking it isn't *fair*.'

'Well then, honey—'

'Beth,' Stacey said, interrupting, 'do you know what's going on with Gaby? And Melissa?'

Beth sighed. 'You must ask them yourself,' she said carefully.

'Aren't you being plain priggish?'

'No,' Beth said. 'You can accuse me of that if you want – Claire certainly would – but I think I'm respecting your own relationships with both Gaby and Melissa. I'm also saying that if you want anything to happen to ease your plight, you're going to have to make an effort yourself.'

'Did you lecture Claire like this?'

'I tried not to.'

'So you think I've got to pick up the phone to Gaby and pick up the phone to Melissa and stop wallowing?'

Beth gave her a ghost of a smile. 'Yes to one and two, and I wouldn't dare suggest three.'

Stacey tried to smile back. 'Bethie. Will you be OK?'

'In time. Possibly. Even probably. You can't switch off loving someone just because they've switched off you.'

Stacey gave Beth's nearest hand a brief pat. 'I know. Especially if, like Mum, they had no choice about switching off.'

From upstairs, Bruno gave a few sharp barks. Stacey was off the sofa and across the room in a flash.

'That's Mum,' she said. 'He's brilliant at telling me. She's awake.'

CHAPTER SIX

MELISSA

When Melissa suggested – gently but firmly – that all boards, especially those of public companies, should review their conduct and their performance once a year, the chairman of the huge retail group she had been asked to advise looked as if she had hit him.

'Once a year? *Every* year? It's a preposterous suggestion.'

'When I started Hathaway,' Melissa said, smiling at him, her hands loosely clasped on the table in front of her, 'lots of people told me it was the worst idea I'd ever had. Several people, I remember, described it as outlandish. But that was fifteen years ago. So much has changed in fifteen years, including notions of infallibility.'

The chairman, a lean man in his late fifties, with a set of top-quality golf clubs propped in one corner of his severely uncluttered office, fiddled with his fountain pen. 'I've never thought of myself as infallible.'

'No.'

'My wife certainly doesn't think so.'

'I'm not suggesting anyone's at fault,' Melissa said. 'That isn't the point. Nor is it my aim, in trying to help. I'm just here to explain my methodology to you, in detail, so that you can make an educated choice as to whether I can be of use to you.'

The chairman unscrewed the gold-rimmed black cap of his pen, and screwed it back on again. 'Well, Miss Hathaway–'

'Melissa.'

'Well, *Melissa.* I *did* ask you, even if my arm was twisted by our mutual friend, and I must take the consequences of that. So. Let's cut to the chase. What is, say, your one crucial question?'

Melissa counted to five. The interview was following a familiar pattern, and her responses would therefore be equally tried and tested. To be measured in manner, she had discovered, was the most effective response, even to outright hostility. After five, she said, still smiling slightly, still looking at him, 'How well are you prepared for the future?'

'Excellently.'

'Could you describe . . . ?'

He gestured with his fountain pen. 'Trial stores in America, production shifts out of one Asian country to another, constant innovation in food lines, experiments in homeware collections . . .'

'Excuse me,' Melissa said, 'but are these ideas, or projects in the course of implementation?'

'Ideas, mostly.'

'And is somebody in charge of every area of development?'

'I am,' the chairman said.

Melissa counted to five once more. Then she said, 'May I describe something to you?'

He gestured again. He was, she reckoned, exceptionally good at what he did. It was just that, collectively, the board could assist his flair to make the business so much better.

'Of course,' he said with elaborate courtesy.

'What I would like,' Melissa said, 'is to give to you the backup and the implemented support that you both need and deserve. I propose the following plan, the plan I use for every company I have helped in the last fifteen years, none of which - none - have failed to increase, at least, their output and their profits.'

The chairman put his pen down at last and leaned back, folding his arms. 'Fire away.'

'I start,' Melissa said, 'by interviewing everyone on the board alone, for two hours. After that process is complete, I attend every divisional and board meeting - I live with the company basically. I then tell you all what I see as the strengths of the board, and what I see as the challenges, and then I produce a report of about twenty pages, in which, from past experience, there will be very few surprises. Then, finally, I interview everyone separately again, and to top the whole process off, we have a board meeting. Everyone, all together.'

The chairman said nothing. He was frowning at his own thoughts.

Melissa went on in a deliberately reasonable tone, 'You called *me*, after all. Did you think I'd praise you? Did you think you *needed* a health check? Or . . . ?' She stopped, and waited.

'Bad figures,' he said, slowly and reluctantly.

'Yes.'

He glanced at her. 'Which you knew all along.'

'Yes. When things are going well, nobody thinks about the board. They only do when things start to go wrong.'

He sighed. Then he looked at her properly for the first time. 'An educated choice? Is that what you said?'

'I did.'

'And these interviews . . . ?'

'They take place in my office,' Melissa said. 'It's a neutral space.'

'Neutral?'

'Yes.'

He sighed again and uncrossed his arms. 'When can you start?'

—

Melissa's office was in a small, secluded mews house off the Gloucester Road. In deference to the stables they had once been, the roadway between the two lines of little houses was still cobbled, with a deep central drain, and there was a ceremonial archway leading off the street outside. The office, rented on a long lease, was at the far end, a modest building, painted cream with a dark grey front door. Beside it was a small brushed steel plate which said, simply, 'Hathaway'.

Inside, there was an open-plan space housing a modern coat rack, Melissa's assistant, Donna, and a flight of stairs leading up to the area which had been fitted out like an unthreatening consulting room, furnished with a sofa, and several padded chairs around a painted wooden table. In one corner was Melissa's desk and computer and in another an enormous weeping fig tree in a galvanized container. There were no overhead lights, only lamps, and the sofa had rugs folded over its arms; hanging above it was a large black and white photograph of shadows cast across a sunny city pavement. It was as bland and unobtrusive a setting as Melissa had been able to devise, as well as being eerily quiet. If anyone slammed a car door in the mews outside, whoever Melissa was talking to at the time would jerk upright as if they had heard a gunshot.

Donna had worked for Melissa since the infancy of both Tom and Hathaway. She had come to work, on a trial basis, as a typist with potential, and had steadily morphed into being the most indispensable person in Melissa's life. She had not only grown with the business, but had also, despite being married herself with a pair of daughters, found time to buy Tom's school uniform, and fill the fridge in Holland Street with something he could raid when he came in, late and ravenous, to a still-empty house. Donna knew everything about Melissa's private life, and Melissa had been invited to Donna's daughters' naming ceremonies. At Christmas, Melissa gave Donna a substantial gift voucher, and Donna gave Tom something her daughters had chosen for him. Donna was blonde, and trim, and efficient. Several of Melissa's clients had tried over the years to poach her with lavish offers of an increased salary and unlimited expenses. She declined each one, and reported the details to Melissa afterwards.

'It's like marriage,' she said to Melissa. 'I know what suits me, and this does.'

She was at her desk, blonde hair smoothed back into a tidy ponytail, navy suit jacket draped symmetrically on a nearby hanger, when Melissa reached the office. There was no need, between them, for Donna to enquire if the meeting had gone well, and Hathaway had got the job. It was understood that Hathaway would get a hundred per cent of the business of companies who applied for its services, and they had not yet had occasion to revise that understanding. Sometimes, the initial meeting did not produce immediate results, but in the end, no chairman worth his position could deny that somehow, somewhere, improvements might be made. This time Melissa put her briefcase down, gave the thumbs-up sign, and said, 'It's a huge board. Twenty-seven of them. It's going to take weeks.'

'I'll start timetabling. And liaising with all their PAs.' Donna held out a piece of paper. 'Tom called.'

Melissa looked at it. '*Tom?* Here? Why didn't he call my phone?'

'He rang about an hour ago. This was the message he gave me. I suggested he ring you and he said he hadn't got time.'

Melissa took the sheet of paper. 'Meaning that he didn't want to speak to me.'

'Or,' Donna said, 'that he daren't.'

Melissa looked at the message in her hand. '"*Star Wars.*" What does he mean? We saw *Star Wars* forever ago, when he was little.'

'It's the latest film in the sequence. The usual sci-fi action stuff. *You* know.'

'"I'm going to see *Star Wars* with Jake and Ben,"' Melissa said, reading. '"Then supper at theirs, and I'll stay over. See you Saturday, I mean tomorrow. Have a good evening. Tom xx."'

She looked up at Donna. 'Jake and Ben.'

'Yes.'

'Will's little boys,' Melissa said.

'Yes.'

Melissa closed her eyes briefly. 'Goodness,' she said, faintly.

'I suppose,' Donna said thoughtfully, 'it had to happen.'

'Yes.'

'They *are* his half-brothers. And he wanted me to add the kisses. He specified that.'

'I – just didn't think it would happen like this. That – that he wouldn't be able to face telling me himself.'

'Oh,' Donna said, moving papers briskly about on her desk. 'Don't pay any attention to *that*. That's just boys. Like the men they'll grow up to be.'

'He's always told me everything.'

'You *think* he has, Melissa.'

Melissa glanced at the note again. 'Do you think he has a crush on Marnie?' she said.

'No.'

'Why are you so decided? Why do you say no so emphatically?'

'*You* know the reason.'

'Do I?'

'Yes,' Donna said firmly. 'Yes. Tom adores you, you know he does. But you can't, on your own, be a family for him. Can you?'

'I try so hard.'

'It's not a matter of trying. You do everything you can. But you can't provide a houseful of kids and mess and big meals and noise and all the stuff that goes to make family life. Can you?'

'No. And if he wants that so much . . .'

'He doesn't know if he does,' Donna said. 'He thinks he does because it's different. Because he hasn't got it right now, he has to try. He may hate it.'

Melissa bent to pick up her briefcase. 'But he may not.'

'Well,' Donna said. 'There'll probably be a honeymoon period. There usually is. Meanwhile . . .'

'Yes.'

'There's work to be done.'

'I know, Donna. I know.' She began to move slowly towards the stairs that led up to her own office.

'Are you OK?' Donna said in a different tone.

Melissa didn't turn. She began to climb the stairs with a briskness she didn't feel.

'Yes. Yes, I'm fine,' she said, firmly.

She put a hand on her heart. Donna couldn't see. Nobody could see. There wasn't, in fact, anything *to* see, but she could feel it acutely, a pain of a sharpness she hadn't felt since that long-ago dinner in Paris when Connor Corbett had told her that they were over.

—

The Holland Street house was very quiet. It felt, Melissa thought, intentionally quiet, as if it wanted to emphasize Tom's absence. Friday night had become, in any case, something of a ritualized special night for both of them. Very occasionally a school friend of Tom's would be there, scrupulously polite in the manner of someone playing a role to perfection, but more often than not it was just the two of them, and a takeaway dinner of Tom's choosing, followed by a movie screened on the immense basement television set, which they chose in strict rotation, week after week. Without Tom, Melissa reflected, she would never have seen the *Star Wars* films which preceded the very one Tom was now watching with his young half-brothers, and his father, in some cinema only a few streets away, really, in Notting Hill. Without Tom, there was a dramatic hollowness to the prospect of a long evening of whatever music or food or form of relaxation she might choose. There seemed, suddenly, to be neither point nor savour in being able, for under twenty-four hours, to have nobody to please but herself.

There was, of course, as Donna had pointed out, work to be done. Melissa plugged her laptop into the specially designated socket in the kitchen, and fired it up. The resulting emails all seemed absurdly mundane, and without exception could wait until Monday. People seemed to have a Friday-night habit of technological desk-clearing which filled everyone else's inboxes with material that managed, always, to unsettle the transition from work mode to time off. She scrolled rapidly through what had come in in the last hour and then marked for Monday, or deleted, all of them.

Then she poured a glass of sparkling water, congratulating herself on taking the trouble to add ice cubes and slices of lime, and carried it up to her bathroom, with every intention of running a luxurious bath in which she would lie, eyes closed, listening to Mozart. Or maybe Schumann. Or perhaps Tchaikovsky. Something romantic and melodic anyway, something that would buff away the spikes in her feelings, whose jagged edges she was both conscious and ashamed of. Wasn't it right – yes, *right* – that Tom should want to know his father better? And, of course, his father's family?

She took off her black dress and hung it to air on a hanger by the open window. She put lasts in her work shoes, unclasped the pearls her father had given both his daughters, and laid them, and her pearl earrings, in the velvet-lined box in which they had arrived. Then she peeled off her tights and her underclothes and dropped them in the lidded woven basket for handwashed laundry in her bathroom, and put on a white towelling bathrobe. It had the logo of an upmarket health spa embroidered on it and Melissa had bought it when she took Donna there, for two nights, to celebrate her forty-fifth birthday.

She was leaning over the bath, about to turn on the taps, when her phone rang. She raced to answer it, immediately thinking it might be Tom. But the screen did not say Tom. It said Gaby.

'Lissa?'

'Yes,' Melissa said. 'Yes!'

'This is very last minute,' Gaby said. 'I'm just home and everyone's in a horrible mood. It's a case of real save-it-up-to-be-vile-to-Mummy Friday. And Quin's out, the bastard, at some local conservation evening. Will you save me? Will you and Tom save me and come for supper? We're going to have takeaway Japanese because Japanese is the only food there is even *faint* consensus on.'

Melissa subsided onto the floor, overwhelmed with relief. 'I'd – love to. I really would. But I haven't got Tom.'

'You haven't?'

'No. Tom isn't here tonight.'

'Is he at a sleepover? The only thing to be said for the Henderson household tonight is that nobody extra is here for a sleepover.'

'Yes,' Melissa said. 'Yes, he is.'

'Well, you come. The kids have to improve their behaviour to me if you're there. Come and stop me murdering them. *If* you can bear it.'

'I can bear it.'

'It must be weird,' Gaby said, 'being alone in that house without Tom.'

'It is.'

'I mean you never are, really, are you? Where is he?'

Melissa took a breath. 'He's – quite near you, actually. He's in Notting Hill.'

'Oh!' Gaby said. 'Anyone I know?'

Melissa smoothed down the towelling tie of her robe, along her thigh. 'I don't know.'

'What's their name?'

'It's Will, Gaby, Will Gibbs.'

There was a silence. Then Gaby said, 'Will Gibbs? Tom's father?'

'Yes.'

'Oh, Lissa . . .'

'Yes.'

There was another small pause, and then Gaby said, in a different tone, more collected, more formal, echoing Donna, 'Well, I suppose that was bound to happen. In the end.' And then she added, almost as if making an effort, 'But you come. Come anyway.'

—

Gaby met her in the hall of the house in Ladbroke Road. Despite the stately presence of a mirrored console table and a pair of modern acrylic ghost chairs, the overriding impression was one of elaborate chaos, with school backpacks and random trainers and scarves and fleeces flung down all anyhow, as if their owners had been suddenly compelled to flee.

Gaby said, stepping over everything disdainfully, 'I'm not picking up anything. Not one single thing. They do it to wind me up so the only possible reaction is to ignore it all. Does Tom chuck everything about like this?'

Melissa dropped her car keys into her jacket pocket. 'There's only one of him so the effect isn't quite so dramatic.'

Gaby kissed her cheek. She was still wearing her work clothes, black trousers and an emerald green jacket with black lapels, but she had huge furry slippers on her feet, striped like zebras, with green plastic eyes appliquéd on the toes.

'Yes, I know,' she said, following Melissa's gaze. 'Liam gave them to me last Christmas. They may do nothing for my image but they are divinely comfortable and just what my feet feel like after a day in heels. You, of course, look amazing. And immaculate. It isn't surprising if Tom reacts against immaculate a bit.'

Melissa said, gesturing, 'Oh, Tom . . .' and then she said, 'It was perfect timing, when you rang. I was suddenly feeling like the very definition of spare.'

Gaby indicated the open sitting-room door. 'Let's go in there. The kitchen is a nightmare of kids squabbling over the sashimi as they say I never order enough of that and always too much rice. I could kill Quin for being out.'

The sitting room, huge and high with modern sofas and an enormous abstract painting hanging above the carefully restored fireplace, had the same air as the hall of having been thundered through by a mob in flight. There were garments scattered here and there, a discarded violin in an armchair, drifts of newsprint and magazines across the floor and coffee table, and every cushion looked as if it had not so much been leaned against as jumped on. Gaby waved towards the armchair.

'Just shift the violin. Claudia never plays it; more's the pity as she's quite gifted. I keep meaning to sell it but the list of things I mean to do would stretch from here to Oxford. I brought some wine up. Such a relief, when it's Friday and I can allow myself a drink.'

Melissa lifted the violin respectfully and carried it across to a side table which was empty except for a chessboard with all the pieces lying tumbled across it as if they had been blown over.

'I think it's just this kind of casualness and busyness of living that Tom wishes he had,' she said, laying the violin down gently beside it.

'He won't wish it for long.'

Melissa turned. Gaby was pouring rosé into a mismatched pair of glasses. 'Gaby, he might. He might just fall in love with the whole set-up.'

Gaby straightened up, and held the taller wine glass out to Melissa. 'What's Will Gibbs like these days?'

Melissa came forward and took the glass. 'I have no idea. Probably much the same as he was fifteen years ago.'

'Fatter, greyer . . .'

'Maybe.'

'And more children?'

'I think,' Melissa said, 'that that's the lure. Two little boys.'

'Ah.'

Gaby looked as if she was considering something. Then she said, raising her glass,

'Happy days.'

'Yes,' Melissa said, 'just this one happy-day glass for me. I'm driving.'

'All the more for me, then.' Gaby hesitated a moment and then she said, 'I expect you think I'm an absolute cow about Stacey.'

Melissa looked at her. 'No, I don't.'

'Well, thank you, but I bet you do. The thing is, Lissa, I simply haven't room. My team is complete. In fact there's a guy on it I'll be letting go because there's a girl I need to persuade to stay who's much better than him, and he's really surplus to requirements as it is. So, the bottom line is, I haven't got room for Stacey.'

Melissa said slowly, 'I probably should have asked you first.'

'Maybe.'

'You mean yes. You mean I should have asked you before I started getting Stacey's hopes up.' She paused. Then she said, 'Did she sound as if they were got up?'

'Well,' Gaby said, swallowing wine, 'Stacey and I had the kind of conversation that my old boss would have called sticky. So whatever she was hoping for, I made plain that I wasn't in a position to give it to her.'

'I should never have emailed.'

'As a professional woman, no, you shouldn't. As a friend, of course you should. Have you spoken to her recently?'

'No. No, I haven't,' said Melissa, sitting down in the chair where the violin had been. 'To be honest, Gaby, I couldn't think how to tell her that I was reviewing the board of Steve's company, that I recommended that he be put on it. I expect he's told Stacey, because they have that kind of marriage, but I wouldn't blame her for wondering, right now, whose side I'm on. So, no, I haven't rung her. The only person I rang was Beth. I spoke to Beth.'

'I've had a frantic week,' Gaby said. 'I haven't spoken to anyone. My mother sends me postcards with *Remember Me?* printed on them.'

'And Beth said she had been round to Stacey's.'

'And?'

'It was awful. Awful. Stacey's mother is like another person, a stranger, and Stacey was in an old shirt of Steve's with dirty hair and on the verge of tears all the time.'

Gaby filled her glass again and came to sit on the sofa near Melissa. 'Jesus.'

'Beth said that she wasn't in a fit state even to think of an interview.'

'Well, if her mother suddenly–'

'I don't think it's so much her mother,' Melissa said. 'I mean it is, of course, but it's almost more losing her job like that. The shock of it, the humiliation.'

'As men who've been sacked or made redundant have been telling us for decades,' said Gaby. 'How was Beth?'

'Sad.'

'Angry?'

'She didn't sound angry. She just sounded really, really sad.'

'But,' Gaby said, 'she's quoted everywhere. Professor Mundy's theory of this, Professor Mundy's theory of that . . .'

'But she loves Claire. She still loves Claire. You can't just turn off loving someone.'

Gaby tucked her legs up under her. 'Did you love Will Gibbs?' she said thoughtfully.

Melissa smiled at her. 'No. I really liked him and I really fancied him. But I wasn't in love with him.'

'But Tom . . .'

'I've never felt about anyone the way I feel about Tom.'

'He'll be home tomorrow,' Gaby said, comfortably.

'Perhaps. But he'll be different.'

'Will he?'

'Of course he will,' Melissa said. 'He'll have discovered what it's like to have brothers. He'll have had family supper, he'll have slept in a sleeping bag on the floor probably without anyone nagging him to brush his teeth or eat an apple or wear clean socks. He'll have – secrets. He'll have seen what it's like to live in a family.'

Gaby waved an arm. 'Like this. Permanent disorder.'

'Maybe.'

'Actually,' Gaby said, 'not all houses are like this. If Quin gave a flying . . . button about how the children treat the house, it wouldn't look like this.'

Melissa looked up at the ceiling. 'I can't help wondering . . .'

'What?'

She looked at Gaby. 'I can't help wondering what Will's house is like.'

'Of course you can't.'

'And even more,' Melissa said, 'I wonder what *she's* like. Will's little boys' mother. Tom says she's called Sarah.'

Gaby took another sip of wine. She said, almost absently, 'Is she?'

'I don't even know what she looks like,' Melissa went on. 'Partner to Will, mother to these boys, stepmother to Marnie, and now to my Tom.' She gave a little laugh. 'It's mad, really, isn't it, not to know anything about where Tom is tonight, and be absolutely powerless to do anything about it?'

'You could contact Will.'

'Yes, I suppose so.'

'You get on perfectly well, don't you?'

'Well, yes,' Melissa said. 'As long as he hardly featured in Tom's life, we did fine. But this is different. This involves Will's new family, and his house and - and *her*.'

There was a sudden eruption of noise from the kitchen, followed by thudding feet, and then Claudia burst into the room with Liam in hot pursuit, brandishing a pair of chopsticks in each hand.

'He's going for my eyes!' Claudia shrieked. She dived onto the sofa behind her mother and seized a cushion as a shield. 'He is! He is! He *means* it!'

Gaby looked across at Melissa and raised her glass. 'Family life,' she said. 'See? Frankly, you can keep it.'

CHAPTER SEVEN

GABY

The girl sitting opposite Gaby looked exhausted. She was immaculately dressed, and her hair was twisted behind her head into a neat knot, but she had dark circles under her eyes and her skin was grey. She wasn't, Gaby thought, much over thirty. Thirty-three at the outside. Married with two small children and a difficult commute across London. Her husband worked in sports media and, she said, travelled all the time. He was a sports nut, she explained, and had been when they met, so it was no good her saying she didn't know what she was getting into. This was his dream job. And it was also his choice to live within easy reach of Heathrow.

'We could,' the girl said, 'manage on his salary. Just. We talked about it.'

Gaby continued looking at her, waiting for her to say more. She went on, after a pause, in a rush, 'I thought I ought to tell you. You always say . . .'

'Yes?' Gaby said.

'That we shouldn't hide the fact that we can't cope any more. And I can't.'

'Ellie,' Gaby said, putting her glasses on. 'Can you tell me what you can't cope with, exactly?'

'All of it,' Ellie said quickly.

'Like?'

Ellie made a despairing gesture. 'I set the alarm for five thirty a.m. Five o'clock sometimes, because there's always more laundry and getting breakfast and preparing a special packed lunch for Joey because he's coeliac so he can't eat at nursery school, and showering and dressing and getting the children up and dressed and giving them breakfast and collecting Joey's stuff for nursery school and Bindy's for the childminder and out the door latest by seven twenty because I can drop Bindy off at half past, and then Joey with my friend Sam till his nursery time.'

'Where is Scott in all this?'

'He's great,' Ellie said. 'When he's home. But he's away so much.'

Gaby leaned forward. 'Do you think it will really be better, if you stop work?'

Ellie said sadly, 'It's more that I can't go on like I'm going on.'

'Of course you can't.'

'So I thought if I stopped work for a bit . . .'

'You know,' Gaby said, 'so many girls say that to me. Because the social pressure is still on girls to shoulder the family and domestic burden, it's the girls who drop out of working, and then it's the girls who find it so hard to get back in. I don't want you, Ellie, to be one of those girls.'

'But I can't–'

'I know you can't. Of course you can't go on as you are. You'll go mad. You'll fall to pieces. Does Scott earn more than you?'

Ellie looked faintly startled. 'No, but–'

'But what?'

'He gets a lot on expenses. So it kind of looks like he earns more.'

'Ah.'

'I'm not blaming Scott,' Ellie said with sudden energy.

'Nor am I.'

'Aren't you?'

'I might be blaming the *system*,' Gaby said. 'The system that produces traditionally entitled men like Scott, but I'm not blaming him personally. He's not the problem. *You* are the problem. What you want and what you feel you ought to want. Do you like working? Do you like this job?'

Ellie nodded.

'How much?' Gaby said. 'A lot?'

'Yes.'

'Would you miss it?'

Ellie's eyes filled with sudden tears. She nodded again, vehemently. Gaby took off her glasses. She said, 'Shall I tell you something?'

Ellie waited.

'You're good,' Gaby said. 'In fact, you are very good. Of all the people I've taken on in the past five years, you are among the top three. I don't want you to go. You are a team player and you are a real contributor.'

Ellie fished a tissue out of her dress sleeve and blew her nose. She said, indistinctly,

'Wow.'

'So,' Gaby said, 'I can quite see that your present situation is intolerable. I understand your sense of obligation to family life and your respect for Scott's desire for self-fulfilment. But if I can help it, you are not about to sacrifice yourself either to your children or your husband. Those days of wifely obligation to all the other people in her family are *over*, Ellie. You have all the validity as a working professional that Scott does, even if your appreciation of that is buried under your need and wish to be a good wife and mother. So, the bottom line is – I do not accept your resignation.'

'But I can't–'

Gaby put her glasses back on. 'Wait. Wait just a second. Honestly, Ellie, you're as bad as my children. I haven't *finished*.'

'Sorry.'

'For the next few months, while we see if this works, you are going to work from home. You are going to get up at a civilized hour, take the children to wherever they need to go, come home and clock in, online. A few times a week, or a month, there may be something you need to come in for, a meeting or an event, and I will expect you to be a part of all the video conference calls you are usually part of, so I don't want you in your pyjamas. And I'll expect you to work until it's time to get Joey from nursery school. We'll give it till Christmas, and then we'll see. OK? How does that sound?' She looked across at Ellie and picked up the box of tissues on her desk, holding them out. 'Ellie. Blow your nose.' She shook the tissue box. 'And if you dare to try and say thank you, I will probably change my mind.'

—

Someone had attempted to tidy the hall. One of the ghost chairs was piled with an assortment of the garments that had been scattered across the floor, and Claudia's violin lay on the console table with a Post-it note stuck to it, reading, 'Please sell me.' The writing was not in a hand Gaby recognized. On the floor, at the back of the hall, weighted by a single gumboot, was a piece of paper on which Liam had written, 'Dad and me have gone to rugby practice. Claudia's at Sophie's,' and had then signed his full name at the bottom, Liam Quintin Henderson, as if he and Gaby had never met.

Gaby stood at the foot of the stairs and called upwards, 'Taylor!'

There was no reply, but there was the sound of music, or of a steady beat at least, slightly muffled by a closed door. Gaby kicked her shoes off under the console table where her zebra slippers waited, slipped her feet into them, hobbled a step, stooped, took one slipper off and extracted a red Lego brick from the toe, put her foot back in and began to climb the stairs. She held the bannister, hauling herself up as if she was very tired or very old, until she came to the wide first-floor landing. All the doors were shut and there was the blue knitted elephant that Liam had loved as a small boy on the rucked-up modern rug in the centre of the floor. Gaby picked it up and looked at it. It was missing one eye and someone had clamped a plastic clothes peg to its tail.

'Taylor!' Gaby shouted again.

From behind the furthest door came the thump of music. Taylor shouted something inaudible back. Clutching the elephant, Gaby shuffled down the landing and opened Taylor's bedroom door.

'Why can't you use earphones,' she yelled, 'like everyone else?'

There was an abrupt silence. Taylor was lying on her bed. She didn't move. 'I didn't think there was anyone in but me,' she said. 'Why're you holding Heffalump?'

Gaby looked at the elephant in her hand. 'I met him on

the landing. He was just lying there, poor thing. Why has he got a clothes peg on his tail?'

Taylor sat up slowly. 'Ask Liam.'

'They're at rugby.'

Taylor yawned. 'Liam was so excited,' she said. 'They'll have to play with floodlights.'

Gaby said, 'Have you had supper?'

'Not hungry.'

'Please don't tell me you've eaten three bags of crisps.'

Taylor pulled off the band holding back her hair and shook it out. She said, 'If I had, I wouldn't tell you.'

'What would you *like* to tell me?'

'Nothing,' Taylor said.

'Nothing about your day or what Miss Dixon said about your history project, or what you had for lunch or whether you have made up with Flossie?'

Taylor sighed. She got up from her bed very slowly. 'I haven't,' she said.

'Have you tried?'

'I don't want to try. She put a photo of me on Snapchat I'd asked her to delete. It wasn't a rude one. I just looked really, really rubbish.'

Gaby propped herself against the door frame. She tucked Heffalump against her, as if he was a small, knitted baby. She said, 'I've had, basically, the same three best friends for over twenty-five years. Do you think Flossie might be a friend like that?'

'No,' Taylor said.

'Because of who she is?'

'Because,' Taylor said with emphasis, 'I don't want friends.'

'Ah.'

'What's that supposed to mean?'

'It means,' Gaby said, 'that you don't want supper and you don't want friends and you don't want to answer civil questions about your school day from your mother, so why is she wasting her time on you?'

Taylor bent to pick up her headphones off her bed. 'Steve rang.'

'Who?'

'Steve. Steve Grant. Stacey's Steve.'

Gaby pushed herself upright. 'When? When did he ring?'

'I dunno,' Taylor said. 'Maybe an hour ago. I didn't look. I left you a note in the kitchen.'

'Taylor,' Gaby said, 'what did he want?'

Taylor shrugged. 'To talk to you.'

'And what did you say?'

'I said you would be back by seven.'

'I wonder why he didn't ring my mobile?'

Despite herself, Taylor looked suddenly more engaged. 'Maybe he was ringing from his office landline. Maybe he didn't want the call traced on his mobile.'

Gaby looked at her daughter. 'Good thinking. Something about Stacey. Something he didn't want Stacey to know about.' She stopped, and then she said, in a different tone, 'Friendship isn't easy. Is it?'

Taylor went pink. She made a clumsy gesture which could have been a distant attempted embrace, and could equally have meant nothing much. 'I follow Flossie on Facebook,' she said. 'I know what's she doing.'

Gaby looked at her. 'Of course you do.'

'If you were on Facebook with Stacey and Melissa and Beth, you'd know more–'

From Gaby's bedroom across the landing, the landline began to ring. Gaby held Heffalump out to Taylor. 'Take him for me. That'll be Steve.'

—

When Gaby had accepted her present position, she had made it plain she wasn't going to spend her working life going round the world. Work colleagues had told her that the travel involved in investment banking was, they said with grave excitement, brutal, and Gaby had resolved, there and then, to do it differently. It was lucky that her determination had been appreciated by an enlightened Swedish chief executive, the son of a working mother, husband to a working wife, and father to three ambitious daughters. He had accepted, without demur, that Gaby would only travel when it was vital she attend a meeting in person. Otherwise, she made a point of proclaiming, one of her team would deputize for her. They were younger, mostly childless, and relished the chance. It was never a problem for Gaby to find someone eager to go to Shanghai or Singapore or São Paulo, nor for them to be equally eager to return with the results that Gaby would have achieved herself.

'I am,' she had no hesitation in saying, 'a good delegator. After all, I handpicked my team so everything they do is a reflection on me. So they'd better be good. And they know it.'

So when Sarah Parker came into Gaby's office – a surprisingly modest corner room, crowded with furniture that had accompanied Gaby all her working life – and said that she would prefer someone else to go to France that week to discuss funding for sourcing enriched fuel for research reactors at a nuclear power institute in Grenoble, Gaby was astonished.

'But it's your project! You've done so much work on it.'

'I know,' Sarah said. Her voice, after all these years in England, was still distinctly American. 'And I'd like to go. A lot. I really would. But I just don't want to travel these particular weeks. I just – don't. So I can try and change the meetings to next month, or Martin can go now.'

'Martin?'

'He's worked alongside me. He knows it all. His French isn't wonderful, but it'll be better if he *has* to use it.'

Gaby looked past Sarah through the internal glass wall of her office to where her assistant Morag usually sat. Morag would, in the normal course of things, have alerted Gaby about Sarah's request, so that Gaby could prepare a response. But there was no sign of Morag.

'I bypassed her,' Sarah said. 'She's sorting something out with Ellie and HR. So I just kinda thought I'd surprise you.'

'You have.'

'I won't make a habit of it,' Sarah said. 'It's just – there's a new dynamic in the family and I feel that has to take priority.'

Gaby looked at her. She was holding a file of papers across her chest with one arm, and smiling at Gaby over the top of it. Her dark hair fell in smooth obedient curtains around her jawline, and the hand holding the file had well-kept natural nails and was very wholesome-looking, Gaby thought, very tidy and together. And pretty. Pretty was as much the word for Sarah as it wasn't for Melissa. When you thought of Melissa, the word that came to mind was glamorous. Melissa was groomed and studied, even if apparently carelessly. When they were students together, some of the boys had behaved as if Melissa had cast a spell on them, just by being in the same room. No wonder Will Gibbs, newly divorced sixteen years ago, had been entranced to find Melissa part of the same holiday house party. And no wonder, perhaps, when it came to choosing someone to live with and mastermind family life, he hadn't gone for a Melissa, but for a pretty, capable, responsible, unthreatening Sarah Parker.

Gaby said, 'Would you like to elaborate on this new dynamic?'

There was a tiny pause, and then Sarah said, pleasantly, 'But I think you know about it, don't you?'

Gaby leaned against her desk. 'Try me.'

'Tom Hathaway's name isn't unknown to you.'

'No.'

'Nor is his mother's. Melissa Hathaway.'

'Sarah . . .'

Sarah held up her free hand. 'Just one moment–'

'I'm not playing games, Sarah,' Gaby said. 'If you want to know if I know that Tom is Will's son, and that he spent the night with you last week, the answer is yes. I knew the night it happened. Melissa told me.'

Sarah went on smiling. She said, 'But what you have never told me is that you know Melissa as well as you do. You never told me, when you hired me, that you and Melissa had been at college together.'

Gaby folded her arms. 'I didn't know until well after you started working here that you were living with Will Gibbs.'

'You knew I had a partner and children.'

'I knew that,' Gaby said. 'But I didn't know who your partner was.'

Sarah's gaze didn't waver. 'OK then,' she said. 'But you've never told Melissa, have you? You've never told your old friend that her son's father is living with a senior member of your team. Have you?'

Gaby unfolded her arms. She reached across her desk for her spectacles, and put them on. Then she said, in as conversational a manner as possible, 'Are you trying to blackmail me, for some reason?'

'Of course not.'

'Then I don't understand your air of elaborate intention. What happens between me and my friends is no concern of yours. Your concern is to arrange the funding for Grenoble in the next two weeks.'

'I think,' Sarah said, 'that Melissa ought to know. It looks like Tom'll be at our house every week, right now. He's wonderful with Jake and Ben, and even Marnie was less bratty with him around. But it doesn't seem fair if Melissa doesn't know about me working for you.'

Gaby took off her glasses. 'I know.'

'So why–'

'There was just never quite the right time to tell her. That's all.'

'I really don't want to go to France.'

'You needn't. Send Martin in. I'll tell him it's his big chance, and I'll be meaning that.'

Sarah got up and turned towards the door. She was wearing ballet flats, of the kind Taylor and Claudia wore, except that Sarah's hadn't got scuffed toes. She said, her back to Gaby, 'Who's going to tell Melissa then? You or me?'

—

Steve Grant had booked a window table in a restaurant on Canada Square that specialized in modern European cuisine – 'Whatever that is,' he'd said to Gaby – and told her that he would meet her there.

She kissed him briefly, sat down, ordered fish to eat and water to drink as if he were hardly part of the encounter at all, and then said, 'I gather things are bad at home.'

'Terrible. Losing her job was one thing. Her mother's dementia is quite another. And she only lost the one because of the other.'

'Why don't you order?'

'Because,' he said in the level, reasonable tone he found he was using most of the time at home now, 'I haven't had a chance.'

'Well . . .'

Steve held the menu up towards the hovering waiter. 'Risotto and green salad please. And Diet Coke.' He glanced at Gaby. 'Salad for you?'

She shook her head. 'I hate salad.'

'I know,' he said, 'just testing. My little joke. There aren't many jokes in my life at the moment.'

He offered Gaby a basket of Italian breads. She shook her head again. He said, 'Gaby, I need your help.'

'I thought you were going to demand to know why I didn't offer Stacey a job.'

He took a breadstick and snapped it. 'If you thought that, I'm amazed you agreed to see me.'

'I'm in a new phase,' Gaby said. She took a swallow of water. 'It's a phase of facing up to everything, telling everyone everything, generally behaving in a way that leaves everyone else to deal with the fallout because I'm not doing any previous editing.'

'Goodness,' Steve said. 'What brought this on?'

'Just life. And circumstances. And getting caught out by the consequences of trying to be professional at the same time as trying to be kind. It doesn't work.'

'So, in that case,' Steve said, 'why didn't you even have a conversation with Stacey about what to do when she lost her job?'

Gaby put her water glass down. Then she looked directly at Steve. 'I didn't want to.'

'You–'

'I didn't want to for several reasons. One, she might be brilliant at private equity, but it isn't the same as investment banking. Two, we are the same age, and equally experienced, so I couldn't expect her to be subordinate to me. It would be awkward for both of us. Three, my team is complete, and I have someone particularly good at exactly the level Stacey might have considered, and that someone happens to be the partner of the father of Melissa Hathaway's son, which is a fact I didn't know until after I hired her, and have chosen, for the best reasons, not to reveal since. All in all, the reasons added up to not wanting to talk to Stacey about it.'

'Ah,' Steve said. 'All too difficult.'

'Yes. Too difficult. You can sound sarcastic if you want to, but you know about too difficult yourself. You're living with it.'

'Too right.'

'Steve,' Gaby said. 'Before I get really angry and shout at you in a public place, will you please tell me what it is that I might help you with?'

Steve put the pieces of breadstick down. 'Stacey,' he said, in a quite different tone.

'I know. I haven't been to see her.'

Steve waved a hand. 'Not that. She's made herself pretty unavailable, I know that. But all the energy's gone out of her, all that wonderful get-up-and-go, all that enthusiasm. She goes out to get food and walk the dog, otherwise she's just at home with someone who often doesn't even know who she is. Just at home. I don't know what she's doing. I don't know how she passes the time. It's as if she got hit on the head, or something. I tell her about my day, and she's very polite about that, you know how she is, and then we watch the news, or a movie, and then someone from a local care agency comes in to help get her mother to bed and give her sleeping pills, and by then Stacey's wiped out. Not just tired, flattened. Sandbagged. She sleeps like someone's knocked her out.'

'Doctor.'

'What?'

'She needs to see a doctor.'

'She won't,' Steve said. 'I've tried. I even asked our doctor and she said patient confidentiality meant she couldn't do anything without Stacey's consent.' He picked up the breadstick again and began to break it into equal, small pieces. 'Gaby, will you see her? Will you come and see her?'

'Couldn't she come here?' She gestured around the restaurant. 'It might remind her of what she's missing.'

'I don't think she'll leave the house. Will you come to the house?'

There was a fractional hesitation, and then Gaby nodded. 'Of course.'

He swallowed. 'Thank you.' And then he said, 'I feel so guilty.'

'For having a job?'

'Yes.'

'And getting a promotion?'

'You can't imagine,' he said, 'what her reaction was, when I told her. It never occurred to me she'd be fired instead of getting what she'd asked for.'

'You knew,' Gaby said tentatively, 'that Melissa recommended you.'

'Yes.'

'And you told Stacey that?'

Steve looked miserable. He leaned sideways so that an immense white soup plate containing a tiny amount of risotto could be set down in front of him. 'No,' he said simply.

'No?' Gaby repeated.

He glanced at her. 'I couldn't,' he said. 'Not on top of everything else.'

'But Melissa thinks you told her! Melissa thinks yours is the kind of marriage where there aren't any secrets!'

Steve looked at his risotto without enthusiasm. 'Not any more,' he said.

—

'Would a whisky help?' Quin asked Gaby.

They were on the kitchen sofa together, in front of the television, which was set into the wall like a picture. A late-night news programme was running, with the sound turned off. It gave Quin a feeling of power, he said, to be able to mute all those glib politicians at the touch of a button.

Gaby yawned. 'No thanks. Anyway, it's only Wednesday.'

'Just thought it might help.'

She rolled her head against the sofa back to look at him. 'It helps telling you how utterly fed up I am,' she said.

'Good.'

'You know how I feel when life and work start leaking into each other. And usually, I'm pretty good at keeping them separate.'

'As one who falls into the lesser, and therefore neglected, half of that equation, I would heartily agree with you.'

Gaby hit him lightly on his arm. 'Stop that. You knew what you were getting into.'

'Ah,' he said, 'except that one never does know, until one is right *in*.'

'But you like it.'

'I've got used to it.'

'Please, Quin, take me seriously for a minute.'

He turned to look at her, full on. He had pushed his own rimless glasses up on top of his head where his hair, like Taylor's, stood up in a small, unruly fuzz. 'I am now very serious.'

'I think I sorted a few things at work today. Martin is thrilled and terrified about going to France alone, which is just as it should be.'

'Good. Poor bugger.'

'*Lucky* bugger.'

'Being thought lucky when you are terrified is poor.'

'So,' Gaby said, counting items off on her fingers. 'Work, once I've got those pathetic box-tickers in HR to agree about Ellie working from home, will be OK.'

'Phew.'

'You said you'd be serious.'

'Gaby,' Quin said. 'This is quite boring. We've been through all this at supper, so the repetition isn't very fascinating. And when things aren't fascinating, I have to liven them up a bit. Anyway, I know what all this is leading up to.'

She rubbed her nose with the back of her hand. 'Do you?'

'Yes,' he said. 'You have promised to talk to both Melissa and Stacey, and neither conversation is going to be in the least bit easy, and you basically don't want to have either. Do you?'

'No.' Gaby's voice was small.

He leaned across the gap between them and kissed her cheek. 'Usually,' he said, 'out of hard-won experience, I'd say at this point, well, don't. But in this case, in this instance, as it concerns two of your closest friends in the world, you just have to.'

He got up from the sofa and stood looking down at her. He was smiling.

'Sorry,' he said.

CHAPTER EIGHT

BETH

'Should I,' the girl reporter asked anxiously, 'call you Professor Mundy or Doctor Mundy?'

They were in Beth's crowded business school office, with its medley of tables and chairs, the former like her desk in Wilkes Street, invisible under stacks of books and piles of paper.

Beth smiled. 'I'm both.'

'Yes, I know, but–'

'My professorship is the senior appointment.'

The girl nodded. She was Hong Kong Chinese, a ferociously hard-working MBA student and, in her current capacity, reporting for the graduate students' online newspaper. It was hard, Beth reflected, to persuade focused girls like her to broaden their interests to embrace anything cultural, let alone anything remotely *fun*. You might persuade a girl like Linda – a deliberately Westernized version of her Chinese name – to go to a gym, or for a run, but the idea of a rock concert, or clubbing, or even the theatre, would be met with utter incomprehension. Linda was here to work, to gain the highest possible scores in her MBA, and to return home to a well-paid job, and the consequent approval of the family.

Two years in London, even if it did include all tutoring fees and living expenses, didn't leave much change out of sixty-five thousand pounds. Young women like Linda were to be regarded with sober respect, Beth told her colleagues frequently.

'They're here because they *want* to be here. These are grown-ups.'

Linda, despite the remarkable agelessness common to her ethnicity, looked both young and strangely unformed. She wore an impeccable grey flannel dress and her improbably glossy hair was tied back with a grey ribbon, but her tiny feet, in their shiny patent pumps, looked like the feet of a little girl. And her hands, moving swiftly over the keys of her laptop, were the hands of a child, small and innocent.

'Just to give you some background . . .' Beth spoke firmly, to distract herself from wondering about Linda's private life, 'I am the oldest woman but one on the teaching staff here and – I say this emphatically – it has been a huge advantage to me, throughout my career, not to come from a fancy family.'

Linda paused. 'Fancy?' she said, with only a quick glance away from her screen.

'Upper class,' Beth said. 'Effortless. I think it has been very good for me to have had to strive.'

'Striving is natural in my culture,' Linda said.

'Particularly for women?'

Linda's gaze shifted. She didn't look up or speak.

'I haven't taught here for all these years,' Beth went on, 'without noticing how many of you young women are intent on staying well below the public and media radar. And how picky you all are about boyfriends. Not just that, either. When I went to a reunion of all the women I'd done my own

MBA with, all those years ago, there wasn't a single one who had managed to succeed in combining a career, motherhood and marriage. Lots of them had two out of the three, and it was invariably marriage that was the casualty. Young ambitious women today – women like you, Linda – have to make very careful marriage choices. Don't you think?'

Linda was typing rapidly. 'My mother is a doctor,' she said. 'I never really knew my father. He left long ago. And I am an only child.'

'And here you are.'

'Yes.'

'It's gratifying to have my point proved,' Beth said. 'Even if I wish it were otherwise.'

'And your doctorate, Professor? What was the subject of your doctorate?'

Beth moved some papers in front of her. 'Organizational psychology.'

Linda looked up. Her expression was respectful.

'It has been believed,' Beth went on, 'for over a hundred years, that you could scientifically manage the workplace so that the people operating machinery could be as seamlessly efficient as possible. But we have moved beyond that with the advance of technology. Organizational psychology is now concerned with humanizing employment. My academic and lecturing efforts are geared to making work fit humans, rather than the old way of thinking, which was the other way about. Linda?'

'Yes, Professor?'

'Linda, don't you want a fulfilling work life?'

Linda looked up abruptly, almost emotional. 'Oh, yes.'

'Well, so does everyone. Everyone deserves it. That's why I

strive to improve work environments, where there is teamwork, and knowledge sharing. That is my creed. That is what I am trying to do. I am an academic but I have increasing involvement with practitioners. We have a lot to learn from one another.'

Linda stopped typing. She looked across at Beth. 'May I ask you a personal question?'

'Of course.'

'May I ask,' Linda said, 'if you have ever shared a bank account with anyone? Would you advise it?'

Beth waited a moment and then she said, firmly, 'No, to both questions.' There was a pause, and then she added, 'I have put properties in joint names with someone else, but I have never shared a bank account.'

There was another, more highly charged pause and then Linda said, almost confidentially, 'My mother says that you should never let go of your money or your friends, because you never know when you might need either.'

'Well,' Beth said. 'Well. There you are, then. Your mother is absolutely right.'

—

When she was alone again, Beth went across to the window and looked out between the buildings to the great grey curve of the river, mud-coloured today under an unhelpful sky. Young women like Linda were inspiring in their seriousness and dedication and depressing in their inflexibility of concentration, a tension she herself had been wrestling with ever since the night when Claire had – so ingeniously, in retrospect – managed to get Beth to drop the bombshell on their relationship.

Claire had not said, in so many words, that Beth's work was not profoundly worthwhile, nor that she did not believe in it. She probably would not have dared. But she had made it very plain that Beth's commitment to her career, and all the demands it made on her time and her attention, was responsible for Claire having no further appetite for being with her. Beth's work, she said, came first with her, and she couldn't bear it. Academic life – and now the research with international companies that backed up her academic findings – had made Beth not just unavailable to Claire, but dull. Dull was the word Claire had used over and over, amplifying it by saying that Beth was no fun, and pompous, and overbearingly always right. She wasn't, she said – not shouting, not upset, but with an almost steely calm – going to spend the rest of her youth with someone who treated her like a charming, but often tediously silly, *puppy*. It wasn't just offensive, given what Claire herself had achieved, it was also extremely unfair, and fairness was something Beth had always set great store by. Hadn't she?

Beth had had no contact at all with Claire for a month. There had been no telephone calls, no texts (although Beth had written, and then deleted, several), no emails. Mutual friends had tactfully, Beth supposed, reported no sightings of Claire, and Beth had deliberately avoided all their usual haunts, going back to Wilkes Street later and later, even paying their cleaner extra to come in and feed and talk to the cats if she couldn't get home – as she often couldn't – to do it herself.

The cats had unquestionably noticed. Their behaviour had become needy and querulous, causing them to mew persistently for attention and then trample across her keyboard or papers when she was trying to work. They scratched at doors if she tried to confine them or shut them out of her study, and leapt onto surfaces crowded with precious fragile things, and paced along the edge of the bath, as if forcing themselves reproachfully into her consciousness at every opportunity. Dishes of favourite food lay untouched on their special tray, and their small, neat paw marks freckled every pale surface. There were even pad prints up the window glass, indicating that in Beth's absence, the cats had made it plain to the outside world that they were imprisoned in a building where they urgently no longer wished to be.

And where, Beth had realized, she no longer wished to be either. Or, at least, she no longer wished to be under present circumstances. It was madness to live with three empty bedrooms on her own when she was frequently too preoccupied to use any rooms except the kitchen and her study. The house, still hauntingly full of Claire's presence, even if her clothes and treasured possessions had gone, felt like a manifestation of her grief and bereftness. She opened the living-room door once, and such an echo of long-ago laughter and parties rushed out at her that she slammed it again at once as if she had seen a ghost.

It was not only bleak, still living in Wilkes Street, it was increasingly untidy. Claire had been the neat one, plumping cushions and burnishing surfaces, as well as replenishing flowers and creating the kind of order that spelled a perpetual welcome. Without Claire, Beth's papers and books spilled out of her study and into the kitchen in a way that made her feel slightly desperate and out of control; the very work that she was so urgently promulgating threatened to overtake everything else and dominate her life as she constantly told everyone it shouldn't. Even her father, recovering from a hip operation, was unable to come south and occupy at least one of the spare bedrooms. If he had, Beth could have told him about Claire's departure. As it was, using his convalescence as an excuse to herself, she said nothing.

She had, in fact, said almost nothing to anyone. There had been a brief conversation with Stacey, expressions of sympathy from Gaby and Melissa, but the preoccupations of their own lives had rather swamped their ability to empathize fully with what Beth was suffering. And, to be truthful with herself, that was how she preferred it. When her heart was less sore, and her wretchedness more manageable, she told herself, she would be happy to see them. But in the meantime she simply had to grit her teeth and endure the absence of Claire, and the strangeness of having a house to sleep in which no longer felt like home.

A sudden shaft of milky sunlight pierced the low grey clouds outside the window, and alighted improbably, like a knife blade, on the surface of the water. Beth thought of Linda, girls like Linda, girls who flew across half the world to spend two years of their youth in a completely alien culture in order to fulfil their aspirations. Linda, for two years, would have no home. Even at twenty-seven, she was probably far from immune to homesickness. And here was she, Beth, homesick for a person, and for the domestic life that person had been the key to. I must stop myself indulging in thinking of her as the one and only, I must just–

On her desk, lying where she had left it, on a pile of telephone notes, Beth's mobile began to ring. She hurried across the room and snatched it up.

'Melissa!'

'Oh, Beth. So good to hear you. Are you OK?'

Beth curled into her office chair and put her head back against its tall padding. 'I'm a lot better for hearing *you*, honey.'

'I've got to be quick,' Melissa said. 'A meeting in five minutes. But can we meet?'

'Of course, but–'

'Can we meet soon?'

'Tomorrow?' Beth said. 'The weekend?'

'Tomorrow. Please. Tomorrow would be great.'

'Lissa–'

'The thing is,' Melissa said, interrupting. 'The thing is, I've discovered something. And I don't know what to do.'

—

Melissa had booked a table in a restaurant in the Aldwych, halfway, she explained, between Beth's work and her own. The table was by the windows, on the edge of the restaurant, a table Melissa said she often reserved if any of her clients wanted to discuss her findings out of an office context, but discreetly. She welcomed Beth with her characteristic fervour, ordered vodka and tonic for both of them ('Your usual – a bit much for a week night, Bethie?') and subsided onto the banquette opposite Beth.

'I want to get what I have to say over with,' Melissa said. 'And then I want to talk about you.'

'Maybe.'

'You've lost weight.'

'Only a good thing,' Beth said.

'Not for the wrong reasons.'

Beth shrugged. 'Tell me,' she said, diverting the topic.

Melissa shook her hair back from her face. 'My Tom.'

'Yes.'

'It all began with my Tom. He's in year eleven, two years behind his father's daughter by his first marriage. She started there a year ago. So, inevitably – and I have to admit, naturally – his father and he came across one another in a school context, and then began to like being in each other's company, ending up with Will watching Tom play for the under-sixteens and so on, till Tom—'

A waiter arrived, fussily serving their tumblers of vodka on the rocks. He held a tonic water bottle aloft. 'Shall I?'

Beth made a gesture. 'All the way up, please.'

'Me too.'

They waited, watching their glasses as the bubbles rose and fizzed.

'They liked each other?' Beth asked when the waiter had gone.

'They did. They liked each other so much that Tom wanted to meet Will's family, not just Marnie at school, but his little boys by his partner. I couldn't stop him. I mean, I didn't *want* to stop him, but it was hard.'

'Of course.'

'So he goes to a film with them all,' Melissa said, 'and he stays the night. And he won't say much – well, nothing at all really, except that he wants to stay again, and then again, and now he goes every Friday and sometimes he isn't back till Sunday, Sunday night, even, and I—'

'Oh, Lissa.'

Melissa checked herself and picked up her drink. 'It isn't that. Or at least, of course it is a bit, but I've just got to get used to it. I've got to realize that he was only ever sort of *lent* to me, that he's got every right to see his own father and all that entails. But that's not what I wanted to tell you.'

Beth took a sip of her drink. 'So painful,' she said sympathetically.

Melissa nodded. She put her glass down again. She said, 'Of course, Tom mentions Will's partner. I mean, he was bound to. He clearly rather likes her, but he's very anxious not to talk about her too much in front of me, you can see that. So I don't ask him but I don't flinch when he says her name.' She glanced at Beth. 'She's called Sarah. Sarah Parker. She's American.'

Beth waited. She turned her drink round and regarded it intently.

Melissa said, 'I Googled her.'

Beth sighed. 'Of course you did.'

'I knew she worked. I'd gathered from Tom that she worked in Canary Wharf. What I didn't know, until I Googled her, was that she not only worked for Gaby's bank, but that she worked for Gaby. On Gaby's team. My son's father's partner has worked for Gaby for over three years, and Gaby hasn't said a word to me. Not one word.'

Beth looked up at her. Melissa appeared to be close to tears. She said, almost desperately, 'Did *you* know?'

—

The cats had overturned a vase of dead chrysanthemums on the kitchen table across a printout of a lecture by a fellow academic that Beth had been planning to read. A light bulb was gone in one of the industrial metal lamps that she and Claire had chosen together, and the mug in which Beth had made tea sixteen hours before was where she had left it on the side, its contents strangely repellent now that they were cold.

Beth put down her work bags, and, still in her coat, set about clearing up the flowers and drying her papers with a dirty tea towel. It had been such a mixed evening, with the pleasure of Melissa's company dimmed by the misery of Melissa's distress, all compounded by her own inability to explain or justify Gaby's decision. Beth had found herself constantly emphasizing that Gaby's motives could only have been for Melissa's protection, and that her, Beth's, advice was to see Gaby face to face and ask her directly. Melissa explained that they had spent an evening together only a few Fridays ago, and Gaby had had every chance to confess that Sarah Parker worked for her, and had deliberately not done so. 'Quite enough of that,' she had then said. '*Enough*. You *did* know, you can't help and I must find my own answers. So. What about you? I really want to know, Bethie. What about *you*?'

Beth had just stared at her plate. She thought about it now, how she had glared fixedly at her uneaten sea trout and wilted spinach, and wondered if this was the moment to open the emotional sluice gates, but had decided only seconds after that she would feel worse later if she indulged herself now. So she said, instead, still looking at her plate, 'The problem now, Lissa, is that Wilkes Street feels so absolutely pointless. I mean, living there does.'

Melissa leaned forward. Her expression was full of understanding. 'Of course.'

Beth gestured. 'It'll get better.'

'Do you want to sell it?'

'Not really. Not so soon after getting it straight, rescuing it, restoring it. I just feel so – so melancholy and weary living there on my own.'

Melissa waited a moment, watching Beth's bent head. She put out her hand and lightly touched Beth's nearest one, to get her attention. 'Then don't,' she said. 'Live there on your own, I mean.'

'Honey,' Beth had laughed, shortly. 'I am so far from being remotely interested in anyone else–' and then they had been interrupted by someone Melissa knew, whose company had been one of Melissa's first clients, and Beth had taken herself off to the ladies' room and looked at herself in the mirror above the washbasin long enough to persuade herself that Claire had been entirely justified in saying everything she had said. When she got back to the table, the man was still there and Melissa was paying the bill, and then it was the usual end of evening confusion of goodbyes and taxis, and Beth had found herself on the way back to Wilkes Street, feeling that many complex hares had been set running, and that nothing whatsoever had been resolved.

She dropped the wet tea towel into the sink and pushed the dead flowers into the overflowing pedal bin. Then she tipped out the cold tea, put the mug in the dishwasher and crossed the kitchen to check her laptop. There was, as there often was, a new entry in her email inbox. She bent forward to see if it required immediate reading or deleting. It was from Claire.

—

Claire had chosen to meet in the basement cafe of a small museum. Ever the coffee addict – her caffeine consumption had been both legendary and humoured in their relationship

– she was sitting in front of a glass pot of greenish tea, with her iPad open beside it on the table. She looked stridently well, in a sharply cut suit that Beth didn't recognize, with gold hoops in her ears. When Beth approached the table, she got up with no apparent self-consciousness, and gave Beth a cursory kiss on one cheek. 'Thank you for coming,' she said, and resumed her seat.

Beth pulled out a chair opposite. 'Of course I came.'

'How are you?'

'Brilliant,' Beth said. 'Wonderful. Never been better. How do you bloody *think* I am?'

Claire was sitting very upright. She picked up her teacup and held it in both hands.

'It's good manners to ask.' She spoke as if speaking to someone hard of hearing and fragile.

'Then the same good manners,' Beth said, 'might prompt you not to be so supremely insensitive and heavy-handed.'

Claire shrugged. 'D'you want coffee?'

'That's more like it. More natural. Not "Would you like some coffee?" but "D'you want coffee?" Why aren't you drinking coffee?'

'I've given it up.'

'For any reason?'

'I needed to make some changes.'

'I see.'

'Coffee seemed like a good place to start.'

Beth waved an arm to attract the waiter's attention.

'Coffee, please. An Americano. Black.'

'Some things don't change then,' Claire said. 'How's work?'

'Very good, thank you. How's yours?'

Claire gave a little smirk. 'Ditto.'

'Well, that's good then.'

'Yes.'

'Is that green tea?'

'It is.'

'I thought,' Beth said slowly, 'that you detested green tea.'

Claire gave her cup a private smile. 'Not any more.'

Beth leaned back in her chair. 'Well, having got over the small talk, can I ask why you wanted to meet?'

'When your coffee comes.'

'Can't we talk while we wait?'

'No,' Claire said. She put her cup down very precisely on its saucer. 'I don't want to be interrupted.'

'Heavens. What can you possibly be about to say?'

'It's nothing emotional.'

'Nothing–'

'It's not,' Claire said, 'about someone else.'

'How am I supposed to react to that?'

'Any way you like. I'm just telling you that I haven't asked you for this meeting in order to tell you that I've met someone else.'

Beth peered at her. 'Do you expect to be congratulated for that?'

'My God,' Claire spat, with a sudden flash of temper. 'You don't change, do you?'

The waitress appeared and put a thick white cup of coffee down in front of Beth.

'Thank you,' Beth said, and then to Claire, 'Now tell me.'

Claire bent her head. 'In a moment.'

Beth thought of saying, 'When you have composed yourself. Of course,' and bit the words back. She resolved to say nothing until after Claire had spoken again.

'Sorry,' Claire said.

'Accepted. Although there is nothing to be sorry for. We haven't seen each other for over a month.'

'A month . . .'

'Four weeks and five days. Since you came to Wilkes Street to collect your things.'

'How are the cats?'

'Maddening.'

'Perhaps,' Claire said, 'I can take them.'

'Take them? Take them where?'

Claire paused. She studied her fingernails – unpainted – and then she glanced at Beth. 'To my new flat.'

'Your rented flat?'

'No,' Claire said, 'not there. But I've found a flat, another flat. A flat I want to buy.'

Beth had picked up her cup. She put it down again. 'Ah.'

'I wanted to see you,' Claire said, 'because I've found this gorgeous flat. On the river. Not far from Blackfriars. It's got a balcony looking downstream over the water.'

'Sounds lovely.'

'I want to buy it,' Claire said. 'I want the equity out of Wilkes Street. I wanted to ask you if we could sell Wilkes Street so that I could use my share to buy the flat. Or at least make a down payment.'

Beth smiled at her. 'I don't want to sell Wilkes Street.'

'But couldn't you, say, buy me out of my share?'

'I can't,' Beth said amiably, 'afford to.'

Claire regarded her. 'Are you getting your own back, refusing to sell?'

'I wouldn't be so petty. But I don't want to sell, and I haven't enough money to give you your share.' She paused. 'I don't want to remind you too much, but I paid for Wilkes Street almost entirely. Your share, as you put it, is what I chose to give you. I chose to put Wilkes Street in our joint names.'

'Am I supposed to thank you?'

'No. Not at all. I don't want to rain on your parade, but now is not the right time to sell Wilkes Street either for market or personal reasons. Decisions about selling up might legally be joint but they aren't morally.'

'But do you *like* living there alone?'

'No,' Beth said, 'I hate it. I was telling Melissa the other night how utterly pointless it feels.'

'So,' Claire said, her temper flaring again, 'these are just dog-in-the-manger reasons for not selling? You just want to thwart me in any plans I have for my future.'

'No, honey,' Beth said quietly. 'If I had the money to give you, you would have it. But I haven't. Everything I had went into Wilkes Street and I can't bring myself to put all that investment, emotional as well as practical, on the market just yet. I'll tell you when I can, but it isn't now.'

'But what will you do, rattling about in that house all on your own?'

Beth picked up her cup again. She said, looking at Claire over it, 'Take lodgers. Plenty of room for lodgers.' And then she added, 'Melissa got me thinking.'

CHAPTER NINE

STACEY

The dementia nurse had said that it didn't matter if Mum refused most solid food these days. Stacey could give her wholewheat cereal with milk, or mashed avocado and banana, or homemade chicken soup, if pale mush on a spoon was all she would even contemplate. She was wonderful, the dementia nurse, endlessly supportive and sensible and sympathetic, but she had ever-growing numbers of families and patients who needed her, and although she said, 'Ring me any time, day or night,' Stacey didn't like to. She and Steve had, after all, their own house and enough money. Janice was supporting plenty of people who had much less. Those were the people who rightly needed Janice; those were the people she meant. So Stacey found herself asking only practical questions when Janice came, and studiously avoiding saying, 'I don't even know what I feel about Mum any more, and that's killing me because there never was a more supportive mother in the past than my mum. But I can't bear, I really can't, what she has become now.'

Steve knew. Of course he did. Even if she held back from saying it, her feelings and her efforts not to show them were glaringly plain to someone who knew her as well as he did.

And it was evident – and unspoken – to both of them that he had no idea how to help her beyond what he had said he would do, and did most faithfully. He wanted her, she knew, to step back from her anguish and her guilt, and let him help to rescue her. Of course he wanted his house and his life back, but both those things paled into insignificance besides his wanting *her* back, his Stacey, his companion and intimate friend. He was enduring this terrible new existence – you couldn't call it a life – because Stacey insisted that was how things had to be, but nobody could be expected to endure the unendurable forever, without something giving. What form that giving would take, Stacey couldn't quite see, any more than she could see herself letting go of her profound and lifelong obligation. She tramped round the supermarket twice a week, buying organic chickens and avocados for her mother, and ordinary stuff for herself and Steve, knowing all the while that she was behaving without what Mum would once have called her common-sense head on, and being quite unable to stop.

She went to the shops when Mum was asleep in the afternoons, in front of the blaring television. If Stacey turned the television off, Mum woke up and stared wildly about her, as if a lifeline was missing. So Stacey would leave Bruno in charge, the door to the hall open, and the front door double locked, and sprint to the shops, clutching a random selection of plastic bags, none of which she would have considered using for one second in the past, but which now seemed to constitute part of her demonstration of commitment to this new and entirely unwanted way of living.

If she was quick, and resolute, and stuck rigorously to the items on her written list, Stacey could achieve a supermarket shop, door to door, in twenty-five minutes. As she put her key in the lock she could hear Bruno's claws on the hall floor inside, and his welcome ritual included, she was sure, an element of relief at her return. Of course, it wasn't fair to ask a dog to share the burden. But the fact was that a dog – or this particular dog – was of more use to her than anyone now. He never flagged in his role of guardian and companion to Mum. And what was more – you could see it in his eyes – he was glad to be of use, glad to have a job that he could do well. Often, having hauled the shopping inside, Stacey would sit on the hall floor, still in her coat, and hold Bruno hard against her, inhaling his reassuring smell. She did not, she knew, hold Steve like that these days. These days there were many, many things about their lives which were not the same.

This particular day, however, there was something palpably different. Coming up the street towards her house, bumping the heavy supermarket bags against her legs, Stacey saw that someone was leaning against the railings outside her house. It was a woman, peering as everyone did now, at the phone in her hand; a small, blonde woman in glasses. She didn't even glance up until Stacey was close enough for her to be aware someone was approaching.

Stacey stopped and stood there, burdened and astonished. 'Gaby!'

Gaby slipped the phone into her coat pocket. She said, 'Would you like to say, "Not before time, you so-called friend," and get it over with?'

Stacey shook her head. 'No—'

'Stace, I'm sorry. I'm really, really sorry.'

'Don't . . .'

Gaby moved forward and bent to relieve Stacey of some of the bags. 'Let me help.'

Stacey said, 'Fish in my pocket. For the key.'

'Your dog's going mad.'

'He would. It's what he does, when I come back.'

'I thought,' Gaby said, finding the key, 'that you wouldn't be long. Steve said you were badly housebound.'

'Steve!'

'Yes,' Gaby said. 'Steve and I had lunch last week. Didn't he tell you?'

'No.'

'Well, I'm telling you. I'm telling everyone everything right now. I only wish I'd started long ago.'

Stacey surrendered a couple of bags. She said, with force, 'Me too.'

Gaby opened the door. Bruno, insane with tension, hurtled out onto the pavement and flung himself at Stacey. She staggered back, saved by a lamppost, and dropped a bag. Gaby came running back to help, gathering up potatoes and satsumas. Stacey, leaning against the lamppost and fending off Bruno's anxious leaps and licks, shouted, 'Leave it!'

'But I–'

'Go away!' Stacey yelled. 'Just go! What do you ever do that doesn't just make things worse?'

Gaby straightened up, holding the bag. Then she walked steadily into the house and put it down on the hall floor and returned to the pavement. Stacey was still there, propped against the lamppost, Bruno at her feet. Her eyes were closed and she was still holding the rest of the shopping.

'I came to say sorry,' Gaby said. 'I came, in good faith, to say sorry and to try and explain what had happened, and what my thinking had been. But I can see that I was wasting my time.'

Stacey, immovable against the lamppost, said nothing.

'I promised Steve I'd come,' Gaby said. 'I said I'd come, and I have. I probably should have rung first, but as I thought you'd be at home, there didn't seem much point and it *felt* better, somehow, just to turn up. But it was clearly a mistake. On top of all my other mistakes. So I'll go. It seems the only thing to do.' There was a pause and then she said, 'Bye, Stacey,' and Stacey heard her heels going purposefully down the street, down and down until she turned a corner and they faded away.

—

It was only later that day – much later in fact, when Steve and Stacey were moving wordlessly round each other in their bathroom, with toothbrushes and towels – that Stacey said, indistinctly through a mouthful of peppermint-flavoured foam, that Gaby had been.

Steve was vigorously towelling his face. He paused, and lowered the towel so that he could look at Stacey in the huge mirror that covered the wall above the twin basins in their bathroom.

He said, emphatically, 'Good.'

Stacey spat into the basin. 'You would think that. Since I gather you put her up to it.'

Steve didn't speak. He shook out the towel, turned to sling it over the glass side of the shower cubicle, and went through to their bedroom, still without a word.

Stacey finished flossing her teeth, ran a comb through her hair, hitched up her pyjama bottoms and padded through after him. He was sitting up in bed with his new black-rimmed reading glasses on, flicking through the *Evening Standard*. Stacey got into bed under her side of the duvet. 'What's my horoscope for tomorrow?'

'I have no idea.'

'Won't you look it up for me?'

'No,' Steve said.

Stacey turned to look at him. He was not a sulker, and he usually kept whatever temper he had well under control. He didn't look angry, actually, now. He just looked removed. Stacey said, 'It's no good Gaby coming crawling around having treated me like she has.'

Steve said nothing. Stacey went on, 'I was flabbergasted to see her. I dropped the shopping. But then – then I told her to go away. I didn't want to hear all her false excuses.'

'False?'

'Of course they'd be false.'

Steve put the newspaper down. 'How do you know they were false if you wouldn't even let her explain what they were?'

'Her tone was all wrong. From the start. You know how she is, facetious and everything. She didn't *sound* sorry.'

Steve took his reading glasses off. He was still not looking at Stacey. He said, 'So Gaby came up here on a working afternoon to try and explain, and you sent her away before she had even started?'

'You knew about it, you and she–'

'Stacey,' Steve said, 'let's stick to this afternoon, shall we?'

'I shouted at her. I shouted at her to go away.'

'Very constructive.'

'Don't speak to me like that!'

Steve leaned over to put his reading glasses down on his bedside table. He said, 'I rang Gaby to make an appointment to see her. We had lunch together so that I could ask her two things. One, why she hadn't even considered helping you with a job, and two, would she please come and see you, and explain to you herself, and maybe help you in some other way.'

'*Help* me?'

'Yes.'

'Steve,' Stacey said. 'What do you mean, *help* me?'

At last Steve turned to look at her. He looked suddenly like a stranger to her, a healthy, attractive, purposeful middle-aged stranger.

'You need someone to help you out of this situation. It's doing you no good. It's doing us even less good. If it were making a difference to your mother, I'd be in two minds about going on like this. But it isn't. It's all getting worse and worse and more and more pointless. I thought if Gaby, who is very practical, could see the situation for herself, she could start to help you find some kind of solution. As well as clearing the air, I hoped you could both come up with some ideas for the future. That's why I contacted Gaby. That's what I asked her to do. For you. For us.'

Stacey was hunched over her knees as if examining the weave on the duvet cover at close quarters. 'I won't be treated like this,' she said, in a low voice.

Slowly, Steve got out of bed. He stood looking across at Stacey, wearing, as he had for years in bed, boxer shorts and a white T-shirt. He said, without particular heat, 'Nor will I.'

'You haven't—'

'Stacey,' Steve said, interrupting, 'Stacey. I am going to New York next week, for five nights. There are two of us suitable to go, and I said quite frankly to Gian Carlo that I really needed to get away. I do. And you need to do something, too. You need to go and find Gaby and apologize to *her*, and then hear her out.'

Stacey went on staring at her knees under the duvet.

'I'm not going to do anything melodramatic,' Steve said. 'I'm not going to sleep in the guest room. But I'm going down to watch television for a while. OK?'

Very slowly, Stacey nodded. She heard him go through to the bathroom and find a bathrobe, and then his footsteps, muffled, as he went down the stairs. Very carefully, she lifted the duvet and slid down underneath it, lying as still as if she were very cold. She lay on her side, her eyes open, and stared into the shadows of the room. What, oh what, had she done?

—

She had clearly lost weight, quite dramatically, but she didn't feel any better for it. She had never been exactly thin, but her clothes and her body, in the past, had at least looked as if they belonged together. She had never been a beauty after all, and had once caught sight of a work assessment that described her as 'pleasant looking', but she had definitely, and successfully, once made the most of what there was. But now, standing in front of the long mirror in her bedroom in her favourite suit – black and white flecked tweed with black leather piping – the sight was appalling. The skirt hung limply on her as if it couldn't be bothered to try and accommodate itself to someone of so irrelevant a size, and the jacket stood away from her neck and shoulders, gaping and alien.

She slid a hand inside her waistband. It was loose, but not that loose. Had her hips and thighs shrunk? What had happened? She didn't *feel* thinner after all, she just felt lumpy and bloated, saturated with all the wrong things, misery especially. She threw the suit jacket on the bed and stepped out of the skirt. Standing there in her underwear and a silk camisole from her previous life, with bare feet and unbrushed hair, she regarded herself in the mirror with something close to both revulsion and despair.

It was Janice who had sent her upstairs, Janice the dementia nurse, who had brought Mum a remastered DVD of *Gone with the Wind*, starring Vivien Leigh, which Mum was now utterly engrossed in. Stacey had told Janice that she had an appointment in Canary Wharf and Janice had said she was pleased to hear it, and why didn't Stacey book herself in at the hairdresser and try on some of her old work clothes?

'You want,' Janice said cosily, 'to make a nice impression at an interview.'

Stacey had not contradicted her. She had not explained that she was not going for an interview. At least, she told herself, she could spare Janice the awkwardness of responding to the truthfulness about going to Canary Wharf to make an apology.

'You're under a lot of strain,' Janice would say, if she knew. 'You're not to beat yourself up about it. I'd like to see you have a bit of a life of your own anyway.'

Janice had arranged for a fellow dementia nurse to come in for the afternoon while Stacey went to Canary Wharf. She made this arrangement – as she did every arrangement – sound both utterly normal and no trouble at all to organize and fulfil. What she would think of Stacey, staring at herself in the mirror with revulsion, was strangely consoling. She would not be repelled by either the sight or the situation. To her, there were no surprises in people's capacity to behave in a strange or shocking way. Stacey picked up her jacket and skirt and put them back on their hanger. Janice was, in so many ways, to be emulated, not least in her refusal to allow her outlook to be distorted by human difficulty. Stacey carried her suit on its hanger across to the cupboards that she and Steve had had designed for their bedroom when they first moved in, to put it away. She would, as she suspected Janice would suggest she did, work through all her professional clothes until something, in some combination, would remember that it and her body had once had something in common.

She hadn't actually spoken to Gaby. She had rung at a time when she could be fairly sure that Gaby would be in a meeting, and left a quick message to say that she would make an appointment through Morag. Morag of course had been very warm on the telephone, blithely unaware of any problem between Gaby and Stacey, and full of heavy-duty sympathy about Stacey's mother. She had said that Gaby was finished with all meetings by four o'clock the next Tuesday, so why didn't Stacey pop by then and they could have a cup of tea together? Stacey could tell that all the time they were talking, Morag was simultaneously typing and that kind of multitasking busyness gave her the same feeling she'd had at fourteen, at school, when she was the last in her particular group of friends to have a boyfriend.

'Lovely,' she'd said to Morag. 'Four p.m. on Tuesday. Give her my love.'

She unhooked a sweater dress from the rail in her wardrobe. Navy blue. Round necked. Knee length. Always, before, slightly on the tight side. Would that do?

—

Gaby had sent a text, saying that they would meet in a coffee shop near her office. It was a branch of a huge chain, and when Stacey arrived Gaby was perched on a high stool by a counter against the window, engrossed in something on her phone. The heels of her shoes were hooked into the stretcher of her stool and she had pushed her glasses on top of her head so that they held her hair back, like a band. Stacey went to stand silently beside her. Without glancing in Stacey's direction, Gaby said, 'Hello, Stace.'

Stacey said, 'I don't quite know where to begin . . .'

Gaby finished whatever she was doing on her phone. 'Nor me.'

Stacey hitched herself onto the empty stool next to Gaby. 'There might have been a reason for how I behaved last week, but there wasn't an excuse.'

Gaby sighed. She put her phone face down on the counter top. 'I know.'

'Gaby–'

'D'you want some tea?'

'In a minute. After I've said that I think I went – I've gone – a bit bonkers.'

Gaby turned to look at her. She said, with emphasis, 'I would have, too. In your place.'

'It was insane,' Stacey said, 'to think you could possibly help with a job. Melissa should never have suggested it, and I should never have got worked up about it.'

Gaby nodded. She said, a little unsteadily, 'I'm never very good when people are lovely.'

'I'm not lovely. I just gave myself the most god-awful fright. I'm still stuck, but I'm not quite so blinkered, crazy, stuck.'

'We ought to be in a bar,' Gaby said. 'We ought to have real drinks, to cry into.'

Stacey dropped her coat off her shoulders. It was astonishing to see her knees, flesh-coloured in new tights, below the hem of the sweater dress. She hadn't seen her knees in weeks. She said, 'We haven't got together since I lost my job.'

'It doesn't mean I haven't thought about you.'

'I know.'

Gaby said, 'Are you sure you don't at least want a cup of tea?'

'No,' Stacey said. 'No. What I want is to tell you about that afternoon. What happened that afternoon after Jeff fired me. I haven't told anyone.'

'Not even Steve?'

'No.'

'Why not?'

'He was so full of his own promotion that evening that somehow there was never the right moment, and then all the Mum crises began and went on and there's never been a chance to . . .' Stacey stopped.

'To what?'

'To tell anyone how devastating it was. How – how I thought I'd stopped being me and been handed some completely strange other person instead.'

Gaby turned her whole body to face Stacey. 'Tell me now.'

Stacey swallowed. 'I sat on a bench–'

'Did you? Where?'

'In St Paul's Churchyard,' Stacey said quietly. 'I crammed all the stuff from my desk just anyhow into the first empty bin I could find, and then I just sat on a bench and – and thought I couldn't breathe, I was in such shock, such delayed shock, that I often wonder if I'm over it yet, or whether something in me isn't damaged, broken forever.'

Gaby reached across and put a hand on Stacey's knee. She said, urgently, 'Are you missing this? Is being back somewhere like this making you feel that this is where you belong?'

Stacey looked at her for a long moment. Then she said, 'No. Actually.'

'No?'

Stacey looked round her, at the other people in the coffee shop, at the people going purposefully past the window, in Canada Square. 'Not this,' she said.

'So I'm off the hook?'

Stacey gave her a half-smile. She said, 'You always were. It was just – me feeling trapped. So trapped.'

'Like you did that afternoon?'

'There was a woman,' Stacey said. 'A woman at the other end of my bench. She wasn't in a burkha or anything, but she had a headscarf on, and a big sad cloth bag, not a handbag, and she was phoning her whole family to tell them she hadn't got the job she'd gone for. As a shelf-stacker. She offered me some water. She told me to go home and get on with it. She – she admired my handbag.'

Gaby glanced at it and smiled. 'Nice bag.'

'She said that. She said it in – in quite a meaningful way.

As if women like her with nothing but a shopping bag to carry their stuff in wouldn't stand a chance of being even a shelf-stacker. She said that the supermarket people knew, just by looking at her, that they didn't want her. Wrong clothes, she said, wrong bag. She sounded angry, not sorry for herself, as if she was saying what am I not *getting* about this work thing in London, what don't I understand?'

'Poor her,' Gaby said. Her voice was quiet. 'Poor you.' She slipped off her stool. Even in high heels, she was very small, standing on the floor looking up at Stacey on her stool. She picked up her phone and her bag. 'Come on,' she said. 'This place won't do. Let's find somewhere where we can talk properly.'

Stacey hesitated. 'I've only got till six.'

Gaby was already heading for the door. 'Me too,' she said.

—

Janice's carer friend said that there'd been no problem that afternoon. Mum had watched *Gone with the Wind* again, and had tea and one of the flapjacks Stacey had left out – 'Thank you for that, dear, so nice to have something homemade', and the dog had been as good as gold, 'He's lovely, isn't he?' – and the phone hadn't rung, but then, they didn't, these days, did they, what with everyone having their own mobiles?

She said she was happy to stay on and help settle Mum for the night, after supper, but Stacey said that a nurse came in from the local social-services-approved agency for that, thank you so much, but another visit would be much appreciated as she herself hadn't been out properly in weeks, and it had been wonderful. Janice's friend regarded her. She said, 'My father used to tell us that there was a fine line between generosity and self-sacrifice, and that our mother mostly lived the wrong side of it.'

'He sounds fun.'

'He was. Too much fun to put up with our mother for too long. I've got one mother and three stepmothers.' She nodded towards the sitting-room door. 'Imagine that multiplied by four.'

When she had gone, Stacey went into the sitting room and, as she often did, sat in a second armchair, close to Mum's TV chair, and started talking. Mum glanced at her without particular recognition but without alarm, either, and then went back to watching a nature programme about meat-eating pitcher plants.

'I've been to see Gaby,' Stacey said. 'You remember Gaby? She was the little blonde one I was at uni with. Well, she's now a really big shot in a huge international bank. You'd be amazed to see her, Mum. Tiny Gaby controlling all that money, and all those people. We went to a cocktail place and I had two mojitos. I shouldn't think you've ever had a mojito in your life, have you?'

Mum's gaze didn't waver from the screen. Some kind of climbing shrew had cleverly learned to balance on the rim of the pitcher plant and lick off the alluring sweetness without falling in. Mum's expression was blank. What, exactly, was she seeing?

'We talked about so much,' Stacey said. 'Over an hour of solid talking. And I found myself telling her all kinds of things, like I'd been longing – don't get me wrong, Mum – to go back to work, but I was surprised to find that being in Canary Wharf didn't turn me on as I thought it would. I thought that I'd be gazing at all those busy people and envying them and longing to join them, but I wasn't. I didn't. Isn't that weird? I'd imagined that all I wanted was to be back where I used to be, but something in my head seems to have moved on a bit, and however much I'm dying to feel my own purpose and power again, it doesn't feel right returning to what I used to do. Does that sound insane to you?'

The shrew had now clambered nimbly off the plant and a large flying insect had replaced it and fallen in. There were extraordinary camera shots of the liquid in the pitcher plant engulfing the struggling insect. How had they done that? How had they got a camera *inside* a pitcher plant? Mum's expression betrayed not a trace of wonder or curiosity.

'Mum,' Stacey said, 'can you imagine how I feel? Can you visualize this really strange sensation of liberation?'

Mum suddenly said, with emphasis, '*Good* dog.'

'Yes,' Stacey said. 'Yes. He is, isn't he?' She looked at Bruno, lying still but watchfully by her feet. 'Too good, perhaps. I think I'm going to ring the dog walker we used to use when we were both working, because I think Bruno deserves some time off duty, too. Mum, I'm just going to go and email Steve. He's still in New York. He's in New York till Thursday night, their time. I'm going to email him and tell him I've seen Gaby. It'll please him, that I've seen Gaby.'

She stood up. Mum's gaze remained fixed on the screen. Bruno tensed.

'It's a fascinating choice,' Stacey said to him. 'Either stay here and watch man-eating flora or come downstairs and watch me send an email. Up to you.'

Bruno gave the smallest wag of his tail and settled his chin on his front paws.

Stacey touched Mum's nearest cheek. 'You win,' she said. 'He's chosen to stay with you.'

—

Only weeks ago, her inbox was full, full to overflowing all the time, a perpetual cascade of queries that she had had to fight hard not to see as innately reproachful. These days, after almost an afternoon away, there were only three, and two of those were spam. The third one, she saw with a small but distinct jolt of dismay, was from Steve. He had written it as he got up in his New York hotel, at six fifteen on an American morning.

Their parting, when he left for the airport at the weekend, hadn't been exactly uncomfortable, but it had been formal and wary. He had gone into the sitting room and kissed Mum goodbye, and pulled Bruno's ears, then held Stacey in his arms for a short but not censorious time, and kissed her mouth with purpose rather than passion, and climbed into his waiting taxi without looking back. It had been impossible to tell if he had implied anything with this brisk behaviour, or if she had just imagined that he had. He had texted, as he always did, when he had checked in for the flight, and again when he had landed. He had texted each day to inform Stacey of his schedule, using exactly the language and abbreviations he always used, and signing off each text with a double kiss. But he had not emailed. This message – not very long, Stacey could see, at first apprehensive glance – was the first expression of anything other than practicalities in four days. Only a few months ago, they would both have considered four days to be a very long time to be apart.

Sweetheart,

Unsurprisingly, being away has given me a bit of perspective. So I am writing to give you notice of something that I want us to discuss when I'm back. I didn't want to bounce it on you, hence writing this now.

The thing is, Stace, this isn't working, having your mum with us. I don't know if it's helping her, but it's killing you and it's killing me and it's killing us, as a couple.

Frankly, my priority is us. I want our life together back. And the only way I can see that happening is for your mum to go into a nursing home.

This is what I want us to talk about.

See you early Friday.

Love as ever,

S.

CHAPTER TEN

MELISSA

There were flowers on the kitchen table. Melissa never put flowers on the table, but only in specified – and styled – places in the house, and only white flowers at that. These flowers were orange and red, orange gerberas and scarlet roses, and they had been, plainly, dumped in a jug, a black and white pottery jug that Melissa would only use for, say, milk, and then parked on the kitchen table. As a statement.

Melissa went to the foot of the stairs. An intercom had been installed when the house was renovated from top to bottom, to avoid having to shout from the basement to the upper floor. But since Tom had started his visits to his father's house, Melissa had stopped using it out of an instinct that any device that even hinted at the impersonal was to be shunned. She climbed the stairs to the hall. On a black marble shelf above the modern radiator there stood a glass cube vase crammed with identical, upright white tulips. Melissa put a foot on the lowest step of the stairs leading up to the first floor, and took a breath.

'Tom?'

There was no reply. A faintly discernable thump of drums indicated that he was in his room and had music playing.

Melissa went up the stairs to the first floor. The door to her bedroom was open and this being one of the days her Portuguese cleaner and ironing lady came, there was a pleasingly neat pile of ironing on the long stool at the end of her bed. Beatriz, who ironed every last scrap of fabric in the house, would have left a similar pile in Tom's room, which he would fail to see and, if not specifically instructed to put away, would allow to disintegrate gradually into the tangle of worn and unworn clothes and shoes that covered a large area of his bedroom floor. Beatriz adored him. He was, she said, so polite to her. She didn't in the least mind picking up after him. What else did his mother expect, of a fifteen-year-old boy? *Ai meu Deus*, what are you *like*?

Melissa went on up to the top floor. The door to Tom's bathroom was open and there was one of his navy blue towels on the floor, as well as a crumpled copy of the football magazine Tom swore he had outgrown at least two years before. His bedroom door was shut. Melissa knocked. The music thumped on. She knocked again, louder. There was a fractional pause and then Tom shouted, 'Come!'

She opened the door, cautiously, into the noise. Tom was at his desk, lamp on and correctly angled, with his laptop open and his left forefinger halfway down a page in his French dictionary. Without apparent hurry, he transferred the forefinger to the volume control on the iPod in front of him, and then got up to cross the room and give his mother a leisurely kiss.

'Hi,' Tom said.

She smiled at him. 'Thank you for the flowers.'

He ducked his head. 'Nice and bright.'

'For once, were you thinking?'

He grinned. 'Well, yes.'

She looked past him. 'Homework?'

'Of course,' he said.

'Usually there isn't much of course about it, is there?'

'It's French,' he said, as if that explained everything.

Melissa moved past him and sat on the edge of his bed, beside Beatriz's pile of devotedly precise ironing. She looked round the room. It was apparently unchanged, but to her eye it looked slightly but distressingly uninhabited. She said, 'Did you have fun last night? At Dad's?'

Tom nodded. He went back to his desk chair and sat sideways in it, so that he could see her. 'Jake's got football. At last. He's really suddenly *got* it. And it's all he wants to talk about, all the time. He knows all the players' ages and everything. He's kind of *fanatical*.'

'How old is he?'

'Nine. He'll be ten in January.'

Melissa said, 'I expect you know the exact date.'

'The seventeenth,' Tom said. And then, 'We made a lasagne.'

'We?'

'Sarah made us boys do all of it. Sauce and everything. I had to cut the onions up because of using knives. It was cool.'

'Sarah.'

'She thinks men who can't cook are out of the Ark.'

'Oh.'

'Ben just wants to make cakes. But I like meat and chopping. Thing is, if you get stuff on the floor at Dad's, Henry'll clean it up.'

'Henry?'

'Dad's dog. Well, he's a family dog, really. He's supposed to sleep in the kitchen, but usually he's on my feet at night. Snoring. I never knew dogs snored.'

Melissa said, 'It sounds like fun. The whole set-up.'

'It is,' Tom said. 'It's wicked.'

'Then it was extra sweet of you to buy me flowers.'

'You'd hate it, though,' Tom said, warmly. 'It's chaos. Sarah's quite tidy but Dad and the boys are chaos. And Marnie won't let anyone in her room and Sarah says there's good reason for that.'

Melissa took a deep breath. 'Darling. Are you happier there?'

Tom looked amazed. 'No. Why should I be?'

'I just thought that maybe all the cooking and not having to tidy up, and the dog . . .'

Tom spread his hands. 'It's different,' he said. 'It's not like here. That's all.'

'So you wouldn't—' She stopped.

'No,' he said, 'I wouldn't. I love it, but I wouldn't.'

She bent her head, abruptly overwhelmed with relief and gratitude.

'Mum,' Tom said. 'Don't be such an idiot.'

'Sorry.'

'And don't say stupid sorry!'

Melissa took a deep breath and sat upright. She smiled brightly across at him. 'You can make *me* a lasagne now.'

'OK.'

'I did think of a dog, you know. But I worried about it being here on its own so much.'

'I don't want a dog here.'

'Oh. Right.'

'I don't want a dog. I don't want here to be different. I don't want you to try to be what you aren't.' He stopped.

Melissa said, gently, 'I sense a "but"?'

He said, almost sheepishly, 'But I do want something.'

'Ah. Something you think I'm going to find hard to give you?'

He turned away slightly. He said, 'Don't see why it should be.'

'Try me.'

Tom looked up at the ceiling. He said, loudly, 'I want to change my name.'

'*Change* it? From Thomas?'

'From Hathaway,' Tom said.

There was a small, stunned silence. Then Melissa said, 'Oh, Tom.'

His head whipped down and round to look at her. 'I don't mean get *rid* of Hathaway.'

'Oh.'

'I mean *add* to it. Add Dad's name to it, too. I'll always be Tom. I just want to be Tom Hathaway Gibbs.'

He put a hand out towards Melissa, as if trying to reaffirm a connection.

'That's all,' he said again.

—

The office, down its mews, was, apart from the perpetual distant city rumble, almost silent. It was the end of a long and productive day – meetings all morning, an exhaustive interview with a significant American financial journal in the afternoon – and now Melissa was alone at her desk, Donna having left early for her six-monthly dental check-up. Melissa had finished her notes on the morning's meetings – interviews with the board of a major insurance company – and was now staring at her screen and the website of the UK Deed Poll Office, which promised that a legal change of name only cost the applicant fifteen pounds sterling.

The doorbell rang. As Donna was usually there to answer the door, Melissa initially took no notice. It rang again, for longer. It was, doubtless, either someone selling something Melissa didn't want, or more likely, a neighbour agitating about the way cars had been parked in the mews to whom Melissa would have to explain, patiently, that as she never brought her car to work, she couldn't really help. She spoke indifferently into the front-door intercom system,

'Hello?'

There was a pause. And then a voice said, 'It's Gaby.'

Melissa pressed the button that illuminated the small screen beside the intercom, which revealed Gaby, in her parka and running shoes, standing gazing up at the front of Melissa's office.

'Wait there,' Melissa said.

She ran down the stairs and across the carpeted space to the front door, which Donna insisted was kept double locked at all times. Gaby was standing four or five feet away, her bag on her shoulder and her hands in her pockets.

'Gaby.'

'Surprise, surprise,' Gaby said.

'Come in.'

'I'm on my way home.'

'I guessed that.'

'And I didn't ring because I knew Donna would tell you and I wanted to be sure you didn't scarper.'

'Donna's gone to the dentist.'

'And when I came down the mews,' Gaby said, 'I saw your lights were still on, so I knew you'd be here. That I'd find you.'

'Yes,' Melissa said. 'Well.'

Gaby stepped into the office and dropped her bag on the floor. She looked at Melissa.

'I've got some explaining to do, haven't I?' she said.

Melissa waited. Her mind, still trying to absorb the fact that for fifteen pounds only, Tom could take this first, giant step away from her into his own independent life, was not focusing on having Gaby standing in her office and taking her battered old parka off to reveal a neat work trouser suit underneath.

'I'm afraid I haven't anything to offer you, except tea or coffee,' she said automatically.

'Lissa, I don't want tea or coffee. I want, if you must know, to feel less awful and guilty.'

'About Sarah Parker?'

'About you, and Sarah Parker. I've been wondering how to say it, how to find you to say it to. I got my fingers burned with Stacey, so I don't really want them burned a second time with you, so if you want me just to go, now, or you are so angry you don't ever want to speak to me again, could you just say so at once and get it over with?'

Melissa said tiredly, 'I'm not angry.'

'What a relief.'

'I'm – I'm a bit miserable. About several things, of which you are one. But I'm not angry.'

Gaby reached up to hang her parka on the coat stand.

'I'm very pleased – and grateful – that you're not angry.'

Melissa took a step back. 'D'you want to come upstairs, to the sofa?'

'Only if you want to talk to me.'

'To be truthful,' Melissa said, 'I don't really want to talk to anyone.'

Gaby clasped her hands in front of her. In her trainers, she was almost a foot shorter than Melissa. 'Fair enough.'

Melissa said nothing. She was standing at a distance from Gaby, her arms folded, seeming more cold than antagonistic.

Gaby went on, 'The thing is, Lissa, that there isn't really an explanation. There was no scheming, there wasn't even a reason except that I didn't want to tell you, because it was difficult. When I hired Sarah, I had no idea she lived with Will Gibbs, and when I did discover the connection I thought I'd wait, and then I waited for it to be the right time to tell you, or easier or something, and that time never came, and anyway I'd begun to tell myself that I wouldn't need to tell you because yours and Sarah's and Tom's paths would never cross, and then they did, and I just – funked it. I just funked saying anything, and now I've made it all worse because I was such a wuss. I am so sorry, Lissa; I am really, really sorry. But I haven't got any excuse or explanation or anything, except saying to you that telling you that Will's partner was working for me was just in the mental file marked Too Difficult.'

Melissa was looking away while Gaby was speaking, not at anything in particular, just not at Gaby. When Gaby fell silent, Melissa left a little pause and then she said, in a low voice, 'That's OK.'

'You don't sound as if it is.'

'It is. It really is.' Melissa sighed. 'Water under the bridge, anyway.'

'Lissa, I never meant to hurt you. I may be, as Quin is constantly telling me, unable to live in the fruit bowl without bruising my fellow apples all the time, but you are very dear to me and I *really* hate causing you pain.'

Melissa looked directly at her. 'I know.'

'Good. As long as you are in no doubt.'

'No.'

'Lissa . . .'

'In the great scheme of things,' Melissa said, 'what you did or didn't do falls into the category of puzzling rather than painful, anyway.'

Gaby looked enquiring. 'Meaning?'

Melissa held out a hand. 'Come upstairs with me. Come and look at what's on my screen. And I'll tell you what it signifies.'

In her pocket, Melissa's phone began to ring. She said, 'I'm ignoring that.'

'Don't,' Gaby said. 'Answer it.'

'No.'

'*Answer* it, Lissa!'

Melissa pulled her phone out of her jacket pocket, glanced briefly and uncomprehendingly at the number on the screen, and put it to her ear.

'Hello?' Then she swung round to look at Gaby again, eyes wide. 'Will!' she said.

—

Melissa demurred at the idea of lunch. Or a drink. She would, she said, meet Will for coffee, or something else anodyne like tea, or breakfast. Privately, she also added, in a very public venue, and when she asked herself exactly why she was making all these extremely specific conditions about meeting her son's father, found that she had no reasons to give, only instincts. Which were, she told herself, fastening her earrings that morning, borderline hysterical and not to be admitted to anyone. She was to meet Will for coffee in the lobby of a smart hotel off Whitehall, which suited her schedule that day, and which he had seemed most anxious to oblige her over.

The hotel lobby had a huge central flower arrangement in it, circled by a deeply padded bench, with small tables forming yet another ring beyond it. Will was already there, traditionally accessorized by a newspaper, but alert enough to her punctual arrival to be on his feet by the time she reached him. He was smiling.

'Melissa!' He put the newspaper down, stepped away from the padded seat and took her shoulders in his hands. Then he kissed her cheek. Firmly.

'Hello,' she said.

He dropped his hands. 'You look wonderful.'

'Thank you.'

'And before we go any further, can I say what a really fantastic job you have done with Tom.'

'Please,' Melissa said. 'Don't talk like that.'

'Like what?'

'In that sort of stagey barrister way. Tom is great because Tom *is* great.'

Will gestured as if to an audience. 'Shall I go out and come in again?'

She laughed. 'Maybe.'

'I'm nervous,' Will said. 'Aren't you?'

'Yes.'

'Well, start by sitting down.'

She sat. He lowered himself back to where he'd been sitting. He said, 'Coffee?'

'Tea, please.'

'Earl Grey, if I remember? Or is that irritating too?'

'No,' Melissa said. 'It's accurate.'

'You're so successful,' Will said. 'I'm a bit daunted.'

'A lot of the men I deal with professionally say that. I think it's a kind of flirting. To try and disarm me.'

Will said, 'I'm not up for that.'

'No.'

'I just wanted us to be able to talk about Tom. Now he's beginning to know – or to think he knows – his own mind.'

'Yes.'

Will looked at her. He was greyer, certainly, than sixteen years ago, but not visibly stouter, and his gaze was as merry and curious as when she had first encountered it across a huge candlelit dinner table in an anglicized villa in Provence. He said, 'I don't think you want to help me make conversation, do you?'

She said truthfully, 'I don't know what I feel.'

'About me?'

'About seeing you again. But mostly, about Tom.'

'This name change thing.'

'Yes.'

'Do you hate the idea?'

She began to shrug herself out of her coat. 'Not hate . . .'

He leaned forward to help her. Nice hands. She had forgotten he had such nice hands. Tom had inherited them, but she had stopped thinking of them as being attributable to anyone but Tom.

'But it's thrown you?'

'Yes.'

Will deftly extracted Melissa's coat from behind her and laid it on the bench beside him, on top of his own coat. Then he summoned a nearby waitress and ordered Earl Grey tea for both of them.

'Tea for you, too?' Melissa said.

'I'm trying to drink less coffee.' He leaned forward. He said, 'I don't think Tom should be allowed to do anything that makes you unhappy. He can at least be told to wait.'

She looked at her hands. 'I'm not unhappy, exactly. I'm just thrown. First Marnie comes to Tom's school, then you and Tom get together, then there's Tom's sleepovers and now this. I know, intellectually, that what's happening is all inevitable and natural and organic, but I can't seem to get my heart where my head is. I feel – I feel, kind of *jolted*.'

Will was regarding her. Being looked at like this, with distinct interest and approval, was definitely not disagreeable. After a pause, he said, 'Tom is very anxious not to hurt you.'

'I suppose you've talked about me.'

'Of course.'

'I'm not hurt,' Melissa said. 'Or, if I am, it's by the situation. Not by Tom.'

'Or me.'

The waitress arrived and began the ponderous process of unloading teapots and cups and strainers from her tray. As if she wasn't there, Will said, 'And before you say, how typically male and solipsistic to put myself in the equation, I *am* in it, because I'm Tom's father.'

'And I probably had too many years of not having to take account of that.'

'And now you do.'

The waitress put down a saucer of lemon slices and a pot of sugar sachets. She straightened up. 'Enjoy your tea.'

Melissa glanced up at her. In her twenties, neatly groomed in her hotel uniform, East European probably.

'Thank you,' Melissa said. 'Where are you from?'

The girl smiled. She had corrective braces on her upper teeth. 'Riga.'

Will said, 'I went to a legal conference in Riga once. Lovely place.'

'Thank you,' the girl said politely. She stepped back. 'Have you everything you need?'

'Yes thanks,' Will said. He looked at Melissa again. 'Are you saying you need more time?'

'I don't think so.'

'Because what I think,' Will said, 'what I think will help us all, is to normalize things as much as we can, to have more contact, be mundane, get used to each other. I don't think apportioning blame is particularly helpful, but I should have been more present, more active in Tom's life when he was little, and then all this now wouldn't be such a big deal for any of us.'

Melissa picked up the teapot and began to pour. 'Perhaps.'

'I've got a suggestion.'

'Have you?'

'Yes. Could you stop messing about with the tea and concentrate?'

'I can pour and listen,' Melissa said. 'I'm female after all.'

'You're telling me. But I want you to look at me while I make this suggestion.'

Melissa put the teapot down and folded her hands in her lap with exaggerated obedience. 'Well?'

'I think,' Will said, looking at her in a way that demanded she look straight back at him, 'I think that you should meet Sarah.'

CHAPTER ELEVEN

GABY

'The office, you'll be glad to know,' Gaby had said to Quin the night before, 'is a happy place. Martin has done surprisingly well in Grenoble and has enrolled himself on a ten-week course of French classes on Tuesday evenings two minutes from the office. Ellie has done her first week working from home and the arrangement has wrinkles but it's certainly going to be possible. And Melissa and I are going to celebrate our reconciliation next Friday in a manner that most definitely won't include you, but will, equally definitely, include dressing up and not being in our kitchen.'

Quin said he was glad to hear all that. He'd been cooking at the time, making one of his famous frittatas that involved ingeniously using up all manner of ill-assorted leftovers in the fridge, which he would then, mysteriously and miraculously, manage to cajole all the children into eating. He had always cooked, and equally, had always been able to make the children eat – even Liam, who regarded anything not out of a packet that he could examine first as part of a plot to poison him. Liam liked pale food, pale, soft food. But even Liam would somehow eat his father's frittata.

Gaby had bent over to inhale what was in the wide frying pan. 'Yum.'

'It will be. And I'm pleased that you're pleased because then you'll be easier to live with.'

Gaby kissed his cheek. 'I may not be easy,' she'd said. 'But then I am never, ever dull.'

The sky outside the window of her office the next morning was unquestionably dull. There was nearly always a wind in Canary Wharf, but when the sun was out, the wind seemed only to polish up the glass and steel and burnished stone, so that it all shone to the point of glittering. But on other days, like today, a low grey sky made the wind feel nothing but bad-tempered, whipping up savage little swirls of litter and dust, disarranging hair and umbrellas, blowing impudently up skirts. Gaby stood at her office window and looked at the familiar view with affection, the square dotted with purposeful people, the soulless planting, the gleaming facades of global capitalism opposite. It might all be ethically questionable, or at the very least up for vigorous debate, but at that moment, even under such a sky, it looked to Gaby both nicely familiar and satisfying. It was one of those rare and fleeting moments when she felt comfortably slightly ahead of the game rather than battling breathlessly to keep up with it.

It was early still, not yet eight thirty in the morning. Gaby was usually in soon after eight in any case, but this morning, Morag had informed her, Sarah Parker had asked for a quick meeting before the big divisional meeting at nine o'clock that was regularly scheduled for the first Wednesday of each month. Sarah wanted, of course, to talk about Martin and Grenoble, and Martin's future because of Grenoble, and the possibility of his being put on another case of equal importance. Gaby was going to explain to Sarah that she wanted to see further consolidation of Martin's capabilities before he was given anything more significant, but she was in complete agreement with Sarah that he looked as if he really was at last beginning to fulfil his potential. The meeting was scheduled for eight thirty and would, Gaby reckoned, take ten minutes, fifteen at the outside, which would allow her ten more minutes to refresh her memory of the meeting papers before she went up in the lift, to the penthouse level at the top of the building, and the immense company boardroom with its limitless views across London.

'Gaby,' Sarah said from the doorway.

Gaby turned round. Sarah looked as collected as usual, and was also, as usual, holding a file of papers against her chest, with a pen in her hand. She was smiling.

'Good morning,' Gaby said. She gestured to the chair reserved for visitors. 'Sit down and tell me about Martin.'

Sarah sat. She put her file and her pen on Gaby's desk, in front of her. 'He's done great,' she said, still smiling.

'I'm glad to hear it. And about the French lessons.'

'But,' Sarah said, 'I think that we need to see him build a bit more on what he's done before we hand him anything else.'

Gaby put both hands on the back of her desk chair, but did not sit down.

'Then this is going to be a very brief meeting, I'm glad to say,' she said, smiling herself. 'I agree completely.'

Sarah looked unnaturally composed. 'Martin isn't why I asked to see you,' she said.

There was a tiny pause.

'Oh?'

'I wanted,' Sarah said, 'to ask something for myself.'

Gaby took her hands off her chairback and moved to sit down. Then she leaned her elbows on her desk and clasped her hands together. 'Briefly,' she said. 'I have a meeting.'

'I know. I'll be quick.'

Gaby waited. She looked steadily at Sarah, reminding herself to see Sarah as a valued colleague, not as the putative stepmother of Melissa's Tom. It was not easy. In fact it was fiendishly difficult.

Sarah said, 'I know it was a battle to get HR to agree to Ellie's flexitime, but that was because the request was a novelty and HR doesn't care for novelty. So I think a second case would be easier.' She stopped.

'Come again?' Gaby said.

Sarah shifted in her chair. She was clasping her hands together now, Gaby noticed.

'Gaby, I'm asking for myself,' she said.

'What?'

'I'm asking for some flexitime for myself. I'm asking to work a couple of days a week at home.'

Gaby regarded her. 'Why?'

Sarah gave the smallest shrug. 'The children need me.'

'Do they now. More than they did when they were in pre-school?'

Sarah looked very slightly evasive. 'Jake is playing up at school–'

'Boys do. They just do. Liam does, all the time. And Quin some of the time, at nearly fifty. I thought you had a nanny who took care of them after school.'

'I do.'

'Is she leaving?'

'No.'

'Sarah,' Gaby said, 'what is all this about?'

Sarah was now holding the arms of her chair. 'Gaby, I need to be at home more,' she said, in a different tone.

'Why?'

'Did you ask Ellie why?'

'Ellie was different,' Gaby said. 'Ellie is junior, Ellie earns a third of what you do, Ellie has a toddler and a baby and a travelling husband. Ellie is *not* part of this conversation.'

Sarah took a breath. 'OK. OK, I shouldn't have mentioned her. But my own situation still needs me to make some changes.'

'Why you? Why not Will?'

Sarah said nothing.

'Because,' Gaby pursued, 'Will is part of the problem.'

'No,' Sarah said. 'It's the children. There's so much to do, now Tom comes regularly. I have to be there more, for the family.'

Gaby said, not unkindly, 'Sarah, I can't spare you.'

'But–'

'You are a crucial part of the team. If you start working flexitime, it sends the wrong message to the whole team, just as Ellie's situation sends the right message to her level of the team. You have to show commitment, you have to demonstrate to all the naysayers that you *can* hold it all together. And you *can*.'

'I know,' Sarah said slowly. 'I can. But suppose I don't want to?'

Gaby stood up. 'Then you must make another decision

and I must accept the consequences. Which I'd be very sorry about. Now, I have to go to another meeting.'

Sarah rose too. 'I know,' she said, sadly.

'And I know something else, too,' Gaby said. 'I know something you probably don't know I know. But my new attitude means that I'm not hiding anything from anyone, and everyone will just have to deal with the fallout of my telling them.'

Sarah glanced at her. 'What do you mean?'

'I mean,' Gaby said, moving to pick up the papers Morag had left ready for the divisional meeting, 'that I know Melissa is coming to supper with you all next week, and that prospect, I imagine, is enough to unsettle anyone.' She went briskly across to the door, and then turned to add, 'But sacrificing work is absolutely the *last* thing you should do about it.'

It was a long day. The morning meeting, badly chaired, meandered on for two hours, interrupted by conference calls which appeared to Gaby to be chiefly characterized by their self-importance. The remaining hours of the day were plagued by indecision and bargaining for the sake of argument, and equally afflicted by squabbles among the junior members of the team worthy, Gaby told them exasperatedly, of a primary-school playground. Returning, irritatedly, to her office in the late afternoon, Gaby was intercepted by Morag.

'I've got Claire on the phone, I'm afraid.'

'Claire? Beth's Claire? What does she want?'

'I don't know. It's the third time she's rung today. I told her you were in a meeting but she just rang again. D'you want me to tell her you've left the office?'

'No,' Gaby said tiredly. 'No. She'll only ring again. I'll talk to her.'

The telephone console on her desk was flashing green on line one.

'Hello? Claire?'

Claire's voice was warm. 'Gaby. How good to hear you. How are you?'

'At this moment,' Gaby said, stepping out of her shoes onto the carpeted floor of her office, 'on the grumpy side. One of those days.'

'Isn't it odd, the way you never see them coming?'

'This one needs to be over so if you'll excuse me hurrying you, what did you want?'

'To meet, please,' Claire said.

'Meet? Why?'

'I need your advice.'

Gaby groaned. 'That always means a favour.'

'No,' Claire said. 'Advice. I mean advice.'

'About Beth?'

'Not exactly. But indirectly.'

'Of course.'

'Will you? Just fifteen minutes? I'll come to you.'

'Yes,' Gaby said. 'You will. Breakfast on Thursday.'

'I can't–'

'Then I can't.'

'Whoops,' Claire said, rallying. 'Then I'll change my diary. Breakfast on Thursday.'

'Eight o'clock.'

'You don't change, Gaby, do you?' Claire said, laughing.

Gaby bent to pick up her shoes. 'As a matter of fact, Claire, you'll find that some elements of me have changed very much. Which means I'm telling Beth that we're breakfasting together and I'll probably tell her what we said, afterwards. OK?'

There was a pause. Then Claire said, with an effort at insouciance, 'Of course. Fine by me. Even – even if it doesn't help anyone, especially Beth, actually.'

'I'm tired,' Gaby said, 'of being put on the spot by other people. Your spot, your problem. Do you still want to have breakfast?'

There was a longer pause. Gaby stood waiting, her shoes in her hand, her other forefinger on the button that would end the telephone call.

Then, 'Yes,' Claire said, and rang off.

—

Liam had commandeered his mother for Saturday breakfasts. Saturday mornings, Gaby and Quin had decreed in a rare moment of parental unity, were for the girls to finish – the operative word, Quin maintained, was 'finish' – their weekend homework in order for it not to become a regular Sunday-night bone of exhausting contention, and so Liam, who so far had been made to finish all homework at school on Fridays, seized the opportunity to lean heavily on his mother's conscience. Two Saturday breakfasts in his favoured Notting Hill restaurant in a row were enough, in his view, to establish a significant and emotionally loaded tradition. Gaby would eat fruit salad with mint and basil sugar, and he would tackle a stack of American pancakes with maple syrup and, if he could wangle it, a side order of toffee sauce – plus a banana if that was the price paid for getting his own way over the toffee sauce. The idea of a helping of berries instead of banana filled him with theatrical horror.

'It was as if,' Gaby said to Quin later, 'I'd suggested a double helping of steamed spinach.'

They had Liam's favourite table whenever possible, on the first floor looking down into Pembridge Road. Liam would order – a cappuccino for Gaby, a vanilla milkshake for himself – and then he would devote himself to a highly coloured account of the past week's happenings, as if Gaby had been on the moon rather than home every evening and firmly monitoring his sisters' Facebook accounts on a daily basis.

He sat, sucking noisily on the straw that had come in his milkshake, and recounted, in between gurgles, the dramas of his school week, and the near disasters that he had narrowly avoided. When his pancakes arrived, he always offered his mother one, in a display of manners that Gaby seldom saw at home, but which his friends' mothers seemed remarkably impressed by.

'I won't, thank you, darling, but it's nice of you to offer and very surprising.'

Liam, lifting up each pancake in order to spoon toffee sauce between the layers, said reasonably, 'Manners are wasted at home.'

'*Are* they?'

Liam licked his fingers. 'Nobody'd notice.'

'*I* would.'

'There I'd be, all please and may I and the girls'd just look at me as if I was crazy or pay no attention and it'd all be a real waste of effort.'

'It shouldn't be an *effort*,' Gaby said. 'Being polite should be as natural to you as breathing.'

Liam poured more sauce. 'I don't think about breathing.'

'That's exactly my point.'

'This,' Liam said, 'is quite boring. Can we talk about something else?'

'Like what?'

Liam forked in a ragged mouthful of pancake. 'Like can we have a dog?'

Gaby sighed. 'You know the answer already, darling. It's no, because our lives would make life for a dog very dreary and lonely.'

'Then a cat.'

'Well–'

'Cats sleep all day anyway. Or a guinea pig. Or a hamster.'

'Hamsters die.'

Liam began to load up his fork again. He said, 'So will you, one day.'

'Will you mind?'

He thought for a moment. 'Probably.'

'Thank you, darling. What will you miss about me?'

He put another mouthful in. He said, 'I always know when you're in the house. It's the crashing and banging. Weird, really, because you aren't very big, for a grown-up.'

Gaby was laughing. 'And the girls? Will you miss the girls?'

Liam rolled his eyes. 'There'd be some peace and quiet without the girls.'

'Claud isn't very noisy. Or big, for that matter.'

Liam looked at Gaby's bowl. He said, 'Is that melon?'

'Yes. Would you like some? It's nearly white, it's so pale.'

'I'll think about it,' Liam said, and then added, casually, 'Claud's got a boyfriend.'

'She can't have! She's thirteen!'

Liam licked toffee sauce off his spoon. 'I'm not supposed to tell you.'

'I'm sure not. Why are you?'

'Because,' Liam said portentously, 'I thought you ought to know.'

'Why?' Gaby demanded. 'What are they doing?'

Liam shrugged. 'Texting and stuff. Instagram. She wants him to come to ours.'

'Why hasn't she *asked* me?'

Liam waved his spoon. 'Dunno.'

'Was she *planning* to ask me?'

'Dunno.'

Gaby leaned forward and grasped Liam's wrist. 'Tell me everything you know.'

He sat back in his chair in order to pull his arm out of her grip. He said, 'That's all.'

'Who is it?'

'Who is what?'

'Liam,' Gaby said. 'What is the name of Claudia's so-called boyfriend?'

Liam looked up at the ceiling. Then he looked at the tables either side, at a young man who was also eating pancakes.

'He's eating *bacon* with his,' Liam said, disapprovingly.

'Liam,' Gaby said warningly.

Liam smiled at her. His front teeth had grown in with a considerable gap between them which meant, in a year or two, an orthodontist and braces. Taylor had been quite obliging about her braces because she was a girl, and concerned about her appearance. It was difficult to think of Liam giving two hoots about how he looked. Gaby sighed. She said,

'Darling, I'm not prying, but Claud is only thirteen, and I am her mother and need to protect her, so I also need to know the name of this boy.'

Liam picked up his fork again and stabbed at a pancake. He said, with every appearance of candour, 'I have no idea.'

'Really?'

'D'you know, Mum,' Liam said, just before he put the forkful into his mouth, 'I'm not really bothered. I've told you she's got one. Isn't that enough?'

Gaby looked hard at him. He had toffee sauce smeared on his chin. 'No,' she said.

—

Claire said she would have porridge and green tea, but nothing with the porridge, thank you, except blueberries.

Gaby said, 'I thought you were a coffee and croissants girl.'

'I was.'

'Have you noticed,' Gaby said, 'how wellness and fitness have become the new moral imperatives? Do you think you are influenced by that?'

Claire didn't look at Gaby's cappuccino. She said carefully, 'It's possible to be sensible without being priggish.'

Gaby regarded her. She looked wonderful. Clear skin, shiny curls, bright eyes. It crossed Gaby's mind, with a sudden pang, that she hadn't seen Beth in months. She said, 'I'm cross with you.'

'Yes,' Claire said, 'I expected that.'

'It's hard to be in the company of someone who has made one of my closest friends so unhappy.'

Claire poured tea. 'That isn't why I asked to see you, and

I don't want to talk about it, except to say that there were reasons and they were good ones.'

Gaby pushed her croissant aside and leaned her arms on the table. 'What do you want to talk about, then?'

'Beth.'

'I thought–'

'I'm worried about Beth,' Claire said. 'Whatever you think about my conduct, I'm still concerned about Beth. I always will be.'

Gaby didn't move. She said, staring straight at Claire, 'I think it takes a particular kind of nerve, and a particular kind of callousness, to break someone's heart and then say how worried you are about them.'

Claire put down her spoon. 'I didn't express myself properly. I didn't mean I was concerned about Beth's emotional state. I meant I was worried about the way she's living. About – about the company she's keeping.'

'Are you mad?' Gaby said. 'What on earth are you talking about?'

'She's got lodgers in Wilkes Street now. Melissa suggested she take lodgers. Or so Beth said to me. So she did. She's got three lodgers, kids from Queen Mary's doing post-grad this and that, and she's kind of adopting their way of living and boozing and all that, and Wilkes Street is a tip.'

'Dear me,' Gaby said sarcastically.

Claire flushed slightly. She said, 'Beth values her dignity. She's a distinguished academic and her image is very important to her. And to her theories.'

Gaby folded her arms. 'And how do you know this lurid information?'

'I have a friend,' Claire said steadily, 'who is a junior fellow at Queen Mary's.'

'Your spy.'

'Gaby, there is a *lot* of gossip.'

'Clearly,' Gaby said. 'All very shocking. Professor Mundy kicking her heels up in a Shoreditch bar.'

Claire took no notice. She resumed eating her porridge in small, tidy spoonfuls. Then she said, 'You can jeer at me if you want to. But the situation remains. It isn't – *right* to know Beth is out on the town with a bunch of kids who can't possibly have fun without getting wasted.'

There was a brief silence. Gaby went on studying Claire primly eating her porridge. Then she said, 'So what?'

'Well,' Claire said, putting her spoon down deliberately, 'obviously, *I* can't do anything because I'm the last person she'll listen to at the moment, but you could.'

'Could what, exactly?'

'You could go to Wilkes Street,' Claire said. 'You could go and assess the situation and see if Beth would actually like some help.'

'*Help?*'

'Yes. People often get trapped in situations they'd love to be rescued from, and don't know how.'

Gaby didn't move. 'Claire. Of course I can't go to Wilkes Street on such a mission. Of course I can't. None of us can.'

'But if Beth needs help? Needs a way out?'

'Then she'll ask for it.'

'Oh no,' Claire said. 'That isn't her way. That isn't her way at all.'

Gaby made an exasperated sound. 'I can't go to Wilkes Street,' she said again, but with less conviction.

Claire waited a few seconds and then she said quietly, 'I think you should.'

'But why?'

'How else can you gauge the situation? How else will you know what's going on, unless you can see the way they're all living?'

Gaby narrowed her eyes and uncrossed her arms. 'What are you suggesting?'

Claire spread her hands out on the table and looked at them. Then she folded them in front of her. She said, 'It's nothing to do with me, of course–' and then stopped.

'Go on,' Gaby said.

'Well,' Claire went on, as if with the greatest reluctance, 'that house is Beth's biggest investment. Her biggest asset.'

'And?'

'If – if it's trashed, or something, that will affect her, won't it? I mean, if she wanted to *sell* Wilkes Street, at some point in the future, it wouldn't be to her advantage financially, would it, if it looked like some kind of student lodging?' She paused and then she added, 'I'm thinking of Beth.'

Gaby picked up her long-cooled coffee cup and then put it down again, with a small bang. She didn't look at Claire. 'Of course you are,' she said.

—

'It was so transparent,' Gaby reported later to Quin. '*She* wants Beth to sell Wilkes Street because Beth was nice enough to put the house in their joint names even though Claire only paid for about a tenth of it, and so she cooked up this little scheme.'

Quin was lying along the kitchen sofa in Ladbroke Road,

with the evening newspaper tented over his hips. Gaby was perched on the sofa arm by his feet.

Quin said, 'You've never liked her much, have you?'

'I *tried*. God knows, I *tried*. For Beth's sake. But I could never believe she was good enough for Beth. Too self-involved. I have to tell you that I *really* don't want to go to Wilkes Street.'

Quin picked up the paper. 'Then don't.'

'I mean,' Gaby said, surveying her slippered feet, 'I don't know what I'd say to Beth. I don't have an excuse to go to Wilkes Street. I'd have "arch snooper" written all over me.'

Quin sighed from behind the paper. 'I said, don't go.'

'But if–'

'Someone else can go.'

'Claire came to me.'

'Claire came to you,' Quin said, slowly lowering the paper, 'because you have history together, because of Sarah, and because she thinks you'll talk practicalities to Beth, and practicalities are what she's after. I agree Melissa isn't the person. But what about Stacey?'

'Stacey!'

'Yes. Can't Stacey talk to Beth? Can't Stacey go to Wilkes Street?'

Gaby sighed. 'Stacey's in the middle of this nursing home trawl. She says it's all she does, go from one to another with all the grim ones saying they have a bed and all the bearable ones saying they don't.'

Quin sat up slightly. 'Give her something else to think about, then, won't it?'

'You sound hearty *and* heartless.'

Quin threw the paper on the floor. 'It's because I *have* a

heart that I'm suggesting Stacey as the right person to go to Wilkes Street and you as the completely wrong one.'

Gaby smiled at him. 'Sorry.'

'Stacey's trapped,' Quin said with energy. 'Beth's apparently trapped. Doesn't it make every kind of sense for them to try and free each other?'

'Yes. Sorry. I just didn't want to have to do it.'

'I *know*.'

Gaby slid down onto the sofa cushions and laid her right hand on Quin's nearest leg.

'Something else,' she said, in a different tone.

'What?'

'On Saturday, over breakfast, Liam told me something. I've been meaning to mention it to you ever since.'

Quin took his spectacles off, buffed them briefly against his sweater, and put them on again. 'What?'

'He told me,' Gaby said, 'that Claudia has a boyfriend.'

'Well,' Quin said. 'Yes.'

'You *knew*?'

'Claudia said something last week. They went to the flicks together. In a gang, but they were together.'

'They?'

'Yes.'

Gaby took her hand off Quin's leg. 'Who is he?'

Quin groaned. 'You're not going to like this. Which is why I put off telling you—'

'Tell me. Tell me *now*.'

Quin looked at her. He tried a what-can-you-do smile.

Then he said, 'Tom Hathaway.'

CHAPTER TWELVE

BETH

As part of her determined emotional rehabilitation, Beth had ordered some new clothes. She had, since becoming a full professor, settled into a way of dressing in which she felt both authoritative and most herself, and to this end had chosen a tailor who called himself Felix Rigby Bespoke, in Brushfield Street. She had been fitted for two new trouser suits with waisted jackets and white cuffed shirts to wear underneath them. One suit also had a waistcoat, of a slightly different weave, to go with it, and Felix Rigby himself had urged Beth to add a fedora, and a watch chain with a little scissor charm hanging from it.

Beth had declined the ostentation of the hat and the watch chain, but succumbed to a cobalt blue satin lining in one suit jacket. Then she had bought a dozen oysters from the oyster bar nearby, and walked home past a pleasing juxtaposition in Fournier Street of a shuttered house whose front window was artfully stacked with antlers, and next to it, the uncompromising facade of the Bangladesh Welfare Association. There was also, no distance away, Beth's favourite Indian grocer, who advertised his speciality in bright plastic adhesive letters against the glass – 'Beautify your dish with Ambala pickles'.

It was a Saturday. On Saturdays and Sundays Brick Lane seethed with market life, from the stalls selling Québécois Poutine to the man dispensing coffee out of the roof of a London taxi. Since in the past, on Saturdays, she and Claire had made a ritual of Brick Lane food shopping, it was still safer not to plunge into that human tide now, and risk the poignancy of memories being aroused by the sheer smell of it all, the spices and the fresh coconuts, the frying and the dark heaps of raw sugar in the chocolate shop. It was altogether more prudent to focus on the thought of her new clothes, and carry her oysters in their plastic bag of crushed ice across Commercial Road, down Fournier Street past the antlers, left at the mosque on Brick Lane, and left again into Princelet Street, a walk which formed a square around home and gave an illusion of having been out on a Saturday morning without risking too much nostalgic danger.

Beth let herself into the house. Banker the cat was asleep on someone's knitted beanie hat drying on the hall radiator. There were boots scattered across the hall floor and a rucksack on its side, plus an umbrella balanced on the high-backed modern chair that Claire had had upholstered in burnt orange linen with oversized chrome studs. Beth had suggested that Claire take the chair with her, but Claire, with tears in her eyes, had exclaimed that it had been especially designed for that very space, couldn't Beth even see *that*? To Beth's eye, its blatant stylishness was rather mellowed and improved by being used as an umbrella stand, but the fact that it had been a considered choice of Claire's made it obstinately, maddeningly, precious. Beth picked up the umbrella, shook it, folded it and laid it on the floor under the chair, alongside a pair of neon plastic clogs and a splitting shopping bag of books. Claire would have hated the disorder, as much as she would hate lime green clogs in her hallway. There hadn't been lilies in the black glass vase in weeks.

Beth went through to the kitchen and put her bag of oysters in the fridge. The fridge was full of disorganized items, packets and tubs with curling foil lids, splitting cardboard sleeves of drink cans and yoghurts, torn nets of citrus fruit. The table was clear of used mugs and bowls but littered with papers and cartons, among which Bonus sat, his gaze fixed on Beth as if daring her to tell him to get off the table.

'Get off!' Beth shouted.

Bonus didn't move. Beth picked up the nearest magazine and brandished it. '*Off*, I said!'

In a leisurely manner, Bonus strolled to the edge of the table and lowered himself to the seat of a chair at one end. Then he sat down and resumed staring at her.

Beth went across to the sink to fill the kettle. She said to him, mildly, '*Awful* cat.'

The draining board was piled with approximately washed china, and someone had left a pan soaking in the sink. It had, from the state of the water in it, been used for scrambling eggs, which was, Beth acknowledged, the devil to wash up, but also these days, extremely easy to ignore. She carried the full kettle across the kitchen to plug it in. She had no trouble now in ignoring a pan that would be hard to wash up, just as she had no trouble in reverting to coffee made in her old plunge pot rather than in the designated coffee maker. When her colleague came to lunch later that day, they would eat oysters with unsalted butter and newly baked soda bread, and drink some Albarino, or even a Riesling, as an accompaniment, but Beth wouldn't be fussed about matching the plates or even, possibly, laying the table. She would clear one end of the kitchen table perhaps, but the papers and journals and juice cartons were – such an exasperation to Claire! – almost as irrelevant to her as if they had been invisible. It was such tiny but definite displays of defiance, she noticed, that had made the last few weeks more bearable than those that had painfully preceded them.

Beth took the coffee pot and a mug across the passage to her study. The study looked, she told herself, like a caricature of an academic's lair, every surface laden with sliding piles of paper, every shelf crammed with books. Claire had organized for one wall to be entirely covered with cork tiles to form a giant pinboard, knowing Beth's propensity for mislaying business cards and invitations, and this was now haphazardly dotted with both, as well as with newspaper cuttings and photocopies of articles, furled up round their drawing pins as the paper on which they were printed dried out in the warmth of the room. Looking at it, Beth tried to see the room through eyes other than her own: eyes that found it hard to believe that such ordered and logical thoughts as hers could possibly emerge out of such a confused and chaotic setting. She couldn't do it. Or, she told herself with an inward smile, she didn't choose to do it.

She put the coffee pot down on an American journal of academic business studies and leaned across the disorder to fire up her computer. Her inbox was full of all the usual rubbish, inevitably, but there were three emails of interest, and one from Stacey. Stacey! Beth immediately sat down at her desk, her empty mug still in her left hand, and opened the email.

Bethie, dear,

Are you OK? Are you? I don't know what I am, but there are changes. I only hope they're progress, but I think I wouldn't recognize what that is any more. Are you in later? Could I come round for a cuppa?

Stacey xx

Beth balanced the empty mug on the nearest stack of papers, and pulled the keyboard towards her.

'Yes,' she typed rapidly. 'Yes! Here any time after 4 p.m. All news then. X's. B.'

The front doorbell rang. Beth pressed 'send', stood up and went down the stone passage – that carefully sourced limestone was a daily pleasure – to the front door, stepping over the boots and the rucksack to get to it.

Her lunch guest was standing on the pavement, a Japanese expert on post-war economic power shifts, with a sheaf of lilies in his arms.

'Ren!' Beth said, smiling.

He bowed. He was tall for a Japanese, a northerner, and was wearing – absurdly – a deerstalker hat.

'I am too early.'

'No, no, you aren't at all. Come in.'

He held out the lilies.

'I think I remember,' he said, smiling himself, 'that these were what you liked?'

—

Stacey, Beth thought, looked better. She was wearing her own clothes, not cast-offs of Steve's, and her hair had the unmistakable bounce of not having been blow-dried at home. She put her bag down next to Dr Fushimi's lilies and turned to give Beth an embrace which spoke more, Beth thought, of warmth than of neediness. Then she said, 'You look better!'

'I was just thinking the same of you.'

'Thank you for letting me come.'

'Saturdays,' Beth said, 'are good days for impulses. I tend to work on Sundays because the world seems to leave me alone more, on Sundays.'

Stacey looked round the hall. She said, 'You're working?'

'Oh yes.'

'And – playing, a bit?'

Beth gestured at the items on the floor. 'The lodgers have improved the playing side of life.'

'The kids–'

'They're hardly kids. The youngest is in his late twenties. One of them is married, with a wife and baby in Preston. Would you like tea?'

'Not especially,' Stacey said. 'Thank you.' She indicated Banker, on his radiator. 'So you've still got the cats.'

Beth said, 'I've still got most things.'

'The house . . .'

'The house, the cats, all the furniture Claire didn't want. What about you?'

Stacey put her hands in her pockets.

'I feel awful,' she said, hunching her shoulders.

'Your mother.'

'Yes.'

'She went into a nursing home.'

'Yes.'

'Stace–'

Stacey held up a hand. 'Please don't. Please don't give me all the excellent reasons why that was a justifiable thing to do. It isn't why I came. It isn't why I emailed. It's happened, but it's beside the point.'

Beth went past Stacey and opened the door to the sitting room. It was where, these days, the lodgers watched television, and the result was palpable.

'Goodness,' Stacey said, from the threshold.

'Different, huh?'

'Well, yes. I mean, it's the same room but . . .'

'Messier?'

'Yes.'

'More accessible? Less of a stage set? More ordinary?'

'All those things.'

Beth moved into the room and retrieved a couple of cushions from the floor. 'Where would you like to sit?'

'Anywhere.'

'Or you could lie. The lodgers lie on the sofas all the time. As you see. When I was growing up we had something called a settee, in the front room, and you sat on that with your knees together, and if my mother had dared to put a newspaper under your feet, she would have. I like seeing people lolling. It makes up for all those Sunday afternoons on the settee.'

Stacey sat down on a low grey sofa and leaned back. She said, 'I haven't been in this room since your party, your housewarming party.'

Beth tucked the cushions she was holding either side of her. 'There now. Comfy?'

Stacey laughed. 'Of course!'

'Good to see you laughing.'

'Bethie. Can you laugh sometimes now?'

'Yes.'

'Is it – the lodgers?'

Beth looked surprised. 'No. Why should it be?'

'Aren't you having quite a good time, with the lodgers?'

Beth sat down in a leather tub armchair which she and Claire had bought from a fledgling furniture designer in Hoxton.

'They're a nice crew,' Beth said. 'Two men and a girl. PhD theses and some teaching to make ends meet. One of them goes back to his family in Preston every weekend and the girl has a boyfriend in Brighton, so she's only here in the week anyway. They only eat stuff out of plastic pots, it seems to me, but they're no trouble. The cats have calmed down like anything since they came. And I probably have too. I don't look after them, or anything, I wouldn't want to, but I definitely prefer the house with life in it.' She looked at Stacey and grinned. 'I don't mind a bit of mess, after all.'

'No,' Stacey said.

Beth looked at her, slightly sideways. She said, 'Stace?'

'Yes?'

'What is it? Is it your mother?'

Stacey shook her head.

'Then what's the matter with you?'

Stacey said reluctantly, 'I'm here – on a mission.'

'Ah.'

'There was a kind of anxiety . . .'

'Go on.'

'About you being – exploited by your lodgers,' Stacey said. 'Taken advantage of. You know.'

Beth gave a little laugh. 'Led astray?' she said, comfortably.

'Well, not exactly.'

'But enough to send you round here. Was it Melissa?'

'No.'

'Gaby?'

Stacey shifted a little against her cushions. 'Gaby rang me.'

'To say?'

'Oh, Bethie – sorry, really sorry, but the word was that you had lodgers who were trashing the house and—'

'Stop!' Beth said. She balanced her elbows on the sides of her chair and laced her fingers together. 'Gaby said this? Gaby said I was under the influence of wild student lodgers?'

'No. Gaby just said she'd been told—'

'Stop,' Beth said again. 'Stop right there.' She looked at her hands and then she looked over them, at Stacey.

'Claire,' Beth said, with emphasis. 'That sounds like Claire.'

—

Scott, the youngest of the lodgers, was eating noodles out of a pot in front of his open laptop at the kitchen table. He was a tall, wiry young man with carefully spiked fair hair and rimless spectacles. He was halfway, he said, through writing a thesis on the sociological effects of cashless payments and e-banking and spoke, his mother being South African, what Beth's father would have called Commonwealth English.

He said to Beth, 'D'you want me to clear out?'

'Why should I?'

He waved his fork. 'Your friend being here and all. D'you want some space?'

Beth sat down on the opposite side of the table. Bonus, she observed, had resumed his sleeping nest on the far end, part screened by a litre carton of orange juice. She smiled at Scott.

'Thank you, but she had to go, anyway. She has a mother in a nursing home who needs visiting.'

Scott said, 'I can't imagine that.'

'Having a mother in a nursing home?'

'My mum isn't even fifty. She had me when she was a student. That's when she and Dad met, in London as students.'

'Stacey's mother wasn't very old when she had Stacey. Dementia seems to be no respecter of age or cleverness.'

Scott put his noodle pot down. 'I'm sorry to hear that,' he said soberly.

Beth nodded. 'Our responsibilities in life shift without warning, don't they?'

Scott looked at his keyboard. 'I wouldn't really know, yet.'

'You will.'

'Mum's only forty-seven.'

Beth smiled at him. 'A child, then.'

Scott said, 'Actually, I was going to ask you . . .'

'Yes?'

'Mum's coming over from Durban the weeks Angie's away. If it's OK with Angie, could Mum have her room?'

Beth stood up and leaned across to pick Bonus up from behind the orange juice carton.

'I don't see why not. If Angie is OK with it?'

'I haven't asked her yet. But you don't mind?'

Beth held Bonus in her arms. He was purring. She said, again, 'Why should I?'

'Well, it's your house. It's your home.'

'Maybe.'

'OK,' Scott said.

'Maybe it isn't a good idea to invest too much in where you live.'

He looked round the kitchen. 'It's a nice place,' he said, laconically.

'It is. But it is only a place, in the end.'

'I don't think Mum felt like that,' Scott said. 'When she and Dad split up, she went back to Durban and he went back to Auckland.'

Beth sat down again, settling Bonus on her lap. 'They were young, though. And probably felt a bit lost. I'm adopted and, strangely, I've never felt lost. I sometimes wonder if being given away at birth got all my lostness in life over with, in one dreadful fell swoop.'

Scott fell silent, as if all this was far too much information to digest along with his noodles. Beth smiled at him again. 'Just a thought. Different things validate, or fail to validate, different people. I'm just not defined by being adopted. Or by being gay, for that matter.'

Scott swallowed. He took his hands off his keyboard and jammed them between his thighs, hunching forward.

'Did you find your birth mother, ever?' he asked, not looking at Beth.

'I didn't want to.'

'OK.'

'There were a thousand reasons, but one was that it would have upset – badly upset – my adopted parents.'

'So,' Scott said, 'you're still angry? With your birth mother?'

'I don't think about her,' Beth said pleasantly.

He glanced up briefly. 'Conversation for another time?'

'Or never, perhaps.'

'So it's OK about Mum staying, is it?'

'If Angie's OK with it too, and it doesn't conflict with my father coming down from Aberdeen, then of course. I'd be glad to meet her.'

Scott ducked his head. 'Cheers,' he said and then added, 'It's cool, being here.'

Beth stood up, gradually, transferring Bonus to the chair she had been sitting in.

'Good. I like having you.'

He removed one hand and gestured at the noodles. 'Even putting up with what we eat?'

She laughed. 'As long as I don't have to eat it, too.'

He grinned. 'Can I ask you something?'

'Of course.'

'Can you tell me how you get egg off a saucepan?'

—

Beth closed her study door behind her and, for a few seconds only, leaned against it. The room in front of her was, like her room at the business school, evidence of her commitment to work. They were both rooms in which, over the years, her essential, most profound and most developed self had been at liberty to become what she had become. She had thought, once, that how she lived was an indication of both what she was and what she hoped to be, but as time went on, the significance of style seemed to diminish every year as a measure of anything that was going on inside her head. It wasn't exactly a carelessness about surroundings and ways of living, it was more a growing sense of proportion about what mattered and what, in essence, didn't. If the supremacy of the life of the mind meant that you left a full coffee pot and a waiting mug among the papers on your desk and gave them no more thought after you had put them there, then so be it.

She crossed the room and picked up the coffee pot and the mug, and put them down on the carpet, just inside the door, where they would be impossible to miss. Then she lifted a collection of shawls and sweaters that had formed a soft, disorganized mound on the back of her desk chair and hung them on the hooks Claire had had fixed to the back of the door intended, she said, for Beth's academic robes. Searching among the papers on her desk, Beth found her landline telephone handset nestling in its cradle and carried it across to the window, which looked out into the yard at the back of the house. The bird feeder Claire had hung in the plum tree was, she noticed, empty, and swung pointlessly in the wind.

She propped her shoulder against one side of the window frame and dialled. The phone rang out four times, and then Claire said distinctly, 'I don't want to talk to you.'

'Please don't hang up.'

'It upsets me,' Claire said. 'It upsets me to hear you. Anyway, I'm going out.'

Beth fixed her gaze on the plum tree.

'This won't take long,' she said.

'I don't want–'

'And *I* don't want–' Beth interrupted.

'Please–'

'Stacey came this afternoon,' Beth said. 'At Gaby's instigation.'

'I was worried.'

'Were you?'

'I didn't like the sound of how things were going, in Wilkes Street.'

'Honey, life in Wilkes Street is much the same only not so tidy.'

'I heard–'

'What did you hear?'

'You'd been seen in a bar,' Claire said, gathering courage. 'You'd been seen–'

'Which bar?'

'Doesn't matter.'

'I think it does,' Beth said, 'so that I know when it was and who I was with and what was happening.'

'No,' Claire said. 'No. The details are irrelevant. It's the impression you gave, the impression of someone not quite in control any more, and you are someone for whom dignity and respect are very important.'

Beth adjusted her shoulder against the window frame. 'Are we talking about me?'

'Of course we are!'

'Then perhaps I could be allowed an opinion about how I conduct myself and how I wish to be seen?'

'I've always tried to *protect* you!' Claire shouted. 'I'm trying to protect you now!'

'Ah,' Beth said. 'So this has nothing to do with the house?'

Claire was silent.

Beth went on, 'This has nothing to do with our conversation about the new flat you want to buy and the absurdity, as you see it, of my rattling around here on my own in Wilkes Street?'

'Beth,' Claire said, in an altogether lower and calmer tone. 'Please.'

'Explain to me, then. Explain to me what you want.'

'I can't. You're so – so *adamant.*'

'I'm adamant about some things, I know, because some things I can't change. I can't change what I earn, for example. As you know, I'm better paid than I would be at the LSE, but not as well paid as I would be at the London Business School. Another thing I can't change is the mortgage, which is still reasonable against the value of the house, but needs paying each month all the same. So, with the lodgers here, I will be able to release sums of money to you now and then – a few thousand here and there perhaps – but in the meantime, you just have to put up with the consequences of a situation which I'm afraid, honey, nobody but you created.'

'That's not true.'

'It's true enough,' Beth said, watching a blue tit discover that the bird feeder was disappointingly empty. 'For the purposes of the present situation.'

'You are so pompous.'

'So you keep saying.'

'How can I put anything behind me, how can I move on, if you refuse to change anything, ever?'

Beth picked a dead fly off the window frame and moved to drop it in the nearest waste-paper bin.

'I'm trying to recover too, Claire. I'm trying to heal as well. But I have to do both in my own time and in my own way.' She paused, and then she said, 'Are you crying?'

'No.'

'I think you are.'

'It isn't the house,' Claire said unsteadily. 'It isn't the money.'

'Isn't it? Isn't it money that made you say what you did both to me and then to Gaby?'

There was a pause. Then Claire said, in a very small voice, 'I made a mistake.'

'What?'

'I'm not doing as well as it looks as if I am.'

Beth closed her eyes. She said, 'Stacey reported Gaby as saying you looked wonderful.'

'Anyone can look good with exercise and no caffeine.'

Beth waited, her eyes still closed. Then Claire said, softly, 'I miss you.'

—

Scott was watching football on television. He was lying full length on one of the sofas with both cats beside him and no light beyond the glow from the television screen. Beth put her head round the door.

'Scott?'

His gaze didn't leave the screen. Liverpool versus West Ham. First half.

'Hi,' he said, absently.

'I'm going out.'

'Fine.'

'I might be late. Really quite late.'

'Fine.'

'Can you remember not to deadlock the front door?'

'Sure.'

'Scott. Did you hear me?'

The crowd roared as Sturridge scored and Scott threw a cushion in the air, in jubilation.

'Scott?'

'I heard you. Don't deadlock the door.'

'Good. Night night.'

She closed the door and crossed the hall to pick up her coat, passing the mirror framed in strange silver twigs that Claire had hung against the panelling. She paused to look in it. Impossible. Impossible to tell if she looked better or worse. Even good or bad. But she did look - well, *galvanized* was the word. She put her coat on and turned the collar up. She had no idea where she was going or who she would meet. She had no idea, even, of which way she would turn, once she was outside the house. All she knew was that she was going *out*, on a Saturday night, alone and free and ready for anything, rather than something, to happen. She opened the door and stepped out into Wilkes Street, and as it slammed behind her it nudged her forward slightly, like a shove into the future.

CHAPTER THIRTEEN

STACEY

A victory for Steve, Stacey reflected, was a quiet thing. He didn't appear to need to have it acknowledged, and he certainly showed no desire to demonstrate triumph. After Mum had been taken to the nursing home – no distance away and with far less protest than had attended her leaving her flat – Steve hadn't even suggested putting the house back to the way it had been before she came. It was as if he had achieved what he needed to in retrieving their way of life together and the rest was entirely up to Stacey.

What was left after Mum had gone wasn't comfortable. Her personal furniture and possessions – the television chair, the bedside table, the pussy willow tea set – all went with her to her clean, bright, blank room with its view over the Regent's Canal and hospital bed. But the remnants – the bolted stairgate, the adapted shower, the illuminated light switches – seemed to Stacey to be reproachful, symbolic of intention and effort that had, in no time, proved too much to fulfil. Even Bruno, released from his duties, hung about her feet as if eternally pointing out to her that he was, because of her decision, now deprived of his useful employment.

Finding the home had been dispiriting at best. And the

best had been only very occasional. She had been appalled, and alarmed, by most of what she had seen, frightened enough to say frequently to Steve that it wasn't going to be possible, it just wasn't, she couldn't contemplate subjecting Mum to those places, to those indignities, the incessant television, the revolving door of changing staff, the smells. Steve had offered to come with her, on her inspections; he'd suggested doing some research so that she didn't have to, but he never backed down, he never said that because of what she'd seen, he'd think again. He wasn't thinking again, that was very plain. He wasn't resorting to threats and ultimatums about Stacey having to choose between her mother and her husband, but he was sturdily immovable in wanting his wife and his life back where they had been. It wasn't, he said when he got back from New York, a matter for negotiation. Mum's condition was a tragedy for her, but that tragedy was not, he said to Stacey, going to spill over into making an equal tragedy of both their lives, and their marriage.

'I don't mind the idea of sacrifice,' he said, 'I don't even mind the *fact* of sacrifice. But it's got to be worth it.'

It was Steve, in the end, who had found the nursing home. Newly built, part of a small chain, right by the canal, and within walking distance of the house. It specialized in dementia care and encouraged residents to take their own furniture and familiar belongings. It was also expensive. Stacey, standing in the unimpeachable space that might be Mum's, said in dismay,

'A thousand pounds a week!'

Steve was looking out at the water, his hands in his pockets.

'We'll manage,' he said, neutrally.

'Will we? How?'

He didn't turn. He said, in the same tone, 'We can start by selling that flat.'

She gave a little gasp. 'Mum's flat?'

'An empty flat in a good location.'

'Oh, Steve . . .'

'She can't live there again. And it certainly can't become some sort of shrine. Selling it will pay for several years here.'

'Years?'

'It may come to that. But by the time the money from the flat runs out, you'll be working again.'

At last he turned round. He said, 'A lot of things need to go back to the way they were. Like you working.'

She gave a little shrug. 'It's – it's confidence, Steve. It takes years to build up and half a minute to lose, it seems.'

'I know.'

'Do you?'

'You *will* find work again,' he said, with sudden force. 'I know you will. Your mum being here will be the first step for you.' He took his hands out of his pockets. 'You'll see.'

—

What she seemed to see most clearly, once Mum was being looked after in Waterside, was that there was suddenly neither point nor justification in being at home. There were a lot of things that could be – should be – done, like re-arranging all the furniture which had been carried up and down the house when Mum arrived, but it was strangely hard to make herself do them. She could make lists, of course, but then there was a tendency to look at the lists, and feel that the energy taken to write them had used up all the resolution there was. She could walk Bruno, she could make appointments – the hairdresser, the podiatrist – she could visit Waterside, but she couldn't shake off the sensation of being still trapped in a void with no evident way out. And it didn't do to brood, either. Thinking about her situation seemed to plunge her into a cauldron of feelings of failure and rejection that brought back that terrible afternoon on a bench in St Paul's Churchyard. If she hadn't, in the end, been good enough at the one thing she had been sure she was good at, and had now failed in the most fundamental role of dutiful daughter to an irreproachable mother, then what kind of person was she?

When Gaby rang to recount her breakfast with Claire, and suggest that Stacey, being geographically the nearest, might go round to Wilkes Street, Stacey had leapt at the chance with almost exaggerated eagerness.

'Of course I'll go! I'll go at once.'

'No,' Gaby said. 'No. I'm not even sure Claire wasn't over-egging it all. Leave it till the weekend.'

'But if the weekends are the problem?'

'I only have Claire's word that they are. It's just to get an idea, you know. Beth is, after all, a grown-up. A *real* grown-up, if you get me.'

'And Claire?'

Gaby said, 'You know what I think of Claire.'

Stacey had felt immediately fired up – full of a sudden energy, she told Steve, that she hadn't felt in weeks.

He said, taking a beer out of the fridge and flipping off the cap, not hurrying himself, 'Do as she says, Stace. Don't go dashing round there.'

'I wasn't—' she said automatically, and stopped.

'Weren't you?'

She looked away. 'It was so nice – to be asked.'

'Of course.'

'To feel necessary.'

He took a swallow from the bottle. 'You *are* necessary.'

'Well – you know.'

'Yes,' he said. 'Of course you mean to someone other than me.'

She had waited until the Saturday before she emailed Beth. She had written several versions of the email before she sent it, trying to be both truthful and, at the same time, nonchalant enough to look less vulnerable than she felt. And when she reached Wilkes Street on Saturday afternoon, it was all rather anti-climactic, with Beth looking so much better and the house seeming comfortably relaxed; a nice young man with a South African accent at the kitchen table, which had one of the cats asleep on it, in a nest of papers. She had tried to relay her mission but it had felt wrong, and clumsy, even as she was speaking, and Beth had got the point, read the subtext at once and had seemed immediately at her most professional and decided, even amused. Stacey had wondered if Beth was hurt by Claire's assumptions and whether Beth felt it was better to be in Claire's thoughts, even for the wrong reasons, than not be in them at all. But she couldn't ask. She had known Beth since they were both nineteen, but she still couldn't ask. She had said, instead, 'What will you do?'

'Do?' Beth said. 'About what?'

'About Claire.'

'I haven't decided. But I might ring her. I might.'

'To . . . ?'

Beth had got out of her chair. She took her reading

glasses out of her pocket and swung them by one arm. 'To tell her that nobody could take me anywhere I didn't want to go.'

'Are – are you angry?'

Beth looked down at her. 'No. Not angry. Why should I be?'

'Well, it isn't very nice, being talked about like this.'

'Stace,' Beth said. 'Compared to being left, it's a walk in the park. Come and meet Scott. He's in the kitchen.'

—

'She seemed fine,' Stacey said to Steve that night. 'In fact, I would say she was better than I've seen her for ages.'

Steve was carefully mixing a salad, turning the leaves and herbs over with slow precision. He had laid the table and put out candles, and polished glasses and bought steaks, which were lying on a wooden board, ready to cook, side by side. Steve was as neat in the kitchen as if he had been a sailor. He said, 'Well, as Gaby says, she's a grown-up.'

'It isn't just a matter of age, is it, being grown-up?'

Steve went on methodically turning the salad leaves.

'I can't say it again, Stace,' he said. 'You're a wonderful woman and a great daughter and you haven't failed. Not as a daughter, not in your career. Beth has made different choices, and lives with different circumstances. You have to stop comparing. You have to stop beating yourself up about everything under the sun.' He balanced the salad servers across the top of the bowl and pushed it to one end of the table. 'Anyway, I want to talk about something else.'

Stacey tucked her hair behind her ears and folded her arms. 'Good.'

'That's more like it,' Steve said.

He unhooked a long striped apron from the back of the door and put it on, crossing the strings at the front and tying them in a competent bow. He picked up the half-empty wine bottle and held it up, enquiringly.

Stacey shook her head. 'I'm fine.'

'There's just one little wrinkle left,' Steve said. 'One small detail that we haven't talked about.'

Stacey pulled a chair out from the table and sat down. 'What kind of detail?'

'Work,' Steve said briefly.

'Work?'

'*My* work.'

'Goodness,' Stacey said. 'Please don't tell me they want to send you to Singapore.'

'Nothing like that.'

'Phew.'

Steve crossed the kitchen and opened the cupboard under the hob to extract the skillet.

'It's about my being made a director. Put on the board.'

Stacey twisted her wine glass round, watching the reflection from the candle flame move behind the liquid.

'I don't think I was very gracious about that,' she said, slowly. 'I was in too much of a state, that night, to behave properly in any way.'

Steve put the skillet on the hob. He said, 'I don't think either of us get top marks for that evening.'

'I wasn't very generous, though.'

Steve turned. 'What did I say about beating yourself up?'

'Sorry.'

He came across the kitchen and pulled out the chair next

to Stacey's. He sat in it, upright in his apron, his hands on his thighs. 'Stace.'

'Yes?'

'I overdid it that night. I wasn't sensitive enough about what had happened to you and I got – carried away.'

'Well,' Stacey said. 'You were allowed to, weren't you? I mean, you'd been promoted!'

'I was embarrassed as well,' Steve said.

'*Embarrassed?*'

'That's the wrinkle.' He leaned forward a little, taking his hands off his thighs and clenching his fists lightly. 'I earned my place on the board . . .'

'I know you did.'

'And it was absolutely a unanimous decision to have me on it . . .'

'I know.'

'But what I didn't tell you was that the decision to promote me was the result, among many results, of having the board professionally scrutinized and reshuffled, and the professional board consultant specifically advised that I should be among the people who were promoted.'

'Well,' Stacey said, smiling. 'That's all good, isn't it?'

'Think, Stacey.'

'What?'

'*Think*, Stacey. How many consultants who specialize in board scrutiny do you know?'

She stared at him. Then she said quietly, 'Melissa?'

'Yes.'

'Melissa.'

'Melissa advised the firm. She revolutionized the board and it's had a great effect. She wouldn't have backed me if she didn't think I was right, but she did, so she did. I don't exactly owe my seat on the board to Melissa, but I might not have it, without her.'

Stacey said slowly, 'And you didn't tell me?'

'No. Not until now.'

'And – she hasn't told me, either.'

'Not face to face.'

'Is there anything else?'

'Like what?'

'Anything else I don't know? Any more little deals or secrets or relationships?'

Steve reached forward to take her hands. He said, firmly, 'Nothing.'

'Sure? I mean, why didn't you *tell* me?'

'I couldn't. Not then. Think back to then.'

Stacey said, 'Remember how ultra-keen Melissa was to find me a job?'

'Yes.'

'All that nonsense with Gaby.'

'Yes.'

'Who knows about this?'

'You and me, Melissa and Gaby.'

'Didn't you have to declare to the firm that you knew Melissa?'

'She was hired long before I knew. I told the chairman, in private, and I don't think he batted an eyelid. Nor did Melissa. She said competence was competence and she was far too practised to be affected or compromised. She's quite different in work mode. Almost scary.'

Stacey slipped her hands out of Steve's.

He said, 'I am really, really sorry.'

'Were you ever not going to tell me?'

'I don't know. All I can truthfully say is that I hated you not knowing.'

'Now I do.'

'Yes. There's nothing else. I haven't see Melissa since before I was promoted. I haven't seen anyone – except, as you know, Gaby.'

Stacey stood up. 'Right,' she said.

He looked up at her. 'What d'you mean, right? What are you going to do?'

She looked back down at him. She wasn't smiling, but she didn't look unreachable, either.

'I'm going to ring Melissa, of course.'

—

Melissa opened her front door wearing a pale grey tracksuit and spectacles. She gave Stacey an affectionate kiss and gestured at herself. 'Sunday gear. Running, and no contact lenses.'

Stacey took off her jacket. She looked towards the stairs. 'Is Tom here?'

'No, actually. Why do you ask?'

'I thought – maybe you ran together.'

'No,' Melissa said. 'I rather wish – but there we are. He stayed over at Will's last night. One of the little boys' birthdays or something. I find I don't ask for the details much, it's better if I don't.'

Stacey stood looking at her. 'Melissa.'

Melissa put both hands up to pull her hair more tightly through its ponytail band. 'I know. It's – all been such a mess.'

'But it needn't have been.'

'Stacey, if you'd just talked to us that day, the day you got fired . . .'

'I couldn't.'

'Well, I understand that, but it meant that by the time we were in touch again, all kinds of things had got themselves into what Gaby calls the Too Difficult file, and we all did things, or didn't do things, that made all our relationships so much harder. *All* of them.'

Stacey sighed. 'OK then.'

'Coffee?' Melissa said. 'Tea? Water?'

'Coffee, please. And water. Could I just ask you one question?'

'Of course.'

'Were you never going to tell me that Steve's firm were your clients?'

Melissa began descending the stairs. 'Want the truth?' she said over her shoulder.

'Nothing but.'

'I was certainly going to tell you. I was waiting till Steve's promotion was confirmed, and then I was going to take you out for a glass of champagne and tell you in absolute secrecy that he deserved what had happened in every way because he is one of the best senior people that firm has in its entire workforce. It never crossed my mind that your work request would be taken as a chance to fire you and your world would fall in, as a consequence.' She paused at the bottom of the stairs and looked up. 'So you see.'

'Yes,' Stacey said, following more slowly.

'You don't sound very convinced. There aren't any *plots*, Stacey.'

'Sometimes, though, revelations feel as though there must have been plots somewhere.'

'Not in my case,' Melissa said firmly. 'I was hired by the chairman. I told him I knew Steve. He said it was of no importance and he had his eye on Steve anyway. Come on, Stacey! In our world, everyone knows everyone. It's very rare that I don't know something about someone in almost every client firm I take on. It's *good* news that I could do something useful for Steve, and therefore you. And in the circumstances, it turned out to be very good news indeed.'

Stacey looked at her. 'Are you expecting me to be grateful?'

Melissa stopped filling the kettle. 'Absolutely not. I just don't want you to be all suspicious and hurt and upset about something that you should only be pleased about.'

'That's me told, then.'

Melissa turned from the sink. 'Stacey. Please.'

'I'm just so *jealous*, of you working,' Stacey said, dropping her gaze. 'And Gaby. And Beth. Beth's work diary is full, she said, for eighteen months. Eighteen months! I'd be glad to have a single work commitment in the next eighteen *days*.'

Melissa put the kettle down and came across the kitchen to take hold of Stacey's shoulders. 'I do get it. I do.'

'I'm like a little kid,' Stacey said miserably. 'I want, I want, I don't know what I want. When I had a drink with Gaby, I was all braced to fall in love with Canary Wharf and everything, and nothing happened. Actually, it was stronger than that because I felt very distinctly that I didn't want to go back into that world, I didn't want to be among all those shiny people just desperate to get shinier. But I don't know what I want to do instead even if I am longing and longing to do *something.*' She glanced at Melissa. 'I didn't mean to behave like a cow.'

'You didn't.'

Stacey gave a little yelp of disbelieving laughter. 'That coffee?' she said, in a steadier voice.

Melissa released her hands. 'Of course. Stace . . .'

'Yes?'

'I mind for you. I really do.'

'I know.'

'It'll happen, I just *know* it will–'

'Melissa,' Stacey said, cutting in. 'What were you going to do today? Without Tom? And if I hadn't come?'

Melissa made a face. 'You'll laugh.'

'Try me.'

'It's so anal.'

'Lissa!'

Melissa leaned against the counter by the kettle. She said, 'Well, what I was going to do was sort through my whole wardrobe, my work wardrobe, clothes, shoes, bags, everything, and throw out all the stuff I couldn't bear to see any more, let alone put on.'

Stacey smiled at her. 'Can I help you?'

'What? You don't want to go through my work clothes as a way to spend a Sunday.'

'I might,' Stacey said. 'I might really like spending time with you doing something like that.'

Melissa looked straight at her. Then she picked up the kettle again.

'OK then,' she said. 'You're on.'

—

Steve looked at all the carrier bags in the hall. There were five of them, all full – five glossy, upmarket carrier bags.

'What's all this?' he said, suspiciously.

Stacey was on the floor, allowing Bruno to have the full welcoming ritual at his own level. She didn't glance up. 'Oh, just chuck-outs of Melissa's.'

'*All* of them?'

'Yes. There was a lot to chuck. She buys quality for sure but quality in quantity. I got the impression that she was feeling a bit new-broom-ish. Wanting to clear out before starting off again.'

Steve picked a black velvet scarf out of a bag, looked at it, and dropped it back in again. 'But why's it all here? Why did you bring it all back with you?'

Stacey gave Bruno a final pat and got to her feet. 'Because our charity shops need good stuff more than hers do, in Kensington. The charity shops near her are more like boutiques than anything. You should see the labels.'

'I don't know anything about labels.'

'Liar,' Stacey said affectionately. She paused to kiss him. 'You affect to be bemused by women's labels but you know plenty about men's.'

He caught her in an embrace before she could move away.

'You seem very cheerful,' he said, teasingly.

'I had a lovely day.'

'Trying on Melissa's clothes?'

'No,' Stacey said, not pulling away from him for the first time in months. 'No. I didn't try on anything. Except her shoes. Oh my God, Steve, you should see her shoes! No, we just sat on her bed in a sea of clothes and talked and at lunchtime we had a picnic of smoked salmon and bagels.'

'On her bed?'

'Still on her bed. And then we watched a movie I'm not even going to tell you the title of because I don't want to give you the ammunition, and then we had tea and shared a chocolate brownie Melissa had bought for Tom, and then he came back and I saw him for ten minutes and then I drove home with the spoils.'

Steve tightened his arms slightly. 'What did Tom do when he found you'd eaten his brownie?'

'We didn't tell him.'

'That,' Steve said, 'wasn't very honourable.'

'He was full of birthday cake anyway.'

'That's beside the point.'

Stacey looked down at Bruno. 'I ought to feed him.'

'I've done it.'

'Oh,' she said. 'Lovely.'

'The dishwasher is unloaded, the recycling is out, the dog has been walked as well as fed.'

'Wonderful.'

'That's what I thought.'

She looked up at him. 'What else were you thinking?'

He bent and kissed her mouth, without hurry.

'Guess,' he said.

—

Melissa's clothes, spread round the top floor, in the rooms that were once supposed to be Mum's, looked impressive. Skirt suits and trouser suits, scarves and coats, shoes and bags, and all, having belonged to Melissa, immaculately kept. There were no missing buttons or descending hems, there was no fraying or scuffing. The shoes and bags had been polished, the coats had been brushed.

'There's nothing the matter with anything,' Melissa had said, surveying the heaps before they bagged them up, 'except that I can't wait to see the back of them.'

Stacey was sitting on Melissa's bed, her lap full of scarves. 'For any particular reason?'

'No.'

'Sure?'

Melissa picked up a dark brown handbag and looked at it.

'Tom spends a lot of time at Will's house,' she said. 'And Will rings me. He rings me a lot, now. Sometimes every day.'

'What has that got to do with your clothes?'

Melissa put the bag down. 'Restlessness,' she said emphatically. 'This whole new development unsettles me. I don't know what to do.'

'Do you know what you *want* to do?'

'Not even that.'

'Join the club!' Stacey said. They were laughing, both laughing. And then Melissa started gathering up her discarded possessions, armfuls of them, and Stacey said, in mock outrage, 'Honestly, Melissa, honestly. All this just so that you can go shopping again!'

And Melissa had stopped suddenly, her arms laden with clothes, and looked at Stacey without a hint of contrition.

'I know,' she said, 'I know. Shopping. The most satisfactory displacement activity in the world.'

Now here they were, all the things Melissa had worked to pay for, and had now discarded: wool things and silk things, leather and cotton things, sober-coloured, beautifully designed and made *things* that had once meant something in

Melissa's life and were now spread round Stacey's top floor in a way that, despite the hangover of happiness from the day before, seemed unquestionably melancholy. It didn't just seem sad to Stacey, looking at those clothes that had once held the promise of achievement of some kind for Melissa, but also, at another level, plain wrong. It was wrong to think of all the labour and craftsmanship that had gone into Melissa's cast-off clothes and bags and shoes not continuing the validity and intensity of life with which they had begun. It was just wrong to think that these possessions, which had been undeniably an indication of status to Melissa, should not be given the best opportunity to do as much – or even more – for someone else.

Stacey picked up the nearest handbag. It was navy blue, made of slightly grainy leather, with heavy brushed-steel fittings and steel studs on the bottom so that it would sit, sturdily, on the floor, without scratching the leather. Inside, Stacey noticed, there was not only a breath of Melissa's scent, but pockets and a lining of grey suede. It was a wonderful thing. A carefully, handsomely crafted wonderful thing. You would look at that, sitting beside a woman at a meeting, and think, 'Nice bag.'

Nice bag. Stacey had a moment of extreme stillness, quite forgetting to breathe. A memory of the afternoon in St Paul's Churchyard came clearly back to her at the same moment that an illuminating idea flashed into her mind, unformed but compelling. She heard herself give a little gasp, and then a little cry. Nice bag!

CHAPTER FOURTEEN

MELISSA

The meeting room was full. The chairman and chief executive of the accountancy firm Melissa was advising had said that the initial invitation to hear her speak had only gone out to the board and senior managers, but the clamour of protest from the rest of the company had been so vociferous that they had moved the venue to the biggest meeting room in the building and this, they said proudly, was the result.

Melissa knew that they wanted to be congratulated for such a turn-out. They were hugely relieved to find that the doubtful business of applying for Hathway's help in the first place had proved so well justified and, weirdly, wanted Melissa herself to applaud them for being so bold and so enterprising. In her turn, she would liked to have been applauded herself for agreeing to address this audience in the first place. It wasn't the kind of thing she did, after all. It was what Gaby did, often: Gaby was perfectly well practised in standing up in front of an audience and lecturing them on what was needed to change in a modern workplace to make it more progressive, more diversified. But Melissa preferred to work in a much less visible way; quiet scene-shifting that could happen without drama or noise was far more to her taste. And she wouldn't be here now, in this meeting room full of accountants, with a prepared speech about the abiding gap between most company policies on women employees and those women's experience of everyday working, if it hadn't been for Will.

The chief executive of the accountancy firm had been at university with Will. They had shared a flat as students, and another when they were studying for their law and accountancy exams. The chief executive was Marnie's godfather and the friendship had survived both their divorces as well as the acquisition of new partners. At a rugby game at Twickenham – Harlequins versus London Welsh – Matthew had told Will about his firm's decision to consult Hathaway and Will had confessed his connection with Melissa. Then, a little later, celebrating a resounding Harlequins victory, Matthew had asked Will if Melissa would ever consider speaking to his firm, as part of their gender diversity programme, and Will, halfway down his third pint, had said that he could but ask.

So he had asked, over a glass of wine in the bar of a Kensington hotel, and Melissa had initially said no, of course not, that wasn't her style at all, and then, gradually, the no had segued through maybe to a reluctant yes. And so here she was, simultaneously exasperated with herself and elated, in dramatic new shoes and a severe grey trouser suit, standing in front of a room packed with accountants, women as well as men, with Matthew and his chairman in the front row next to Will. It had not felt dignified, or indeed cool, to ask what Will was doing there, so she hadn't. She had, in fact, barely acknowledged his presence. Her own audience, she had made plain from the outset, comprised the women in the firm, especially the younger ones.

Gaby had said, on the telephone, 'Just be yourself. As few notes as possible, don't wave your hands about too much and do *not* touch your hair, ever. Make one major point and two minor ones – it's all you'll get across, even to a bright audience. And they'll all, men as well as women, notice your shoes.'

Melissa looked out across the room. There was a definite buzz of anticipation; she could feel it herself. She put her notes down on the plexiglas lectern that had been provided, and stepped to stand beside rather than behind it. If this was stage fright, it was definitely exhilarating: exhilarating enough for her to think, at some level, that if they were all going to look at her shoes, then they might as well have a good view.

'Good evening,' Melissa said. Her voice sounded remarkably like itself. She smiled at them all. 'And thank you for having me.'

She folded her hands in front of her and shook – rather than pushed – her hair back. Then she said, 'I'm going to start with a statement. A statement that I'm in a position to make because I've been a mother myself, for fifteen years. It is not children that hold women back in their careers, it is something else. And that something else is that men get far more *help*. In a recent study of almost 700,000 employees, 38 per cent of the men received five promotions as compared to 29 per cent of the women. And I want to add to that. I want to refer to the results of research recently published in *Sociology* magazine. In that study, of 4,000 couples in the UK with young children, the risk of those couples divorcing before their children started school was reduced by 80 per cent – *80* – as long as the mother out-earned the father by at least 20 per cent.'

She paused. Small eruptions of cheering were happening here and there in the room, little whoops of support. And in the front row, his eyes fixed on her face, Will was clapping.

—

In the taxi going home, Melissa felt distinct elation, the kind of sheer, slightly wild excitement that she hadn't felt in years and then only in situations that hinted at as much danger as they did promise, like deciding to start Hathaway, or being asked out for the first time by Connor Corbett. When she had spoken, during her talk, about the persistence of sexual advances by men in office life, there'd been a concerted and suddenly confident cheer from the young women in the room, and the bland approval on the faces of the men in the front row had suddenly frozen into abrupt neutrality.

'Every male boss I had in my career before Hathaway,' Melissa said, 'would hit on me. Every one. And when I rejected them, as I inevitably did every time, I knew I would be punished as a way of them denying, or coping with, their shame.'

At the end of her talk – twenty-five minutes that felt like five – the applause was loud and long. It was so long, in fact, that it took the chairman several minutes to make himself heard, and deliver his vote of thanks. He was graceful. He thanked Melissa for pointing out what he had long felt himself, namely that it *wasn't* the biology, stupid. He reiterated his firm's determination to maximize the potential of its workforce, irrespective of gender. He turned to Melissa and told her that she was an inspiration to men and women alike.

Then Will, unmistakably glowing with emotion and gratified pride, asked her to have dinner with him. She said no.

'Please.'

She shook her head again, smiling. 'No. No, thank you.'

'A drink, then. Just a drink.'

'Not that either, thank you. I must get back to Tom.'

'Just a quick drink.'

'No.'

'Jesus,' Will said admiringly. 'You are quite something, aren't you?'

For the length of the taxi ride, from the City to Kensington, she did indeed feel quite something. It had not just gone well, it had gone gloriously well. Everyone in that room - well, the majority of people in that room - had been, by the end, on her side. She had not only been approved of, she had been applauded. They had liked what she had to say. They had liked *her*. Gaby had always said that having a speech go down well was heady stuff. Heady was the word. Sitting in the taxi with her new shoes kicked off and the night-time lights and sights of London sliding past the taxi windows, she felt nothing short of intoxicated. On a glass of water, and success. When the taxi reached Holland Street, she gave the driver a 25 per cent tip on top of the fare, which he, misunderstanding, tried to return as change.

She made a dismissive gesture. 'No. Really no. It's for you.'

He raised his hand, as if touching the peak of a non-existent cap. 'Well. Thank you.'

'My pleasure,' she said, and meant it.

She went up the steps to the front door, in stockinged

feet, her shoes in her hand, hardly noticing how cold the stone was. In the hall, Tom's padded jacket and scarf were tossed on a chair and his trainers had been kicked off at the foot of the stairs. Beside them lay an empty soda bottle and a twist of coloured paper that had obviously once been wrapped round the kind of sweets that Melissa had tried, over and over, to explain contained nothing but tooth-decaying empty calories. Tonight, the sight of evidence that Tom was at home did absolutely nothing but lift her spirits further. She stood in the hall, holding her shoes, and called his name.

'Tom! Tom?'

He was apparently in the kitchen. She could hear the sound of the kitchen television, and the lights that illuminated the basement stairs were on. Still clutching her shoes, and her briefcase bag with her triumphant speech in it, she padded down the length of the hall and then down the stairs to the kitchen. All the ceiling and ambient lights were on, as was the television, and Tom was sitting at the central island, where he had left her flowers, with his headphones on and his face illumined further by the glowing screen of his iPad. Melissa, smiling, went silently across the room, dropping her shoes and bag, and lifted one headphone away from his head enough to say into his ear, 'Hello!'

He swung round, smiling and completely unsurprised.

'Hi! How'd it go?'

'Fantastic.'

'Really?'

'Amazing,' Melissa said. 'Brilliant. Better than I could have hoped for.'

Tom took his headphones off and got up. He put his arms around her. He was, by a fraction, taller now than she was.

'Cool,' he said. 'Congratulations. Was Dad there?'

'He was.'

'He was really excited about you speaking.'

Melissa pulled away very slightly. 'Was he?'

'Course he was! He got you the gig, because of Matthew and all that.'

Melissa looked at him. The skin on his forehead, under his carefully arranged hair, was very bad, but he looked great otherwise – healthy and assured. She detached herself gently. 'What are you watching?'

Tom shrugged. 'Dunno. Didn't notice.'

'Shall we turn it off, then? Did you eat?'

Tom looked suddenly self-conscious. 'Yes.'

'Why do you say it like that? Did you eat something that would appal me?'

Tom said carefully, 'We ate pizza. *And salad.*'

'We? Who came back with you? Rufus?'

There was a short pause and then Tom said, 'No.'

'No? Not Rufus? Who then?'

Tom picked up his headphones and examined them. Then he said, 'Claudia.'

Melissa looked at him. 'Claudia? Who's Claudia?'

'Claudia Henderson,' Tom said.

There was another pause and then Melissa said, 'You mean – *Gaby's* Claudia?'

'Uh-huh.'

'Tom.'

Tom put his headphones on, with the earpieces behind his ears. 'Yes, Gaby's Claudia,' he said, loudly.

'You mean . . . ?'

Tom shrugged. 'Yes,' he said.

Melissa hitched herself onto a stool by the counter. 'Goodness,' she said, faintly.

'It isn't goodness,' Tom said. 'It isn't anything. We're – we're just kind of hanging out together sometimes.'

'I should certainly hope so!'

'Mum,' Tom said. 'Don't do this.'

'Don't do what?'

'Don't do this kind of heavy mother stuff. I'm fifteen.'

'Claudia is thirteen!'

'So?' He remembered his Shakespeare. 'So was Juliet.'

'Does Gaby know?'

'Quin knew Claudia was having pizza here with me.'

'But . . .'

'But what?'

'Are you, I mean, if you're thinking of Claudia as a girlfriend . . .'

'You mean,' Tom said, folding his arms, 'sex. Don't you?'

Melissa looked at him. She nodded.

Tom said, 'If we were, do you think I'd tell you?'

'I'd – hope so.'

'If we were, I don't think I'd tell anyone.'

'Gaby ought to know.'

'There's nothing *to* know!' Tom shouted suddenly.

'Good.'

'God,' he said. 'Do all kids have to go through this with their parents?'

Melissa looked down at her hands. 'Sorry.'

'So you should be,' Tom said. 'I needn't have told you anything. I needn't even have mentioned Claudia. What have you got against Claudia, anyway?'

'Nothing. I think Claudia is lovely.'

'She is. She's cool. I don't know what's the matter with me seeing Claudia.'

'There's nothing the matter,' Melissa said. 'Nothing. It's just that Claudia is Gaby's daughter. It's – a surprise.'

'Well, get used to it,' Tom said, rudely. 'You know now.'

'Does Gaby know?'

'Why don't you ring her? Why don't you get in a mummy huddle with Gaby and have a good old session about us?'

Melissa put out a hand towards him. 'Tom. Darling. I'm sorry. I said I was sorry before, and I meant it.'

He sighed. 'You make such a big deal of everything.'

'I don't. You know I don't. What else have I made any kind of fuss over?'

He straightened up, slid his headphones down to rest them around his neck, and said, 'Sarah.'

'Sarah!'

'Seeing Sarah,' Tom said. 'I know Dad asked you ages ago and you said you would and you haven't. You don't want to, so you haven't. You even cancelled coming to supper.'

'No, I don't want to,' Melissa said, sadly. 'And can't you understand that?'

His lower lip went out fractionally, as it used to when he was small. 'But *I* asked you, too.'

'I know.'

'Look,' Tom said loudly and abruptly. 'I didn't ask to be born. I didn't ask you and Dad to have a fling because you were both on the rebound, and have me. I'm the *consequence* of you both fucking up whatever relationships you were in. I'm not the reason, I'm the result. So in my book, which you mightn't like, because it doesn't suit how you see yourself, you *owe* me. You both owe me. And so I'm asking. I'm asking you, Mum, at least, at the very least, to make an effort to get on with Sarah. So please ring her. Please just ring Sarah and make a plan to meet her. She's OK. Sarah's OK. And, after all, Dad likes her enough to have had Jake and Ben with her. OK? OK?'

Melissa took some moments to nod. But nod she did. 'Of course.'

'Probably,' Tom said, sensing victory, 'I'll screw up just like you have. But I hope I'll listen to my kids. I hope I will.'

'Please don't spoil it all by getting pompous,' she said weakly.

He picked up his iPad. 'I'm going up. I'm going to talk to Claudia.'

Melissa said bravely, 'Skype or Facebook?'

'Maybe.'

She looked directly at him. 'I really don't want to be the kind of mother you don't want.'

He bent forward to kiss her. He said, not unkindly, 'Then don't be,' and then he went out of the kitchen and up the stairs, leaving her shoeless in the brightly lit kitchen with the broken remains of her evening.

—

Later, she went up to Tom's room. He was fast asleep, wearing a T-shirt and jogging pants, in a welter of sound and little winking lights from various technological devices round his bed, a sight that was simultaneously reassuring and disturbing. She tiptoed round the room, turning off what she could, opening the window a chink, pulling his duvet over his sleeping form. And then she bent to kiss him, and felt a rush of something so powerful and warm and right that, even in her jangled state, she knew to be her driving emotional priority. For a moment she stood in the doorway after she had kissed him and looked at his tousled head on the pillow, and reminded herself, sternly, that one day that head would belong emotionally to someone quite other. It might be Claudia, or Claudia could just be the beginning. Children, she reminded herself with a firmness she felt Beth would have urged, are lent to us only. They never belong to us. They belong only to themselves. The sight of Tom, deeply asleep on the lavish bed she had worked to buy for him, was a reminder that he was his own person, his own man. And if she wanted his reciprocal love, she was going to have to earn it. Just as she had earned his bed.

Downstairs again, in her bathroom, her phone told her she had a text message. It was from Will. It read:

> **You were spectacular. Please ring.**
> **Any time, any day. I'm waiting. W. x**

She looked at the message. It seemed to her remote now, detached from what was really of importance. She stood there in her bathroom, under the carefully designed mood lights above her washbasin, and pressed 'delete'. Then she scrolled through her contacts directory to find Sarah Parker's number.

—

Sarah Parker was waiting for her in the downstairs bar of the building allocated for use by Friends of the Royal Academy. She was at a small table in a corner, by a glass door that led to the garden with its planting of tree ferns from New Zealand. Sarah wasn't looking at her phone or reading the evening paper, she was simply sitting there with a bottle of mineral water on the table in front of her, and when Melissa approached her, she looked up, but she didn't smile.

Melissa sat down on the banquette next to her, but at a carefully judged distance.

'Hello, Sarah,' she said, and smiled.

Sarah continued not to smile back. She said, neutrally, 'Hello.'

Melissa made a gesture at her clothes. 'I'm afraid I've come straight from work.'

'So have I.'

'Of course.' She indicated the bottle. 'Are you drinking water?'

'Obviously,' Sarah said.

Melissa stood up again. 'Excuse me a moment.'

She went across to the bar. There was a girl behind it in a white shirt and a narrow black skirt, polishing glasses. Melissa said, 'Could I have a vodka and tonic?'

The girl began to busy herself with the competent business of slicing a lemon and clattering ice cubes into a tumbler. Melissa watched her with extreme concentration in order to quell the turbulence that had flared inside her. Tom had said Sarah was OK. Tom seemed to like her. Tom had suggested Melissa let Sarah choose where they meet.

'You'll see, Mum. She's fine. She's just – kind of normal.'

But Sarah wasn't being normal. She wasn't making any effort to be normal. She was pointedly drinking water and being – well, unhelpful and furious. Fury was what came across, plain rage at Melissa, at what Melissa was or at something she had done. She took a deep breath to steady herself, and turned from the bar. She walked back to Sarah.

'Are you sure you won't have a drink drink?'

Sarah didn't speak. She merely shook her head. Then, as if to make a point about her own self-control, picked up her water glass and drank deeply from it.

Melissa went to get her own drink and carried it back to the table. She sat down again and pushed her hair behind her ears. Then she said, as a statement rather than a question,

'Sarah.'

Sarah put her glass down and turned deliberately to look at her. 'What?'

'What,' Melissa said, 'is the matter?'

'You tell me,' Sarah said coldly.

'I would if I knew what to tell you.'

Sarah made an angry little gesture. 'Feigning innocence on top of everything else only makes me madder.'

Melissa looked down at her lap. Beth would say, breathe. Breathe, and wait. Then she said, as steadily as she could, 'This meeting is because of Tom. We don't particularly want it, either of us, do we? But Tom wants us to meet, Tom wants us to be on polite terms with each other, so that is why we're here. When I rang you, I thought that is what we agreed.'

Sarah folded her hands in her lap. Then she said, 'But there's something else on your agenda, isn't there? Tom is just a decoy.'

'Absolutely *not*.'

Sarah looked at Melissa's bag on the banquette next to her. 'And if I were to look at your phone? If I were to read your texts and listen to your messages?'

Melissa put a hand on her bag. She said, with incredulity, 'Do – do you mean *Will*?'

Sarah didn't flinch. 'Of course I mean Will.'

'But–'

'Don't tell me he isn't in touch with you. Don't tell me there aren't sneaky little meetings. Don't tell me he didn't get you to address Matthew's firm on precisely the topic that I am really qualified to speak on. Don't tell me you aren't letting him know he might have another chance with you.'

Melissa couldn't immediately respond: coherent speech was impossible.

Sarah leaned forward a little, her hands still folded in her lap. Her accent grew defiantly American. Her voice was low but forceful, and her words came rapidly, pouring out of her as if they had been restrained up to that moment with great difficulty.

'I'm not having my life screwed up by some spoiled blast from Will's past. I've worked so hard to make the life we have, our kids, accepting Marnie – who's no breeze as a stepchild, believe you me – making a career in this country, a home for Will . . . When Tom came back into Will's life, I thought nice kid but there'll be more to come and boy, was I right, was I unprepared for Tom's awesomely successful mother to waltz back into Will's life and want a piece of *our* life, our *family* life, because she ain't got one of her own even though she makes a ton of money and spends enough on herself to turn any guy's head with the result, especially a guy with three kids at home, and a rediscovered son, and a full-time working partner and his fiftieth birthday coming up. I thought I could handle it, I thought I could deal with this mid-life-crisis-fantasy guy thing, but I reckoned without you, didn't I, I reckoned without you pulling Will away from us, offering just the chances, the freedoms, the crazy stuff that a guy like him still wants even if he knows he has to put it behind him.

Using Tom, you can pretend you're just doing what's best for your boy, can't you, but I see through that, *I* see what you're trying to do, and I want you to know that even if you succeed, even if you get what you think you want, *I'll* have sussed you all along, *I'll* have noticed every move in your game. And you'll have to live with that knowledge, won't you, in your fancy house with your fancy career. You won't have got away with a *thing*.'

By the time she'd finished, and drawn back a fraction, Melissa had recovered some composure. Staring straight at Sarah, she slowly shook her head. 'You're wrong,' she said.

Sarah snorted and glanced at the ceiling.

'It *is* about Tom,' Melissa said. 'It's only about Tom. Tom is, whatever happened or will happen, the love of my life.'

Sarah said nothing. She went on looking away from Melissa, as if waiting for her to acknowledge that she was right.

Melissa went on, 'There was some flirting, I won't deny that. But nothing serious, nothing that could possibly threaten you or your life with Will. And I had no idea that you were in the running to speak to Matthew's firm, till now. If I had known, I wouldn't have even thought of accepting.'

Sarah picked up her water glass again. 'You expect me to believe you?'

'Yes,' Melissa said. 'It's the truth.'

Sarah said, 'Why aren't you drinking your *vodka*?'

'I don't want it.'

'Oh dear,' Sarah said. Her voice was sarcastic.

'I just want you to believe me that I may have allowed the situation to become something it shouldn't have been, but my only concern, in the end, is Tom.'

'So Will begging you to ring him is *nothing*?'

'I haven't rung,' Melissa said. 'I deleted the message.'

'How noble,' Sarah said, setting her glass down with a bang. 'How *decent*. At last.'

'It's true,' Melissa said. 'He should not have sent such a text. I should not have let him think he could send such a text. That's wrong. And I'm sorry. But it's over.'

Sarah bit her lip. She suddenly seemed to crumple. She said, far less coherently, her voice catching, 'No, it isn't.'

It was Melissa's turn to lean forward. 'What d'you mean?'

Sarah began to hunt in her bag for a tissue. 'You *know* what I mean!' she said angrily.

'It's nonsense.'

'Not in his mind. He's kind of carried away, wanting the past back, dazzled by what you've made of yourself.' She found a packet of tissues, extracted one and blew her nose hard. She said, furiously and sadly, 'You just *know* when your guy's dreaming of someone else, don't you?'

'It's nonsense,' Melissa said again, more helplessly. 'It really is. He'll always be Tom's father, and I'll always be grateful for that, but it's Tom who matters to me. Just Tom.'

Sarah blotted below her eyes. 'Are you dating anyone right now?'

'No,' Melissa said.

'Don't you want to?'

'On and off. Right now, it's off.'

Sarah sniffed. She eyed Melissa. 'Do I believe you?'

Melissa shrugged. 'I can't keep saying it's true, but it is. It's true that I might have been careless and a bit flattered, but no more than that. And it's true that all I care about is Tom.'

Sarah began to gather up her bag and coat from the banquette beside her. She said,

'So you'd still see Will if meetings between the two of you made Tom happy?'

'No,' Melissa said. 'Not now.'

'So, what do I believe after all?'

Melissa sat straighter. She watched Sarah struggle into her coat. She said, in as calm a voice as she could manage, 'I've had enough of this, Sarah.'

'*You've* had enough–'

'Yes. I have. You accuse me of motives and conduct that never even occurred to me and now you try and trip me up with my own priorities in order to make yourself the victim of a personal situation you can't control. Will you *listen*? I don't want Will, except as the father of my son, and on reasonable terms to make that work. Do you hear me? I don't want Will in any other way whatsoever, and I'm not going to keep apologizing for giving any other impression. I'm not responsible for the current predicament you and Will are in and I'm not trying to take anything that is yours. So don't make me your convenient scapegoat. Just – don't.'

Sarah stood up. She slung her bag on her shoulder and pulled a pair of gloves from her pocket. She said, in a quieter voice, 'I expect we'll work something out.'

—

Wednesday nights meant that Tom was having a squash lesson with Rufus, after which he would come home and raid the fridge. It was, this Wednesday, perhaps a good thing that Tom wasn't at home when she returned after her meeting with Sarah, because there would be time for her to wrestle her responses to his inevitable curiosity – even if he didn't articulate it – into some kind of acceptable order.

She dropped her keys in the black marble bowl where she always left them, automatically removed a dead flower head or two from the arrangements beside it, took her shoes off, and climbed the stairs with her shoes in her hand. Her bedroom and bathroom, usually so restoratively calm and orderly at the end of a day, looked today as impersonal and bland as rooms in a hotel, as if their appearance had had nothing to do with anything she might have chosen or decided. With dogged fastidiousness, she put shoe trees in her shoes, took off her work suit and hung it up, put her jewellery in its accustomed trays and boxes, pulled on the velour tracksuit she wore around the house and finally, her feet in slippers and her hair in a ponytail, stooped over the basin in her bathroom to take out her contact lenses. Only then, all personal rituals having been laboriously accomplished, did she descend to the kitchen to check the fridge for Tom's homecoming raid, and put the kettle on to make tea from an infusion of lemon and fresh ginger in a glass teapot especially designed for the purpose. All the while she was silently chastising herself for her habits, and the patterns of life that had evolved – or she had permitted to evolve – as a substitute, probably, for . . . what?

She ought to ring Gaby. They needed to have a conversation about Tom and Claudia. Surely they did. And the fact that Gaby, in her new phase of telling everyone everything at once, had not immediately been on the telephone to Melissa was evidence that she, Gaby, was as mysteriously thrown by this new alliance as Melissa was. Was it because Claudia was only thirteen? Was it because the children had known each other all their lives, or because Gaby and Melissa had been friends for more than twenty-five years but had never, in all those years, apparently considered a romantic liaison between any of their offspring? Whatever it was, Melissa couldn't think about it now. Nor could she think about the bizarre, even grotesque, meeting she had just had with Sarah. At this moment, standing slicing ginger root in her kitchen, all she could do was hope that by the time Tom got home, he would be too consumed by hunger to ask her questions, and she would have, somehow, come up with an acceptably anodyne way to recount what had happened.

In her tracksuit pocket, her phone announced that a text message had arrived. No doubt it would be from Tom, who was comfortingly assiduous about texting her his constant changes of plan. She pulled her phone out of her pocket. The text was from Stacey.

> **Lissa, your clothes went down a storm.**
> **Have had brilliant idea for future.**
> **Need your advice. Ring soonest. Excited!!**
> **Stace xx**

CHAPTER FIFTEEN

GABY

Claudia appeared completely unruffled. She had done her homework, and her latest history and literature essays had been awarded an A and a B plus. She was sitting at the kitchen counter with her glasses on, learning her part for a dramatized class reading of *Twelfth Night*, in which she had been cast as Viola. When Gaby spoke to her, she put her finger on the line of text she was learning, and slowly looked up. 'What?'

'I said that I didn't know you had a boyfriend.'

'You wouldn't,' Claudia said reasonably. 'I didn't tell you.'

'Why?'

'Well,' Claudia said, in the voice she used for spelling something very obvious out to Liam, 'he's just someone I hang out with and he's someone I've known all my life, like you have, so it's –' she paused and made quotation marks in the air with both hands, letting her Shakespeare pages flutter over '– no big deal.'

Gaby, also in her spectacles, came to sit on the stool next to Claudia's. She said, importantly, 'Claud.'

'Mummy dearest.'

'Your Facebook page says you have a boyfriend. So does

his. Say he has a girlfriend, I mean. You and Tom Hathaway or Tom Hathaway Gibbs or whatever he is now, appear to be, officially, what my generation would call An Item.'

'Maybe,' Claudia said. 'So?'

'So why didn't you or Tom say a word to Melissa or me?'

Claudia took her time finding her place again in her text. Then she said, 'There was nothing *to* say.'

'You are thirteen.'

'Fourteen in ten weeks.'

'As your mother,' Gaby said, 'I have to know about your relationships because I have to advise and protect you. As I have said to all of you, over and over, I am not interested in being your *friend* – heavens knows, you have thousands of those – but I am very interested indeed in being your *parent*. So, Claudia, I need to know, especially as you are thirteen, about your relationship with Tom, and exactly what that involves.'

'Oh God,' Claudia said to an invisible audience. 'She means sex.'

'She does,' Gaby said. 'You've had periods since you were eleven.'

Claudia continued to look away. 'Melissa doesn't talk like this to Tom,' she said. 'She talks about love and feelings.'

'I am not Melissa,' Gaby said, 'I am your mother and I don't want you messed about either physically or emotionally by some boy who isn't, I'm afraid, Claud, old enough to know his arse from his elbow.'

Claudia sighed. 'And here I was, thinking you'd be pleased!'

'Part of me is. Nice boy. Known him all his life. Very nice mother. Same wavelength. *All* that. But none of that is my concern. My concern is *you*. I don't want, to be completely upfront with you, Tom Hathaway experimenting with his inevitable boiling cauldron of boy hormones, on *you*. So at best I want to prevent it, and at worst I want you to be as well prepared as you possibly can be. See?'

Claudia closed her Shakespeare and bent her head. Then she said, reluctantly, 'OK.'

'Has he tried anything?'

'Shut up.'

'Has he kissed you?'

Claudia nodded. Her face was obscured by her hair.

'Anything else?' Gaby demanded.

'No,' Claudia whispered.

'Sure?'

'No!'

Gaby took Claudia's nearest hand. 'Look at me, Claud.'

'Can't.'

'This is just the beginning, poppet. You have decades of this ahead, decades. Don't screw up the future by giving in to anything, Tom or your own feelings, too soon. Stick with Viola. Really. And tell me as much as you can, all the time, because, Claud, I am on your side. I truly am. It doesn't feel like that, I know, right now, but I have to look after you, and you have to let me.' She got off her stool and dropped Claudia's hand.

'Where are you going?' Claudia said, in a much less confident voice.

Gaby bent to drop a kiss on Claudia's head. 'Upstairs. To talk to Taylor.'

'Taylor!'

'Yes,' Gaby said. 'How would you feel if you were fifteen

and had never had a boyfriend, and your kid sister suddenly got one, just like that?'

—

For once, Taylor's music wasn't on. Her door wasn't even shut, it was open, just slightly, enough to reveal Taylor propped up on her bed, wearing a onesie patterned like a lilac leopard, reading a book. A physical book. As far as Gaby could remember, Taylor had not picked up a physical, paper book since she could read for herself and had loudly declined bedtime stories. She was not only reading, she was not alone, either. Quin was lying across the end of her bed, his shoulders against the wall, also reading.

Gaby pushed the door wider and regarded them. 'Am I interrupting?'

Taylor didn't look up. 'No,' she said.

Gaby took a step or two into the room. 'Is it OK to ask what you are reading?'

Without looking her mother's way, Taylor held out the book so that Gaby could read the title on the spine. It was *Jane Eyre*.

'Goodness,' Gaby said. 'I didn't know you had ever even tried to read Charlotte Brontë.'

'There's a lot,' Taylor said, returning to her reading, 'that you don't know about me.'

'Clearly,' Gaby replied. She looked at Quin. 'What about you?'

'Bernard Cornwell,' Quin said.

'That I would have guessed. Can I sit down?'

Taylor waved a hand. 'Anywhere . . .'

'I can only see the floor.'

Quin straightened and got up. 'Sit on the bed. I'm going down to make some coffee anyway. I was just keeping Taylor company.'

'I didn't,' Taylor said, still apparently reading, 'ask for anyone's company.'

Gaby sat at the foot of the bed, where Quin had been lying. As she settled herself, he put a hand briefly on her shoulder and squeezed it. She glanced up at him.

'Don't do that,' Taylor said.

Gaby patted her daughter's feet. 'Aren't we even allowed to be sympathetic?'

'I can take sympathy,' Taylor said. 'But if you're sorry for me, I'll *kill* you.'

Quin turned in the doorway. 'Exactly what would you like us to do, sweetheart?'

Taylor put *Jane Eyre* over her face. Then, from behind it, she shouted, 'Nothing!'

Gaby gestured to Quin to leave.

'How are things with Flossie?'

'Don't know,' Taylor said from behind her book.

'At half term,' Gaby said, 'would you like to come in to the office with me?'

Taylor lowered her book. She said, as if completely baffled by the offer, 'No?'

'I'd like you to, though.'

'Why?'

'So,' Gaby said, 'I can show off to you. I can show off my office and my team and the boardroom where we have meetings and the chief executive and chairman want us all to know that they have planes to catch.'

Taylor let her book subside onto her stomach. 'Why?'

'Because there's a life after school. There's another life after your family one and your school friends one. You know how hippy dippy my childhood was. You know how I didn't fit in with all that barefoot bonfire carry-on. It didn't hurt me, it was very loving and all that, but it wasn't what I wanted. I've got what I wanted, more or less, by not doing what I was brought up to do. Maybe you're the same. Maybe you need to live in a way that isn't the way Pa and I run this house. I'm just suggesting you come and have a look.'

Taylor sighed. She unzipped her onesie far enough to be able to reach in and scratch her right shoulder, and then she said, 'I don't care about Tom and Claud. It's just – it's just that she didn't even have to *try*.'

'I know. So unfair.'

'I'm so tired,' Taylor said, 'of things being unfair.'

Gaby squeezed Taylor's ankles. 'That's life, chicken. Unfair, unfair, unfair.'

'I – will come to your office.'

'Good.'

Taylor lifted *Jane Eyre* off her stomach and laid the book down beside her, on her duvet. She said, 'Do you stop getting fed up with people when you're older?'

'No,' Gaby said.

Taylor eyed her. 'Who're you fed up with at the moment? Pa?'

'Not exactly.'

'Who then? Anyone?'

Gaby took her hand off Taylor's ankle. 'Well . . .'

'Yes?'

Gaby looked down at her hands. 'Melissa,' she said, and then, 'Not because of Tom. Because of Sarah.'

—

'What are you doing?' Quin said.

'Writing.'

'I can see that. But it's after midnight. Who are you writing to?'

'Taylor.'

'*Taylor?* Why Taylor? You see Taylor every day.'

'Exactly,' Gaby said.

'Can I see it?' Quin said, after a pause.

'What?'

'What you've written.'

'Of course,' Gaby said. 'There's nothing secret.' She looked up at him. 'I know I get ratty, but I get what you do.'

'Hm,' Quin said, but he smiled. He pulled out the chair next to Gaby's and sat down. He said, 'A recent Mumsnet survey found that over half the working mothers polled said staying at home was much harder than going out to work.'

Gaby prodded him with her pen. 'There you are then. Gold stars all round.' She held out the sheet of paper she had been writing on. 'Here it is.'

He made no move to take it. 'Read it to me.'

'Why?'

'I like looking at you reading it. In your specs.'

She glanced at him suspiciously. 'Why are you being nice to me?'

'I *am* nice.'

'No reason?'

There was a fractional hesitation. 'No reason,' he said.

Gaby held her letter up to read it. '"Dearest Taylor . . ."'

'Not darling?'

Gaby ignored him. '"Dearest Taylor. However annoying certain things are in the family right now, I want to say something to you that I hope will be a small comfort and encouragement. And it's this. Try to focus on work rather than falling in love. That may seem a classic mother-not-understanding thing to say, but it's work that will keep you going through love and children and marriage, it's work that will actually provide more *fun* than almost anything else that happens to you. I expect you'll think that I would say that, wouldn't I, so I'm going to say something else, too. Whatever you choose in your life as your priority has to be *your* choice, not mine, and if you decide to ignore everything I've advised you, I'll still be here, on your side, forever. And that's a promise. Best love, Mum."'

'Very touching,' Quin said.

'I mean it.'

'Yes,' he said, 'so do I. That's a lovely letter.'

'Really?'

'Really.'

She leaned forward and kissed him. 'Thank you.'

'We don't do thanks, do we?' he said. 'We just do what has to be done. Whatever that is.'

She began to fold her letter. 'Quite,' she said, happily.

—

There was an envelope on her desk in the office. An envelope was a rare thing to see these days, as Morag sorted the physical post, and in any case, most communications arrived electronically. This envelope had her name on it in an unmistakably American hand, and it had been placed on her keyboard, where she could not possibly fail to see it.

Gaby hung up her parka and ran her hands through her hair. She would not, she told herself, be in any hurry to open the envelope, and to that end, would first fire up her desktop screen and check her emails, which is what she always did first thing anyway. The emails were, on the whole, predictable and manageable, at least by Morag. The one that wasn't was from Melissa. It was the kind of email that Gaby would have disliked getting even if she hadn't been conscious, guiltily and for almost a week, that she should have rung Melissa and talked the matter through when she was first aware of it.

'Aware' was the word Melissa used. 'I'm sure you are aware,' she had written, 'of what Tom and Claudia think they are doing.' It was annoying on several counts, most of them irrational. Melissa seemed to have expected Gaby to pick up the phone, even though she hadn't done it herself. She also seemed – to Gaby, at least – to imply that whatever was going on was somehow a result of Claudia's arch minxiness, and that Tom, left to himself, would have made a superior choice. Definitely an *older* choice, anyway. 'I wonder,' Melissa had written unwisely, 'how much any of this was Tom's idea, seeing as how obsessed with sport and dogs and learning to cook he seems to be?' Melissa sounded, Gaby thought, almost affronted. How *dare* she even *think* about being affronted? How could any mother of a boy who was lucky enough to be looked at twice by someone of the calibre of Claudia be anything other than humble with sheer gratitude? Gaby said a rude word, loudly, to her computer screen.

She got up and went distractedly across the room to her viewing spot, down across the square. She didn't seem to be seeing it with any coherence. She was consumed, instead, with a ferocious and sudden urge to rush home and take Claudia with her on a plane to San Francisco or Bali, anywhere that was far, far away from horrible, fumbling pollutants like Tom Hathaway Gibbs and his disgracefully blinkered mother. Nobody should touch Claudia. Nobody should be anything other than amazed and entranced by Claudia. Nobody should even begin to *think* that their gormless child had one single right to a second of Claudia's attention. She was breathing hard, she realized, and her fingernails were digging painfully into her palms. How *dare* Melissa? How bloody *dare* she?

She swallowed. This wouldn't do. Quin would tell her that tiger mothers were more concerned with themselves than they were about their cubs. Tom Hathaway was a nice boy, after all. Melissa, being Melissa, was probably in a complicated state about him growing up and away, on top of his rediscovery of his father. Melissa, despite her immense professional success and competence, had an abiding appetite for fairy dust and soppiness, and looked at Tom with an indulgent adoration that Gaby knew her own children seldom saw. She must pick up the phone and talk to Melissa. She and Melissa must stand together, firm but understanding, just as she had been when she'd talked to Claudia and written to Taylor. She was, as she had said to Claudia, a *parent*, Claudia's parent. The relationship between Claudia and Tom could go on as long as there was no deception and no lying. Especially no lying. She was sure Melissa would agree.

She went back to her desk and sat down. The envelope waited beside her keyboard, where she had moved it. With an effort at control, she picked up the letter opener that a grateful client had sent her from Brazil, the end garnished with a blue topaz from Minas Gerais.

She took the letter out of the envelope and unfolded it. Then she stared at it, as if it contained something that was very hard to take in. Concisely, and without much explanation, Sarah Parker was writing to Gaby to tell her that she was taking advantage of the company's three-month notice option, and resigning from her job.

Gaby stood up and marched out of her office. Then she marched back in again and pressed the button for her direct connection to Morag's desk.

'I need to see Sarah.'

Morag was used to Gaby. 'Please,' she said, pleasantly and patiently.

Gaby said, more calmly, 'I need to see Sarah, please.'

'I'm afraid,' Morag said, equally steadily, 'that Sarah isn't in the office.'

'What do you mean?'

'I mean, Gaby, that Sarah isn't physically here for you to see.'

'Where is she, then?'

'Well,' Morag said, 'I believe she has gone to see Stacey.'

Gaby paused, then she cancelled the phone connection and almost ran out into the outer office. She did what she always did and perched on the edge of Morag's desk, slightly obscuring the computer screen from Morag's view. 'Say that again?'

'Sarah,' Morag said, 'isn't in the office because she has gone to see Stacey.'

'I think you had better explain.'

Morag sat back and folded her hands. 'Stacey's new project–'

'What new project?'

'The clothes and interview-practice one.'

'*What?*'

'You know,' Morag said. 'The idea she had for Melissa's old clothes.'

Gaby put her hands to her head. She said, 'I thought Melissa and Sarah had had the most god-awful row.'

'They had. They did. And then Sarah thought she'd overdone it because she was so stressed keeping this job going as well as everything else, so she decided to make some changes, which included a different work pattern, and Melissa suggested–'

'Melissa?' Gaby said, weakly.

'Sarah apologized to Melissa, and apparently Melissa was very nice about it all and suggested that Stacey could do with another business brain behind her new project.'

'Which is?'

'Oh,' Morag said, 'don't you know?'

Gaby gave a groan of despair. 'Do I look as if I do?'

Morag said, 'It's cool. It's a sort of agency, a charity, that helps women dress and comport themselves successfully for interviews. Especially women going back to work.'

'Very good.'

'That,' Morag said, 'sounds a bit qualified.'

Gaby said, 'Why didn't I know about it?'

'I don't know.'

'Why – why was it *kept* from me?'

'It wasn't. You were just so busy and preoccupied.'

'No I wasn't,' Gaby said. 'No more than usual, anyway. All

this stuff, swirling around, never mind how much Sarah's blithe change of heart and career might *affect* me.'

'She was scared of you,' Morag said.

'*Scared* of me?'

'Yes. How you'd react. What you'd say to her.'

'But – but look at Ellie!'

'Sarah thinks,' Morag said steadily, 'that you'll cut people like Ellie much more slack because they're junior and need help.'

'Well,' Gaby said. 'True. Obviously. I need grown-ups like Sarah to behave like grown-ups.'

'There you are then,' Morag said quietly.

'So she's ashamed?'

Morag nodded.

'Maybe,' Gaby said, 'it's just as well that she *isn't* here. I'm not sure I'd have full control of my tongue.'

'No.'

Gaby got off Morag's desk. She said, 'Martin isn't ready to take Sarah's place. I actually doubt he ever will be.'

'You always say,' Morag said carefully, 'that no one is indispensable.'

'That doesn't preclude them being immensely important and valuable.' She glanced down at Morag. 'What's the name of Stacey's new venture?'

'Peg's Project. After Stacey's mum.'

Gaby gave a little grin. 'Just think if it was *my* mother,' she said. 'She's called Christobel.'

—

Gaby lay in the bath. However late it was, or tired she was, a bath was an imperative. Growing up, there had been too many people and too little hot water for a reliable daily bath, so the moment she could arrange it, Gaby insisted on a nightly soak, even at three in the morning. If the children, or Quin, needed to be certain of finding her, the bath was the place, her hair screwed up in a plastic claw, her specs on, and a business or economics magazine held just above the water, dimpled with damp.

When Quin, in the towelling robe he had been wearing since Liam was born, settled on the corner of the bath by Gaby's feet, she didn't look up from the *Financial Times* Saturday magazine she was reading. She merely said, 'Some days are just remarkable for being over.'

Quin scratched his ear. 'Did you ring Melissa?'

'Yup.'

'And?'

Gaby threw the magazine sideways onto the floor. She said, 'Surprisingly, she said she wasn't that worried now and she thought it would soon be over.'

'Really?' asked Quin. 'Will Claud mind?'

Gaby reached for the soap. 'Remember how many Valentine cards Claud got.'

'Well,' Quin said, 'it's all given you the chance to say what needed to be said, to Claudia.'

'And Taylor.'

'Of course. And Taylor.'

Gaby began to soap herself. 'I just need to be able to say what needs to be said to Sarah Parker.'

Quin looked away. 'Yes.'

She glanced at him. 'Don't you think the abruptness and evasiveness of her behaviour merits a slap on the wrist from me?'

'It's – hard . . .' Quin said slowly.

'What is?'

'Making changes.'

Gaby sat up and leaned forward to twist the plug to open. She said, slightly warningly,

'Quin?'

'Yes?'

'Are you taking Sarah's part?'

He turned his head back. He said, 'Not hers. Mine.'

'What?'

'*I* want to make a change.'

Gaby sat and stared at him, while the water level sank steadily round her. 'You . . .'

'I want,' Quin said, more decisively, 'to make a change. In my life. Before it's too late.' He got off the edge of the bath and flipped a towel off the heated rail nearby. Then he said, holding it out to Gaby, 'I want to sell the shops.'

—

It was after two in the morning before Gaby went round the children's bedrooms. She did this every night, retrieving duvets and pillows, removing phones and iPods, switching off connections and lights. Sometimes the girls, especially, were still awake, but Liam was almost always asleep, sprawled across the bedful of stuffed animals whose feelings, he said, he couldn't hurt by leaving them to sleep without him. Tonight he was on his side, Heffalump between his knees and his head pillowed on a plush turtle with yellow plastic eyes. Claudia, by contrast, slept in an empty bed, her glasses on the bedside table beside her phone and her spectacular collection of nail varnishes lined up like chess pieces. Taylor had two lamps burning still and the floor of her room was strewn with clothing, a single trainer, several plastic carrier bags and a scattering of screwed-up pieces of paper, as if Taylor had tried to draft something and found every version unsatisfactory.

Gaby switched off the lamps and, with the light from the landing, found the pair for the trainer and gathered up the balls of paper. They were apparently printouts of something to do with Taylor's current citizenship project on cultural diversity. Then the sight of her own handwriting caught her eye. She smoothed out the piece of paper. It was her own paper, her writing paper. She was holding her letter to Taylor, written three nights before, and now, screwed up like any other piece of rubbish, on Taylor's floor. She looked at it for a long time and then she tiptoed across the room and put it, smoothed out but still crumpled, on Taylor's desk. She looked at her hands in surprise. They were shaking, violently. Out of instinct, she pressed them against her heart, partly to still them, and partly to ease the sudden pain.

CHAPTER SIXTEEN

BETH

Beth's assistant, Eileen, had been with her all her years at the business school. She was married, with grown-up children, and never spoke about any of them, in exactly the same way that she never asked Beth a single thing about her private life. Beth gave her book tokens at Christmas and on her birthday, and Eileen, in return, kept Beth's professional diary and made the necessary arrangements with an impersonal zeal that Beth much appreciated. Eileen was always asked to every lecture, and every book launch, as a matter of courtesy, and seldom came. If she did, she would sit in the back row or stand at the edge of the crowd long enough for Beth to register her presence, and then she would slip away, home to north London and the house she shared with a husband called Maxwell about whom Beth knew nothing beyond that he worked in a bank.

In the mornings, Eileen left a printout of important emails and any significant items of physical post on Beth's desk, with small neon paper flags to indicate the need for immediate action. That morning there was nothing out of the ordinary, in fact nothing that wasn't, in its way, rather pleasing, such as yet another offer from a distinguished business school in Lausanne – which had been courting Beth to join its staff for over two years – and a substantial amount of fan mail as a result of a lecture she had given and a speech she had made to the senior management of twenty significant manufacturing companies. It was, Beth thought, briefly dwelling on an especially glowing compliment, a very good start to another working week.

At the bottom of Eileen's tidy pile was an old-fashioned letter bearing the letterhead of a firm of solicitors Beth had never heard of. It would, Beth thought initially, be a request for a promising student to be subsidized for an MBA course, or an invitation to speak, or, as sometimes happened, a need to have some aspect of business practice confirmed as being in common, rather than legal usage. But it wasn't. The letter was addressed, formally, to Professor Elizabeth Mundy, and across the top was typed not only the address in Wilkes Street, but also Claire's full name as co-owner of the property.

Beth put the letter down for a moment and stared ahead, unseeingly. Then she made herself pick it up again, and read it.

> Dear Professor Mundy,
>
> We have been instructed by our client, Miss Claire Faraday, to inform you of her intention to apply to the courts for an order under section 14 of the Trusts of Land and Appointment of Trustees Act 1996, in respect of the above property.
>
> It is our client's wish, and need, that the property, which is co-owned with yourself, should now be sold.
>
> The intention was that the property in Wilkes Street should be a home, rather than an investment, but as the

purpose for which the property was required has now ended, it is our view that the courts, when applied to under the Act cited above, may order an immediate sale.

In order to avoid such a process, which could well prove protracted, we are writing to request that you reconsider your refusal to sell. Compliance would be to the benefit of both parties.

Yours faithfully.

Beth put the letter down again. She sat there for a while, her head bent, waiting to feel more coherent. It occurred to her, randomly and to no purpose, that this is how Stacey must have felt, sitting on a bench in St Paul's Churchyard, the afternoon she was sacked, wondering if she could even breathe. Beth tried breathing. Shallowly, she could manage. She squeezed her eyes shut and then opened them unnaturally wide. A question formed in her brain, not a directly relevant question but a loud, insistent one, clamouring to be heard. Had Claire actually been *this* kind of person, all along?

She waited for a moment, and then she picked up the letter and made her way slowly to the door. She paused again, transferring the letter to her left hand, and with the right, opened the door to the corridor outside.

Across the corridor, in a small glass-walled cubicle, Eileen was typing. Eileen had, she realized, opened the letter and had put it on her desk, unflagged and at the bottom of the pile. Quiet, competent, discreet Eileen had not known what to do with such a bombshell any more than Beth did, so she had opted for the most neutral action she could think of.

Beth crossed the corridor and stood in the open doorway to Eileen's cubicle. Eileen went on typing, but with a sudden tautness that betrayed her consciousness of Beth's presence and what it portended.

'Eileen,' Beth said, quietly.

She didn't look up. She had taken, recently, to wearing spectacles for computer work, rimless spectacles that caught the light in an eerie fashion and gave her face a kind of halo.

'Eileen,' Beth said again.

Eileen stopped typing and whisked her hands into her lap. She couldn't look at Beth.

'Oh, Beth,' she said, in almost a whisper. 'I'm so sorry.'

'About?'

Eileen gave a little gulp, and raised her head. 'All of it,' she said.

—

In the kitchen at Wilkes Street, Scott's mother, Nadine, had made herself at home. She was, she told Beth, very much a homemaker, she couldn't help herself: give her a hotel room and she'd make it hers in ten minutes. And Beth's kitchen was just crying out to be a kitchen again and not an overflow office with a fridge in it. Scott's father, she said confidingly, had detested her domesticating instincts. He'd grown up north of Auckland, after all, and got claustrophobia if you even suggested being out of sight of the sea. Would Beth mind if Nadine just kind of took the kitchen in hand a bit?

Beth didn't mind at all. She had wondered if the letter from Claire's solicitor would make her feel violently possessive about Wilkes Street, but discovered that her intense preoccupation with Claire's betrayal had made almost everything else, including the house, irrelevant. If Nadine wanted to clean the kitchen floor and banish the cats from the table and polish all the granite surfaces, then she was welcome. A bright checked tablecloth and a jug of forced yellow roses from Kenya might not have been Beth's first choice, but she found that the effect of both was undeniably cheering. It was also orderly and purposeful. Even the cats seemed to be aware that some form of domestic control was being reasserted, and it was to everyone's benefit.

Scott, Beth was pleased to see, wasn't even thinking of apologizing for his mother. On the contrary, he was proud of her efforts, and the contribution she was making. He said Beth should try the results of Nadine's baking and when he watched television in the evenings, he no longer lay on the sofas to do so, but sat on them with a cat on his lap, looking strangely alert.

Beth did not mention the letter to anyone in Wilkes Street. Nor, when they had their weekly telephone call, did she tell her father. Stacey called to tell her about Peg's Project and Beth, catching the energy and excitement in Stacey's voice, said that she was delighted to hear about it, and if she could be of help in any way, she'd be only too happy. Melissa, phoning to recount the row with Sarah Parker and the remarkable day that had given rise to Peg's Project, said, 'How are you, Bethie?' and Beth said, 'I'm doing fine, honey. One of the kids has his mother staying for a few weeks, so I'm even coming home to hot food,' and Melissa had laughed and said that, speaking personally, that's what restaurants were for. Beth asked if Melissa had heard from Gaby recently, and Melissa's voice had taken on the tone of intense sympathy.

'I think she's up to her ears in family stuff and personnel problems at work.'

'Family stuff?'

'Well,' Melissa said, 'my Tom had a bit of a thing for Claudia for ten whole minutes.'

'And?'

'It seems to be over. On Tom's side anyway.'

'I hope it didn't create trouble,' Beth said. 'Between you and Gaby.'

'Oh no,' Melissa said. She sounded remarkably breezy. 'In fact, we hardly spoke about it at all. What about *you*, though?'

Beth took a determined breath. 'I am fine. Absolutely *fine*.'

'You sound so purposeful, Bethie. I'm so glad to hear it. I really am. No sight or sound of Claire, I do hope?'

'None.'

'And Wilkes Street?'

Beth had instinctively straightened, standing in her study whose waste-paper bin, she noticed, Nadine had emptied. 'We're fine, here, honey. A full house, as I said.'

'And no plans?'

Beth smiled into the telephone. 'No plans.'

In the kitchen, Nadine was dicing a butternut squash, for soup. Last time she had made it, she had sprinkled Parmesan cheese on the top and added a shining spoonful of truffle oil. Beth and Nadine and Scott and Phil from Hull had sat at the kitchen table, their elbows on the checked cloth, and eaten the soup with real respect. It was, as Nadine had promised, excellent soup. And when it was finished, both the men had got up and stacked the soup bowls in the dishwasher, without being asked.

'Respect,' Beth had said to Nadine.

Now, chopping up the chunks of squash, Nadine offered Beth a cup of tea.

'I won't, thank you.'

Nadine said cheerfully, 'I'd take the offer while you can, if I was you. I'll be gone in three days.'

Beth was startled. 'Gone?'

'I came for two weeks,' Nadine said, 'and I've been here for almost three. Time to go home.'

'We'll miss you,' Beth said, meaning it.

Nadine began to scoop up double handfuls of squash, to dump them in a saucepan.

'I've had a great time.'

'It seems to me you've done little except sort my house.'

'It needed doing.'

'I've not,' Beth said, 'much of a house-proud disposition.'

Nadine poured water from the kettle into her saucepan. She said, 'We aren't all. And you shouldn't try. You're brilliant at other things.'

'But once I thought, you know . . .'

'Things were different then, weren't they? I'm not a brain-box like you, but I think we all have to do what we're designed to do. Obey our instincts. When it all fell apart with Scott's father, all I wanted to do was get back to South Africa and plant a vegetable garden and make my own kitchen curtains. You don't want any of that. So you shouldn't do it.' She put the pan on the hob and adjusted the heat. Then she added, 'What do you want? You're the same age as me and a big shot in your world. Seems to me you could do pretty much what you want.'

Beth sat down by the table and put her elbows on it. 'What do *you* think I should do?' she said, seriously.

Nadine put a lid on her saucepan. Then she turned round and leaned against the counter beside the hob. She was wearing jeans and a green and gold Springboks rugby shirt of Scott's. She looked, suddenly, about sixteen.

'Well, Beth, if I was in your position, I'd just make the most of my freedom.'

—

'Can you talk?' Beth texted Gaby.

'10 mins. Will call you,' Gaby texted back.

Beth was in her office, standing by the window. In half an hour, she was due to give a tutorial – What Has Changed in the Working Consciousness? – to a group of final-year students, and although she knew what she would say, indeed was well rehearsed in the theme of the class, she was beset by restlessness. Behind her, on her desk and table, lay the usual piles of books and papers that needed sorting. She was the only person who could do this task but she couldn't make herself, any more than she could make herself cross the corridor to Eileen's cubicle and smooth all the jagged edges left by their unsatisfactory conversation two days earlier. All she could do, she discovered, was drum her fingers against the rain-spotted glass, and fidget. Texting Gaby had been an unthinking impulse. Why Gaby? Why, indeed, text anybody? And why, as a result of that texting, was she waiting for Gaby's call with all the tense fervour of an expectant lover? When her phone actually rang, she snatched it up with ridiculous eagerness.

'Gaby.'

'Beth? Are you OK?'

Beth pressed her phone hard against her ear. 'I have no idea,' she said, almost laughing.

'If it's any comfort,' Gaby said, from Canary Wharf, 'me neither. And I have a meeting in fifteen.'

'I have a class.'

'Busy busy. Aren't we? Do we love it, though?'

'Work?'

'Yes, work.'

'Work,' Beth said, 'is where we feel most creative and innovative. It's exciting. We make friends at work.'

There was a short pause, and then Gaby said, 'It's also the most frustrating part of our lives. Exasperating.'

'Do you want to talk about it?'

'Actually,' Gaby said, 'no. Not even to you. I've had a go at candour and in my experience, it doesn't work. Nothing seems to affect the – *randomness* of other people.'

Beth relaxed her grip on her phone a little. She said, '*Tell* me about it.'

'Your turn,' Gaby said. 'Do you want to talk?'

'No. I want to scream, but that's different.'

Gaby laughed. 'It doesn't get easier, does it?'

'Change is never easy. This is what we're going through, change.'

'Did you text,' Gaby said, 'to have a quasi-philosophical conversation about the journey of life?'

Beth said simply, 'I just had this urge.'

'OK,' Gaby said. 'But – are things falling apart?'

Beth pressed her forehead against the window. 'Our future – working future – will be increasingly defined by innovation,' she said, in a more formal tone. 'We'll have to combine mastery of our specialities with an ability to connect with other people, and their other competences.'

'Oh God,' Gaby said. 'Don't be all professional with me, *please*, Beth.'

'It's just my way of coping with temporary chaos, honey.'

'I have to go to my meeting.'

'And I to my class.'

'Beth,' Gaby said suddenly, her tone altered, 'is Melissa seeing someone?'

'Well, there was a resurgence of Tom's father . . .'

'No,' Gaby said, 'not Will. There's been some kind of drama there. But she's suddenly quite different, kind of – kind of *skittish*. And she's stopped being all tiger mother about Tom. Just like that. *Dratted* Tom, actually.'

'What?'

'No time to tell you now. Can we meet?'

Beth took her forehead away from the glass. 'Yes,' she said. 'Soon. When I've unpicked a few knots.'

'Hollow laughter to that ambition, sugar,' Gaby said, and the line went dead.

Beth dropped her phone into her pocket and glanced at the clock on the wall. She had five minutes before her class, which she was going to start, she decided, by asking the students – all mature, all intelligent and motivated – if they had ever, in workplace situations, felt that they were being taken for granted. Then she opened her office door and crossed the corridor.

'Eileen.'

Eileen stopped typing. 'What can I do for you?' She spoke in the neutral tone she used to convey information.

Beth put her hands in her pockets. 'Have lunch with me,' she said.

Eileen looked startled. '*Lunch?*'

'Or dinner. But I think lunch might suit you better.'

Eileen – pale, composed Eileen in her rimless glasses –

went pink. She looked down at her keyboard. 'I'd love to,' she said.

—

The estate agent's office in Curtain Street was dotted with primary-coloured low armchairs, as if to create the illusion that what took place there was not, in fact, all about money. Beth chose a yellow armchair and was brought tea and a fridge-chilled bottle of sparkling water by an elaborately friendly girl apparently dressed for a cocktail party. When Beth was joined in the purple armchair beside her by a young man in a suit and dramatically patterned tie, she was feeling sceptical to the point of regret.

The young man held his hand out. 'I'm Shaun.'

Beth didn't take it. 'And I am Professor Mundy. To you.'

'Sorry.'

'No need to be sorry,' Beth said. 'Just don't let either of us pretend that this is about anything other than what it is.'

Shaun sat rather more upright in his chair. He said, 'I don't know what that is yet, though, do I?'

'Whether I want to buy a house or I want you to sell a house?'

'Yes.'

Beth put her hands on the arms of her yellow chair and waited until they were quite still, and then she said, 'The latter.'

'Then I know where I am,' Shaun said, and smiled.

Beth didn't smile back. She said, 'But I don't, yet.'

Shaun said, in a much less practised tone, 'Are you selling against your will?'

'Let's just say that from my perspective, the timing isn't ideal.'

'Ah.'

'I've come to you because I want impersonal, swift, professional service. And a good price.'

'May I ask where the house is?'

'Here,' she said. 'Shoreditch.'

'We have seen a 22 per cent rise in property values in Shoreditch in the last year or two.'

'It's a good house,' Beth said. 'Four bedrooms.'

'In?'

'Wilkes Street.'

Shaun looked straight at her. 'The renovated one? Next to the old factory?'

'Yes.'

'A *very* good house,' Shaun said emphatically.

'Yes,' Beth said again.

Shaun looked at the floor. Then he glanced back at her. 'I'm sorry,' he said again.

Beth gave a little shrug. She said, 'You could walk into it. Everything works.'

'I'll confess,' Shaun said, 'I put a broken desk chair in your skip once. During the renovation.'

'We did everything.'

'Plainly.'

'I expect someone else found a use for your chair.'

'And now we,' Shaun said, falling back into sales mode with some relief, 'must find a new and profitable use for your house.'

Beth winced, very faintly. 'Please.'

'So we'll start with a valuation.'

'Of course.'

'Although I can say, straight off, seeing what I've seen, that we're looking at well north of one. Nearer one and a half, maybe.'

Beth gave no indication that she had even heard him, let alone registered what he had said. She was looking at her fingertips. She said, 'After a valuation and all that, a brochure?'

'Well, we only print brochures now if clients specifically request them, because so much of London property changes hands with online advertising these days.'

'I do want a brochure,' Beth said.

'Of course, if you–'

'Although, on second thoughts, a good online presentation would do. It is simply that I want details of the house and the fact of its being sold to be made very evident.'

Shaun smiled at her. 'Oh, it will be,' he said. 'That's our speciality. We get in everywhere, to everyone.'

Beth smiled back. At last. 'I'm not really concerned with everyone, Shaun. I just want the information made very plain indeed to one particular person.'

—

Eileen had chosen a prawn salad. She wasn't really eating it, Beth noticed, but kept neatly moving bits of it about, cutting up a tomato slice or wedge of avocado to give an impression of busyness, and enjoyment. She had declined a glass of wine and opted for tap water only, which sat in its unsmudged glass beside her, as untouched as the salad.

'Eileen,' Beth said, 'you're not eating.'

Eileen put her knife and fork down. 'It's lovely. It really is.

Prawns are my favourite. I just – don't seem to have much of an appetite.'

'Any particular reason? Like, this is the first meal we've eaten together in all these years?'

'I never expected . . .'

Beth put a hand out and laid it on Eileen's wrist. 'I know you didn't. It was me. I should have asked you. I should have done a lot of things differently, like not taking you for granted.'

Eileen removed her hand in order to bring her napkin up to her eyes and blot underneath them. 'Please don't go and be nice to me.'

'I'm cross with myself,' Beth said. 'Won't you let me say so?'

Eileen lowered the napkin. 'No need for that. You didn't know what you'd have to deal with if you'd asked me anything.'

Beth was holding her own water glass. She put it down with deliberation. 'What is it, Eileen?'

'All I can say,' Eileen said, sniffing, 'is that working for you has held me together. I don't know what I'd have done without the job.'

'Oh my dear,' Beth said.

Eileen gestured at her plate. 'It's awful, not to eat this. It's lovely, really lovely.'

'Forget it. Forget it, please. It's just a salad.'

'Maxwell left,' Eileen said suddenly. 'He left me four years ago. With the bank's receptionist from the Holborn office. And then Becky lost her job and came back home and she's got a boyfriend, a married boyfriend, so we aren't seeing eye to eye about that. And, well, Peter's got a job in Brussels, and he's living there with a girl from the Congo who won't come to England because she says we're all racists, and so Peter never comes, either, and I can't go there because she won't meet me. Even though *he's* white and British. There's no logic to it, but the result is that I haven't seen him in over two years. So you see, Beth, coming to work has saved my sanity. Booking your flights and circulating your speeches has been the one thing in my life that I could rely on.' She stopped as suddenly as she had started and then said, in confusion, 'I never meant all that to come out, I never meant to burden you with all my problems.'

'It's not a burden,' Beth said.

'And just because you know doesn't mean you should feel that you've got to do anything about any of it.'

'I wouldn't patronize you like that.'

'I knew you were gay,' Eileen said, 'I knew from the beginning. And I never thought Claire was good enough for you. But what can you do about love? I thought I loved Maxwell. I did. I suppose, in a way, I always will, certainly to the extent that I don't seem able to look at anyone else. Whatever he's done, he could always light up a room for me. He made me laugh. Did Claire make you laugh?'

'A lot,' Beth said. 'At the beginning.'

'It isn't right,' Eileen said. 'What she's doing.'

'No.'

'But,' Eileen said, leaning forward abruptly and pushing her plate aside, 'it might just open a door for you.'

Beth laughed. 'Financially, you mean?'

'No,' Eileen said indignantly. 'Of course not. But I shouldn't be talking to you like this.'

'Why not?'

'Well, it isn't – it isn't any of my business.'

'Eileen,' Beth said. 'Don't be daft.'

'That's what Maxwell used to say to me.'

Beth regarded her a moment. Then she said, 'Eileen. What can I do for you?'

Eileen folded her napkin and put it down precisely across her side plate. She said, with authority, 'Let *me* advise you. Let me suggest something.'

Beth spread her hands. 'Anything.'

Eileen sat back and folded her hands in her lap. She looked more like the Eileen that Beth was used to. 'Take a look at that offer from Lausanne again,' she said. 'Just take a proper look.'

—

Nadine had left a large bouquet of mixed flowers, still in their pink tissue sheath, and a bottle of South African Merlot on the kitchen table, with a thank-you card filled with characteristic exclamation marks. There was, said the card, soup in a pan on the hob and a cold roasted chicken in the fridge as well as prepared vegetables that would only need a blast in the microwave. Nadine had even laid the table for supper, for three people, with water glasses and side plates. Her busy, cheerful presence hung in the air still, but Bonus was back on the kitchen table, curled up behind the flowers, his eyes firmly closed.

Beth thought about making tea. Then she thought about pouring a glass of wine. But she suddenly felt that both activities might somehow dispel the sunny energy that still lingered in the room. So she went into her study instead, dropping her bag on the floor, looping her jacket haphazardly onto its hook and observing that Banker was, surprisingly, asleep on her desk chair. Her study, Claire had often pointed out, was the one room that the cats took great trouble to avoid, even racing past the door as if a particular bad cat karma lurked within.

Beth stooped over Banker. 'Hi there.'

He gave a sleepy chirrup in response, but didn't stir.

'Where am I going to sit, I wonder?'

She turned aside and began to shift a stack of journals off a nearby chair and onto the floor. It struck her that those journals, once on the floor, would simply stay there; she would cease to see them. In time, perhaps, the same comforting oblivion would blot out other painful preoccupations, too, like cupboard doors being closed on an untidy interior.

She pulled the second chair across the floor, next to the one Banker was occupying.

'Look,' she said to him, 'I still can't reach my computer.'

He yawned and stretched out one languid paw. Then he retracted it and tucked it tidily away underneath himself. She bent over him. Whatever his outward nonchalance, he was purring.

'What,' she said, her face almost on his fur, 'am I going to do with you two, if I do decide to go to Switzerland?'

CHAPTER SEVENTEEN

STACEY

The warehouse space in Farringdon was shabby. It was the right size – a biggish room for the clothes and accessories, and a smaller one for personal interviews – and had good light and a promising reception area, but the floor was scuffed, as if heavy industrial items had been dragged across it, and the walls were scarred. But, Stacey told herself, its condition was reflected in the rental price. It was perfectly easy, in such a location within walking distance of both the Angel and King's Cross stations, to pay almost sixty pounds per square foot. And this place, with its huge windows and helpful layout, was half that.

She had been, for the last week or two, fizzing with ideas. It was like being alive again, truly alive, waking in the morning with the sensation that it was indeed, and at last, worth getting out of bed again. She not only got out of bed, she then ran, most mornings – not in her old running gear but in new clothes that she had, symbolically, bought for the purpose. And then she came home, showered, saw Steve off, breakfasted, walked Bruno and climbed the stairs to the top floor where the better room – the one that was to have been Mum's sitting room – had become her office.

Mum's remaining furniture – the TV, the leatherette sofa, the cabinet of elaborate china – had been moved into the bedroom, and the door had been closed on it all. Mum was visited every other day, and appeared to know no one. She was always in her armchair by the window, cleanly dressed with brushed hair, gazing at the canal view with no indication of seeing what she was looking at. Stacey would kiss her and sit down beside her and take her hand, and her gaze never wavered from the window. It might be uncomfortable to admit it, but this passive, mute, staring Mum was much easier to deal with than the disconcertingly confused Mum of a few months earlier. Bruno's disturbed charge had given way to someone altogether emptier – therefore, sadder – but undeniably more manageable. If Mum didn't piteously seem to want something Stacey could never give her, Stacey's own role in their relationship became blessedly clearer. Sitting by the window, holding Mum's hand, Stacey could think aloud in a way that was more, even, than just a relief.

She had told Mum about the search for a suitable space.

'The thing is, it's got to be big enough to get all the clothes and stuff in, but not so big that it's daunting. It's crucial that it isn't daunting. I mean, none of the women we want to help will *want* to be there, will they? Nobody likes taking charity, do they? You'll remember that. You hated it, didn't you? So I'm reckoning on this whole scheme being very attractive to volunteers – and I'm going to need loads of them – and absolutely the reverse to the people who will use it. So I've got to find somewhere that's welcoming and unthreatening and easy to get to, because I imagine that people might come at the last minute, mightn't they, as an impulse, right before an interview.'

This place, in Farringdon, felt very possible. There *had* been a wonderful space – warm brick walls, wooden floor – in a converted Victorian school building, but it had been too expensive, and Stacey had worried that the groovy young businesses in the rest of the building might have put off the sort of people she wanted to attract: the young and the low-skilled, the immigrants and the poorly educated, the people for whom paid employment seemed to be situated on the far side of a map that they had no idea how to read.

Steve had said that he had never seen her so full of zeal. Enthusiasm, yes; commitment, certainly; but not zeal. He had been onside from the beginning, helping her to make a business plan, estimating start-up costs, suggesting possible supportive companies – fashion houses, cosmetics firms – and potential trustees without which, she discovered, she could not register Peg's Project with the Charity Commission. The application forms that every stage required were formidable, and the number of bureaucratic hoops to be jumped through seemed endless, before something as simple as a cast-off handbag of Melissa's becoming a confidence-boosting accessory to a job-seeking interviewee could be anything like a reality.

It was odd, Stacey thought, standing on the unswept floor of the possible space in Farringdon, how determined she felt. As long as she kept her central purpose in mind, and the image of the woman who had offered her water in St Paul's Churchyard, she felt that whatever the obstacles were, she would get there. Get there, and make it work. And feel, in consequence, well, relieved and guiltless at last – and fulfilled.

She looked round the space and tried to imagine it with clean windows and painted walls and some kind of wood flooring laid over the battered concrete. There was a perfect blank wall for mirrors; there was a reception area just begging for sofas and a coffee machine; there was an ideal room in which to talk comfortably about how to conduct oneself in interviews. Smartening it up could be one of the first tasks she gave to Sarah Parker, who had so surprisingly sought her out and explained that she could no longer reconcile herself to the ethics of banking, and in any case needed something to do that was far more flexible.

Stacey had immediately telephoned Gaby. Of course, she had to leave a message, and when Gaby finally returned her call, she sounded as if Sarah's decision was of no real regret to her at all.

'She'll be great for you, Stace. To be honest, it's easier all round if she doesn't work for me any more. She's terrific, but she was becoming tiresome as a colleague.'

'Will I find her tiresome?'

'No you won't. Not in the charity sector. And you won't have these children in the mix, either.'

'What do you mean?'

Gaby sighed. 'I'll explain,' she said, 'when I've got more energy. For now, all you need to know is that there are no hard feelings on my part, and she'll be really useful to you.'

Stacey took her phone out of her pocket now to dial Sarah's number. Perhaps she might be free to come to Farringdon straight away. She was two digits into dialling when the phone rang with an incoming call. 'Tim Talbot' the screen said. Stacey stopped dialling and put the phone to her ear.

'Tim?'

'Stacey!' he said. His voice was full of excited warmth. 'How are you?'

'I'm fine.'

'Where are you? Can you talk?'

Stacey looked down the length of the room. Tim Talbot had been the colleague who had wanted her to take her dismissal to board level. She had a vision of him chasing after her to the lifts that day, his tie loosened, his top shirt button undone.

'I can talk,' she said.

'Something's happened.'

'What?'

'A big thing,' Tim said. 'Last Friday. But the announcement has only just been made to us all. Jeff Dodds has left the company.'

Stacey's mouth fell open, involuntarily.

'Stacey?' Tim said. 'Are you there?'

'I'm still here.'

'Did you hear me? Did you hear what I said? Jeff Dodds has gone. Instantly. Cleared desk and everything. Just like you, in fact.'

'But – but why?'

'Reading between the lines of the announcement – all platitudes as you can imagine – I think he was sacked. Some bad decisions and general bad management.'

'I can't believe it.'

'I know. I know! I had to tell you.'

'Thank you, Tim.'

'And,' he said, his voice gathering enthusiasm, 'that's not all!'

'Isn't it? But—'

'There's more,' Tim said, 'much more. There's a definite consensus on your team, your old team that is, to get you to come back. It's not just that we miss you, Stacey, but we aren't, quite honestly, doing as well without you either. So we're going to approach the board with a proposal that you should, for the sake of the company obviously, but for all our sakes as well, be reinstated. And of course I need your assent to that – even though I know it's a given, I have to be able to say that I've formally asked you. So this is me, Stacey, formally asking if you'd like your old job back, in a nutshell. OK?'

—

The churchyard looked much the same as it had all those months earlier. Different flowers out, of course, different drifting people wandering the paths or sitting on the benches, but the same sooty pigeons were pecking about for crumbs and the immense bulk of the cathedral gave the whole place the same reassuring air of sanctuary. The bench where Stacey had sat that day was occupied by a young black man, stretched out along its length, his trainered feet crossed and his eyes serenely closed as if he were in a rural orchard rather than the middle of a city. Stacey chose the next bench along, empty but for two schoolgirls eating crisps, and sat down, exactly the same takeaway coffee in its heatproof collar of cardboard in her hands.

She had surprised herself – and, plainly, Tim – by saying that she must think about his proposal.

'Jesus,' he said. 'Stacey. I thought – I thought you'd bite my hand off.'

The reply, 'A month ago, I would have,' rose to her lips and got no further. Instead, she said, 'So many things have changed, Tim, that I'm not quite where I was when I left. I'm not saying anything, either way. I'm just saying I'll have to think.'

'Oh, Stacey,' he said, his voice heavy with disappointment.

'I know. I've spent a lot of the last few months saying exactly that to myself.'

'I never expected this.'

'Nor me.'

'Will you – will you be long in deciding?'

'A day or two,' she said, 'no longer. Promise.'

'We miss you,' he said, sadly.

'It's mutual.'

'You can't imagine how unanimously thrilled everyone was—'

'Tim. Don't. Don't go on. I have to think.'

'OK,' he said resignedly.

'I'll ring you back.'

'Yes.'

'By Friday,' Stacey said.

It was Wednesday, the same day of the week as when she had last been here. She took a sip of her coffee. She wasn't, she thought, even the same person who had sat here in a state of shock, and now she was sitting here in a state of dilemma. But this time she was not just breathing properly, she was, whatever she might tell herself, in control. She had two options now and her task was to choose between them, not from a pragmatic point of view but from – and this had almost never been a factor in taking working decisions – a personal one, too. It wasn't just a question of what would work. It was a question of what would feel right and enriching.

Of course, going back to work was known. To step back

into a salaried world among colleagues who welcomed her promised a return to a pattern of status and demands that had all the seduction of the familiar. She could slip back into those well-oiled grooves without, really, breaking her stride. And yet, what she had left only months ago, would not, subtly, be what she was returning to. The dynamics would, inevitably and organically, have shifted ever so slightly.

She thought of Beth. She remembered the early days, before Claire, when Beth had a flat on the Isle of Dogs and would run to work, keeping shoes in her locker. Beth had, even as a student all those years ago, an overview of what they were all doing at university and what they would all be facing in the world beyond it. Beth had always been able to step back, to exchange the preoccupations of the here and now for something more contemplative and less immediate.

'Don't let it get to you,' Beth had said to her often, at times of academic crisis. 'Don't forget that the psychology of this place, of all universities, is built around stress. They bank on the fact that everyone has something to prove to someone. It fosters the culture of constant achievement. We'll have to battle that all our lives.'

Stacey had heard her, but had not absorbed what she was saying. It didn't matter then. Nothing mattered then but the degree and then the jobs with their steady trajectory of named positions, and the reflection of growing authority in the salary. The money. How much did she care about the money? How much did she measure dignity and freedom by what she was paid?

She took another sip of coffee, regretting the lipstick marks she left on the plastic lid. If she didn't value money, and the choices it could confer, why did she want to help women who didn't have enough even to contemplate a choice? She mustn't, she thought, be squeamish about money. It was a measure, a valuable measure of validity and independence, and as such it should be respected. But if it got taken out of context, if it got exaggerated in its importance and seen as an instrument of power, then it became something else, something both ugly and distorting. And if she, Stacey, were to pull her business suits out of her wardrobe and climb back into both them and the world they represented, would she in fact be doing that because she was deluding herself that a return to a familiar work life was about anything much more than the money?

She squinted up at the cathedral. Its recently cleaned stone glowed in the afternoon light. It was jaw-dropping to think that the image, the idea, the form of this extraordinary building had been in one man's imagination, a man who had lived in a house across the river while this fantastical enterprise grew in reality as he had visualized it. There was somewhere, probably, a record of what Sir Christopher Wren had been paid for designing St Paul's Cathedral, but it was hard to believe, whatever he had been paid, that he had done it for the money. Money could not meaningfully reward genius. But it could prosaically put food on the table and hot water in the tank and shoes on your feet. It could help those trapped by having too little to free themselves enough to join in, even just a bit, with what the vast majority of people took for granted.

Stacey stood up. The man lying on the bench had opened his eyes, and was now staring peacefully at the sky. He looked, whatever he was or wasn't thinking, completely comfortable. Stacey walked past and smiled down at him. He smiled back, easily, showing dramatically white teeth. What did he live off, Stacey wondered, walking on? What did he have to prove to someone, if anyone? And what, while we were about it, did she?

—

Sarah Parker agreed that the Grenville Street warehouse could be made excellent for their purpose with just some cosmetic changes. She seemed to Stacey extremely purposeful, coming in on a Saturday morning, as she was still working out her notice for Gaby, and listing the estimates she would obtain for decoration and flooring. She asked what investment there could be – basically, Stacey's redundancy pay, which would also cover the first three months of her comparatively modest salary – and wrote down the figures without comment. There was considerable competence about her manner, and also, Stacey thought, a palpable tension.

'Have you got time for coffee?' she asked.

'Sorry, no,' Sarah said. She was still writing on a clipboard and didn't look up. 'Boys to collect from football, Marnie from drama class. As if she needs any extra instruction in drama.'

'Do you have to do that? Couldn't Will?'

Sarah went on writing. 'Don't think so.'

'Is he at home?'

'Sure.'

'Then – if I were to ring him?'

Sarah's gaze flicked up. 'You?'

'Well,' Stacey said, 'I've kind of known him, in a way, since Tom—'

'Of course,' Sarah said.

'Does that mean I can?'

Sarah's shoulders suddenly slumped. 'Why not?' she said.

'If it makes things more difficult . . .'

'I don't think,' Sarah said unhappily, 'that anything could make things more difficult.'

Stacey said nothing. She stretched out and lightly touched Sarah's nearest shoulder, then she went into what they were already calling the interview room and dialled Will's mobile.

'Good Lord,' Will said. 'Stacey Grant, by all that's wonderful.'

'Long time.'

'It certainly is!'

'Will, I've rung to ask a favour.'

'Of course.'

'I need to keep Sarah for another hour.'

'Ah.'

'So – perhaps you could collect the children?'

'Of course. No problem.' Will's tone was now elaborately courteous. 'But why isn't Sarah ringing me herself?'

'It's my need to keep her,' Stacey said. 'My decision. It made sense.'

'Stacey . . .'

'Yes?'

'Will Sarah be long?'

'Pull yourself together, Will,' Stacey said, straightening her shoulders instinctively as she spoke.

'Hey,' he said, 'steady on. Sarah announces she's leaving a well-paid job to help you start up some kind of charity and you tell *me* to pull myself together?'

'You know what I mean.'

'Do I?'

'Yes, Will,' Stacey said. 'You do.'

There was a complicated silence, then Will said, in an altogether more subdued tone,

'I'll get the kids.'

'Your kids.'

'Stacey,' Will said, 'don't lecture me.'

'It's not lecturing. Just reminding.'

'Which is what's happening to me every day just now. And it's painful.'

Stacey thought of the as yet unaccounted for blitheness in Melissa's tone these days. She said, seriously, 'I'm sure.'

'Thank you.'

'So, Will, can I keep Sarah for another hour or so?'

'Of course,' he said tiredly, and rang off.

—

'Have a cappuccino,' Stacey urged. 'Or a mocha or something. Have something *heartening*.'

Sarah shook her head. 'I really want a mint tea.'

They were in a booth at the back of a coffee shop, side by side on a beaten-up leather sofa.

'Want, ought . . .' Stacey said, teasingly.

'Please don't.'

'I *know* about ought,' Stacey said. 'I feel, at the moment, that I'm an expert in ought.'

Sarah sighed. She said, almost inaudibly, 'Right now, I'm too screwed up even to think about ought.'

'But not,' Stacey said, 'too screwed up to quit a very serious job.'

Sarah looked down at her lap. Then she said, without looking up, 'That was an impulse.'

'Was it?'

'And then I had to follow it through.'

Stacey leaned forward a little. 'Do you regret it? Would you like to go back? Because if you would, I'm–'

'Not now,' Sarah said.

'Really?'

'Really.'

'Pride?'

Sarah sighed again. She said, 'Only partly.'

'What's the other part?'

Sarah raised her head. 'Why are you asking?'

'Gaby has been a close friend since uni. So has Melissa. And you abandon one of us to seek work with another. What's going on, Sarah?'

There was a long pause, and then Sarah said slowly, and with difficulty, 'I don't want to lose the good opinion of any of you. Not you, not Gaby, not – not Melissa. I went crazy at Melissa.'

'She isn't the kind of woman who bears a grudge,' Stacey said.

'I don't want to lose Will,' Sarah whispered.

'Melissa won't lure him away. She lost her head for a while but she's got it back on again. She won't take Will.'

Sarah glanced at Stacey. Then she said, looking back at her lap, 'But he wants to be taken.'

'He *thinks* he does. Just now.'

'That'll do,' Sarah said. 'That's enough. Just thinking's enough.'

'It won't last.'

Sarah said nothing. Stacey considered her. Looking at her, sitting there in her quietly on-trend weekend clothes, her nicely cut hair, with a house in west London and two healthy children at good schools, it would be difficult to see Sarah, in any wider context, as an object of pity. But she was as trapped by her emotions as anyone, her life circumscribed by her fears and her responsibilities like almost all the other women on the planet.

Stacey said gently, 'Do you want your job with Gaby back, Sarah?'

Sarah shook her head.

'So you don't regret your impulse?'

'I – do,' Sarah said reluctantly, 'but I think the instinct behind it was right. Probably. More than probably. I don't want to work in that sector any more.'

'No,' Stacey said, 'nor do I. I've been quite tempted, but I've decided to take the chance.'

'Brave.'

'Or foolish. We'll see.'

Sarah said, in a stronger voice, 'You have to live with yourself, after all, don't you?'

'Yes,' Stacey said. She stood up. 'Yes. You're the only person you are stuck with, so you might as well make that person someone you can bear to be around. I'm going to order. Cappuccino after all?'

Sarah looked up at her. She was smiling, even if wanly. 'Mint tea, please,' she said.

—

'I reckon,' Steve said, 'that it'll be two years before you can begin to pay yourself anything.'

He was leaning against a bookcase by the built-in television screen, beer bottle in hand.

'I know,' Stacey said.

'And your redundancy won't cover a quarter of that, especially if you include start-up costs.'

Stacey was on the sofa in front of him, surrounded by papers. 'I know,' she said again.

'So what are you going to do?' he said.

'Is this a test?'

He shrugged and took a swallow of beer. 'You turn down the security of employment where your skills are valued and the consequences of exercising them are guaranteed, in favour of setting up a charity whose success can't be evaluated or assured, so I'm just playing devil's advocate.'

Stacey sat back on the sofa. 'What do *you* think I should have done?'

'That's beside the point. You've done what you've done. You've made your decision. I want to know now how you intend to finance it.'

'I shall apply to the bank for a loan.'

He waved the bottle. 'And if they refuse?'

'I shall remortgage the house. Or part of it.'

He paused. Then he said, 'Oh, will you?'

'Yes,' Stacey said. 'It's our house. In our joint names.'

'And it's your mother in care, at a thousand pounds a week.'

Stacey said calmly, 'There are now two competing offers on Mum's flat. We'll manage.'

'I'm sure we will.'

'Less eating out; fewer, cheaper holidays; no taxis.'

'All fine by me,' Steve said.

She waited a moment and then she said, 'Really?'

He nodded. 'Really.'

'But . . .'

'If your heart's in it, then, as I said, it's fine by me.'

'Thank you.'

He gestured with his beer bottle towards Bruno. 'I expect it will be fine by him, too.'

Stacey looked at Bruno, stretched out on the rug between them with one watchful eye open. 'I've got a job for him,' she said. 'In the project.'

—

Mum was in her usual attitude, propped in her adjustable armchair, wearing unfamiliar maroon trousers and an incongruous clip in her hair that was garnished with a fabric primrose.

'Goodness, Mum,' Stacey said, kissing her, 'are they making fun of you?'

Mum gave no sign that she had heard, or even that she had noticed Stacey's arrival. Her hair had been brushed before the clip was put in, and the trousers, whoever they belonged to, were clean and gave off the strong synthetic scent of fabric conditioner. The room was tidy, the window glass shone, Mum's bed, neatly made, bore two turquoise silk cushions that Stacey didn't recognize. It was pointless to get upset about the details, she told herself, a pointless bad habit which had everything to do with residual guilt and nothing, really, to do with Mum's welfare.

She sat down resolutely beside Mum's chair and took her hand. 'Steve sends his love,' she said. 'And so would Bruno, if he could.'

Mum stared out at the clouds, driven past the window on a brisk wind. Her face, Stacey thought, looked almost tranquil, even if it was too blank for complete comfort, and her eyes were, in a strange and ageless way, as innocent in expression as a child's.

'Talking of Bruno,' Stacey said, 'I had an idea for him. An idea for when the project is up and running. Your project, Mum. Peg's Project.'

She paused and looked down at the hand she held. It was ringless as it had always been, as long as Stacey could remember it, and someone had cut and filed the nails and smoothed the cuticles. It was soft in Stacey's grasp, in a way it never had been; soft and limp. Stacey grasped it more firmly.

'I thought I'd take Bruno in with me. To the project, I mean. I thought he might be comforting, like he was with you. I thought he'd take the formality out of things, in case people were nervous. And he'd like it, don't you think? After all, wasn't he the best carer you ever had?'

In her hand, Mum's hand lay passive. There was no change in her expression, no sign that any energy was gathering. Without warning Mum said, suddenly and clearly, '*Good* dog.'

CHAPTER EIGHTEEN

MELISSA

Tom said he didn't want to talk. He was slamming round the house these days, kicking doors open, banging the fridge shut, turning his music up aggressively loud. Melissa watched him anxiously for a week, trying to remind herself that the narrative of their relationship had inevitably changed now that Tom was older, and was no longer as she had been used to dictate it, when he was small.

At first, she had assumed – too easily, she now thought – that Tom had ditched Claudia as being too young and too expected. But Tom's behaviour, the kind of raw, bewildered rage that he seemed to be eaten up by, didn't appear to be the reaction of a boy who had sampled an easy starter relationship as a test to himself, and then, emboldened, had moved on to something more ambitious. Tom looked to her, instead, very much like a boy who was suffering the humiliation of rejection. The sight of him and the probability of what had happened aroused in her the most intense feelings of protectiveness towards him, and a corresponding indignation about both Gaby and Claudia.

She rang Gaby's mobile and got the voicemail message. She rang again, and this time left her own message. She then rang Gaby at work and asked Morag to ask Gaby to call her. Gaby didn't. Melissa asked Tom if he was going to his father's house, as usual, on Friday night, and Tom said of course not, why would he?

Melissa was making tea. 'What about the boys? Won't Jake and Ben be expecting you?'

Tom said rudely, 'When have you ever cared about Jake and Ben?'

There seemed to be no immediate reply – or no civilized reply, at least – to make. Melissa concentrated instead on what she was doing. She took the teabag out of her mug and dropped it tidily in the bin. Then she carried her tea carefully out of the kitchen and upstairs to her almost unused sitting room. Behind her, in the kitchen, an unhappy silence reigned. She felt a stab of pain on his behalf. Poor Tom. *Poor* Tom.

She sat down by the telephone. It might be thought quaint to have a landline still, but in Melissa's mind a landline was valuable for making those calls where a degree of distance and formality were required. It was, somehow, the telephone equivalent of writing a physical letter, in ink, and signing it, and sending it to the recipient by first-class post.

Tom, she knew, had a new form master. He was younger than his predecessor and a good rugby player, Tom said, and his speciality was German literature. His name, Tom told her, irritated at being asked, was Mr Robshaw.

Melissa picked up the telephone and dialled the school secretary. As it was a weekday evening, there was a firm but courteous message saying that the school office was closed until eight thirty the following morning; the emergency numbers were as follows, and for any non-urgent message, could the caller please speak after the tone?

'This is Melissa Hathaway,' Melissa said, 'Tom's mother. I wonder if I could make an appointment in the next week, please, to speak to Mr Robshaw?'

There was a splintering crash from below, in the kitchen. Melissa put the phone back in its cradle and ran to the top of the basement stairs. She called, 'Tom? Are you OK?'

There were scraping sounds, as of shards of pottery being gathered up.

His voice came tiredly up the stairs. 'I broke a jug.'

'It doesn't matter.'

'The grey one.'

'I said it doesn't matter. Are you all right?'

There was a pause and then he said, 'Don't come down.'

'I wasn't going to. I don't mind about the jug.'

She could hear the uneven clatter as he swept the broken pieces into a dustpan.

'I do,' Tom said.

'Darling, can I–'

'Go away, Mum. Just go away. Leave me to deal with my own mess, just *leave* me.'

—

Perhaps it was just as well that Gaby hadn't called back. Perhaps Gaby felt as protective of Claudia as Melissa did of Tom, and if they had spoken, they might have quarrelled. After her encounter with Sarah, Melissa flinched from the idea of any more arguments. They seemed as distasteful, as besmirching to her, just now, as the idea of Will's sudden eagerness did; something that had appeared to be exciting and mildly dangerous had revealed itself to be in fact tawdry and destructive. She had hated the version of herself she had seen in Sarah's eyes: the effortlessly glamorous, supremely successful manipulator of other peoples' fragile happiness, a kind of carelessly malevolent and bewitching modern bad fairy. She was full of self-reproach at what she had encouraged to happen, and she was determined not to seek the reassurance from Stacey or Beth that she was not a trouble-maker after all, not a predatory witch, but someone who was, first and foremost, Tom's mother.

The instinct that was driving her to see Mr Robshaw was, she hoped, clear evidence of that. Mr Robshaw saw Tom for a large proportion of each week and would therefore be able to tell Melissa if he had noticed changes in Tom's demeanour, changes that could be the result of emotional distress. She rehearsed what she would say – no names, no specifics – and practised her emphasis on the fact that she was not a kind of worried well parent making an opera out of a teenage commonplace. Mr Robshaw, even if he was younger than Mr Pettifer had been, wouldn't be *that* young, after all – not too young to understand that she was appealing for his assurance that being a single mother of an only child put her in a position of particular vulnerability. She didn't want him to spell that out, but she needed to know he appreciated it. Just as she needed him to appreciate the depth of her concern.

—

Mr Robshaw was indeed younger than Mr Pettifer had been. He was possibly in his late thirties, and shorter than Melissa, with an open friendly face and an air of barely suppressed energy. He was wearing a schoolmasterly uniform of a tweed jacket over a blue cotton shirt and chinos and he listened with complete attention while Melissa outlined her anxieties. When she had finished, he waited a moment and then he said, 'Can you remember when *you* were first dumped?'

'But I wasn't.'

'I think,' Mr Robshaw said, 'that that was what you were saying might have happened to Tom?'

She smiled at him ruefully. 'Yes.'

'Well?'

'I was much older than Tom. It was while I was working at the BBC, after university, long after–'

'It's misery,' Mr Robshaw said. 'Whenever it happens. However, apart from being mildly more aggressive now and then, I would say Tom is behaving entirely normally. If what you suspect has happened, I don't think that is troubling him. I think it might be something else.' He paused and then he said, 'I don't think I'd be breaking a confidence if I told you that his father has been to see me.'

'Oh,' Melissa said.

'There's hardly a boy in my class with a straightforward family background. And there's hardly a boy, either, who doesn't harbour romantic notions about family life.'

'Tom – Tom changed his name.'

'I know. He told me about it. In fact, I would describe his telling me as being more like announcing. And then he gets to know them all better, and what do you know? What looks like some kind of idyll turns out to be same old same old.'

'I never thought of that,' Melissa said slowly. 'I never thought of the repercussions.' She stopped and then she said, 'Oh God.'

'He'll be OK,' Mr Robshaw said. 'He has two parents who love him, after all. And he has a peer supporter here, in year twelve, who I know he has spoken to. But parental support is key.'

'Even if they're not together?'

'Doesn't do,' Mr Robshaw said, 'to fetishize convention.'

'You're not at all as I thought you'd be,' she said, almost shyly.

He looked at her. 'Nor are you.'

She picked up her bag. 'I should go.'

'I'll walk you out.'

'No, really,' she said, 'I know the way, I'll be fine.'

He walked across to the door and opened it. Then he indicated with his head that she should walk through. He said, quite calmly, 'I insist.'

She went past him into the corridor beyond and waited for him to close the door behind him. Then she said, beginning to walk again, 'I can't shake off the feeling that I'm responsible for Tom's happiness or unhappiness.'

Mr Robshaw fell into step beside her. 'Then you've both got a bit of learning to do. He's got to grow up and you've got to let go.'

She found slightly to her surprise that she didn't feel offended.

'He adores you,' Mr Robshaw said, matter-of-factly, 'and he wants to please his father, and he hasn't worked out how to compromise, yet.'

'But you don't think he's wretched?'

Mr Robshaw stretched forward to open the swing doors ahead of them. 'It's pretty wretched being fifteen anyway, if you ask me. But he isn't worryingly unhappy. He's confused, yes, and he's disappointed, but he's fed up about that rather than destroyed.'

On the far side of the swing doors, Melissa said, almost hesitantly, 'Do you think I'm making a fuss about nothing?'

Mr Robshaw looked directly at her. She suddenly felt unaccountably unsteady.

'No,' he said.

'I'm glad.'

'In fact . . .'

'Yes?'

'I'd like to get you off school premises, actually, before I ask you this, as it doesn't seem quite proper . . .' He stopped.

Melissa wondered if her own eagerness was plain in her face and decided, an instant later, that she didn't care if it was. 'Yes?' she said. 'Yes?'

'I wondered,' said Mr Robshaw, as unremarkably as if he were ordering his daily coffee, 'if you would like to have a drink with me?'

—

On the way to the mews the next day, Donna rang her. Melissa put her phone to her ear. 'Morning! Shall I get milk?'

'Sorry to sound so weird,' Donna whispered into her phone, 'but I'm in the loo and I don't want her to hear me. Claire's here.'

'Claire?'

'She was waiting on the doorstep when I got here. She won't go away. She says she has to see you. I thought I'd better warn you.'

'Goodness,' Melissa said. 'Claire. What can she want?'

'She won't say,' Donna said. 'I'm too lowly to tell anything to, anyway.'

'I'll be two minutes. Put her upstairs.'

'Oh,' Donna said, her voice ripe with sarcasm, 'she's up there already.'

Claire was sitting on the sofa, her legs nonchalantly crossed, reading the copy of *City A.M.* that Donna brought in every morning. She lowered it as Melissa came up the stairs.

'Surprise, surprise,' she said, as if she had practised it.

'Well,' Melissa said. 'It is rather.'

Claire looked round her. 'Nice office. I've never been here before.'

'I don't think,' Melissa said with exaggerated courtesy, 'that I have ever asked you.'

Claire tossed the paper aside. 'Gaby won't see me, I don't really know Stacey – or, let's say, she has taken care not to know *me* – so I have to ask you.'

Melissa put her laptop case down on her desk and began to unzip it. 'Ask me what?'

'What's going on with Wilkes Street?'

Melissa took her laptop out and opened it. 'I have no idea.'

'You must have.'

'Claire,' Melissa repeated, 'I have no idea.'

'So you don't know that it's on the market.'

Melissa touched the cursor pad to find her emails. 'As it's on Buxton's website for all to see, yes, I know that.'

Claire twisted round to face her fully. 'What is Beth playing at?'

Melissa shrugged and said nothing.

'It's half my house, too,' Claire said. 'I have a legal right to know what's going on, you know.'

Melissa said, 'You wanted it sold.'

'I do.'

'And it is on the market.'

'But I haven't been consulted!' Claire cried. 'I don't think that's the right agency, and I'm not even sure about the price. I need to talk to Beth.'

Melissa closed her laptop. 'I can't help you.'

'But you knew, Beth must have told you – Beth tells you guys everything.'

'If I knew anything,' Melissa said, 'I wouldn't tell *you*.'

Claire stood up. 'So you won't tell me anything about Switzerland, either, will you? I've been told she's talking to Lausanne, that they're setting up a new department for her.'

Melissa stood quite still, her hands resting on her closed laptop. Donna had put flowers on her desk, she noticed, dark purple-blue anemones. They had the effect of softening everything around them.

'You don't like me, do you?' Claire said, angrily. 'Any more than Gaby does.'

Melissa looked at her flowers. 'I don't trust you, Claire. That's all.'

Claire stooped to pick up her bag. She looked as if she was bursting to say something but was restraining herself with difficulty. Melissa heard her go down the stairs, say some kind of goodbye to Donna and then slam the outer door behind her. Melissa followed more slowly.

Donna stopped typing. 'Phew.'

'I know,' Melissa said. 'What a start to the day.'

'And it was looking so good up to then.'

'Was it?'

'Yes,' Donna said. She was grinning. 'Your flowers.'

'They're lovely,' Melissa said with sudden warmth. 'Really lovely. *Thank* you.'

Donna grinned wider. 'They weren't from me.'

'What?'

'They were from a man. He was waiting by the arch when I came in, before I got distracted by Claire and all her nonsense. Oh, Melissa, look at your face!'

Melissa had her hands up against her cheeks. 'Was he . . . ?'

'He said his name was Marcus. He said you'd seen each other last night at Tom's school. Right?'

Melissa nodded. She said, faintly, 'Right.'

'He just said – leave these on her desk. No note or message, he said. Just leave them. Romantic or what?'

Melissa slid her hands round to cover her eyes. 'Oh, Donna . . .'

'I could hardly tell him,' Donna said teasingly, 'that you only liked white flowers, could I? Or perhaps you'll make an exception for blue, from the right person?'

Melissa took her hands away. 'Stop it!'

'Goodness,' Donna said, genuinely startled. 'I've never seen you blush before.'

'He's at least a decade younger than me. And shorter. And a schoolmaster. *Tom's* schoolmaster.'

Donna leaned back in her chair. She put her fingertips together. 'So?' she said.

—

'There's nobody here,' Taylor said. She stood holding the front door slightly – but not welcomingly – open. She was barefoot, in black leggings and a giant sweater whose sleeves she had pulled down over her knuckles, the edges as frayed as if she had been chewing them.

'Well, *you* are,' Melissa said. 'And is Claudia?'

Taylor shifted onto her other foot. Only the nails of one foot had been painted, in navy blue. The varnish, Melissa couldn't help noticing, was chipping off.

'Claud's doing prep. As usual. Claud is *always* doing her prep.'

'Taylor,' Melissa said. 'Can I come in?'

Taylor looked truly startled, her russet eyebrows shooting up towards her hairline. But she stepped back, pulling the door open as she did so. 'Course.'

Melissa looked round her. The hall looked as Gaby's hall always looked: disordered in the manner of houses inhabited by people who have more interesting preoccupations than tidying up. In the last week or two, since Marcus Robshaw had taken her to a folk gig in a pub where a friend of his was performing, and to watch the school eights practising on the river down at Putney, Melissa had been conscious of a certain – and not attractive – inhibition in her own life and the way she lived it. She took in the scattered shoes and boots, the clothes on the ghost chairs, the violin with its curling sticky note still attached, lying on the console table.

Taylor said, 'It's a bit of a mess everywhere, I'm afraid.'

'Actually,' Melissa said, 'I was rather admiring it.'

'Mum would pass out if she heard you saying that.'

Melissa glanced at her. Taylor had dragged her sweater sleeves right over her fists, and seemed to be gnawing at one of them.

'You can change, you know,' Melissa said gently. 'If

you want to. I might be naturally tidier than Mum, but I wouldn't want to let my tidiness become – this is my new word – a fetish.'

Taylor lowered her fist and grinned at her. 'Good word.'

'Are you going to make me some tea?' Melissa said.

Taylor nodded. 'If you like.'

'I do like.'

'Claud's in the kitchen.'

'Good,' Melissa said. 'That's exactly who I want to talk to.'

Claudia was perched on a stool, her books and iPad open on the kitchen counter in front of her. She was still in the checked skirt and navy blue sweater of her school uniform, and she had her spectacles on. She looked up when Melissa came into the room, and immediately got off her stool and came running over with every appearance of unselfconsciousness.

'Oh, hi!' she said. She was smiling.

Melissa put her arms round her. She felt as slight as a small child. 'Hi, Claudia.'

'Mum's not back yet.'

'I already told her!' Taylor called.

'I didn't come to see Mum,' Melissa said, smiling back at Claudia, 'I came to see you.'

Taylor was filling the kettle. She said, over her shoulder, 'What has she gone and done now?'

'I expect it's about Tom,' Claudia said, with perfect composure.

'Well, yes.'

'What kind of tea?' Taylor said.

'I don't,' said Claudia in a determined tone, 'want to be ticked off.'

'I have no intention of ticking you off.'

'Really?'

'Really.'

'I thought you'd want to give me a hard time,' Claudia said, going back to her stool.

Melissa took a stool beside her. 'Why do you say that?'

'If you aren't interested,' Taylor said, opening cupboards, 'I'll just make builders' tea.'

'Because,' Claudia said calmly, 'you and Mum want to make a big deal out of something that was never anything much to begin with.'

'But you said on your Facebook profile . . .'

'People don't tell the truth on Facebook,' Claudia said. 'Anyway, no one cares about Facebook any more.'

'Can I join in?' Taylor called. 'Or is this a private conversation?'

Melissa turned on her stool. 'Of course you can join in. Claud?'

'Yes.'

'Could you look at me a moment?'

Claudia sighed. She looked down at her screen and then, very slowly, she turned to look at Melissa. 'I'm looking.'

'I came,' Melissa said, 'to say sorry.'

'Wow,' Taylor said.

Claudia's expression softened a little. She said, uncertainly, 'To me?'

'Yes,' Melissa said. 'To you.'

Taylor brought two mugs of tea across the room and dumped them on the counter.

'Why?'

'Because I thought badly of Claudia and I shouldn't have.

I thought she had dumped Tom and made him suffer and I was angry about that.'

Taylor leaned against the counter. She said, 'She did dump him.'

'*Did* you?'

'He didn't mind,' Claudia said. 'Not really. We were just having a laugh.'

'I believed you,' Taylor said crossly. 'It *was* true.'

'A bit,' Claudia said.

Melissa regarded her. 'Enough to wind Mum and me up, anyway.'

Claudia nodded. She said, 'And Ned, in my class at school.'

'Was that the aim? To make this Ned person jealous?'

Claudia sighed again. Taylor said, 'Can you imagine what it's like having someone like her for a sister?'

'So it was all a game?' Melissa said to Claudia.

'I didn't *plan* it.'

'But it turned out that way. As a game?'

Claudia took her glasses off. Her eyes, without them, were huge and blue, like Gaby's, and no doubt dazzling to Ned at school.

Melissa said, not unkindly, 'I think you're a bit of a minx.'

Taylor reached for Claudia's mug of tea. 'Is Tom OK?'

'That's mine,' Claudia said indignantly.

'Too late.'

'What do you think?' Melissa said. 'Is he OK?'

Claudia lunged for the tea mug and Taylor skipped nimbly out of reach. From the far side of the kitchen, she said, 'Well, he's got what he thought he wanted, hasn't he? Family life and all the dramas and unfairness of it.' She raised the mug above her head. 'Get off, Claud! Make your own fucking tea!'

Melissa said automatically, 'No need to say fucking, Taylor.'

They both stopped and stared at her. Then they began to laugh, and in her head, Melissa could hear herself saying to Marcus later – ruefully, of course – 'Well, I walked into that one, didn't I!'

—

'You're avoiding me,' Will said. He was standing waiting for her on the steps of the house in Holland Street. She had been on a Saturday morning errand to collect the dry cleaning, and when she saw him by her front door, her first thought was that something had happened to Tom.

She stood on the path below the steps, her arms full of sliding plastic and clothes. 'Is Tom all right?'

'Of course he's all right,' Will said. 'Why shouldn't he be all right? He's in the park, teaching Ben to rollerblade.'

Melissa didn't move. She swallowed in relief. 'OK.'

'Aren't you going to ask me in?'

'I don't think so.'

He came down the steps towards her. He looked weary and drawn, and his hair needed cutting. He said, 'What's going on?'

'I don't know what you mean.'

'Lissa,' he said, trying to take some of the dry cleaning from her, 'what have I done to make you change tack so completely?'

She gripped the plastic bags more tightly. 'Please don't,' she said. 'I'm fine holding it.'

'Well, you certainly *look* fine,' he said. 'But I can't make head or tail of how you're behaving.'

She raised her chin slightly. 'Yes, you can.'

He spread his hands. 'Search me.'

'Leave me alone, Will,' Melissa said. 'Go home and appreciate what you've got.'

'But–'

'Go.'

'I know you had a bit of a dust-up with Sarah. And she's not wrong, Lissa, and *I'm* not wrong, reading the signs–'

'You *are* wrong,' Melissa said loudly, interrupting. 'There's nothing for you, except as Tom's father. Nothing.'

Will looked at her for some moments and then he said, as if suddenly understanding something, 'There's someone else. Isn't there?'

Melissa said nothing.

'Isn't there?' Will said again, insisting.

She glared at him. 'No,' she said.

He waited. Then he took a step back. 'I'll take that as a yes, then,' he said.

—

It was an impulse, a complete impulse. She had been at a meeting in the City – a meeting which was not, she deduced, going to end in a commission for Hathaway's services, unless the surprisingly weak chairman could be persuaded – and, with almost an hour spare, realized that she was hardly a mile away from the warehouse in Farringdon where Stacey was going to establish her charity. Melissa felt very wholehearted about Stacey's charity; it was, if she was honest with herself, such a conscience-salving antidote to her shopping habits. They were habits which she already had a strong impulse to moderate after a few weeks in Marcus Robshaw's company because although he evidently didn't disapprove, he equally plainly couldn't see the point. The point, for him, was sharing. He wanted to share, on a scale she had never encountered before. And if that sharing took place while dressed to the nines or wearing bin bags, it was of no consequence to him at all.

Melissa considered telephoning Stacey and alerting her to an impending visit. Then it occurred to her that she would rather surprise Stacey and just turn up, out of the blue, bearing coffee and enthusiasm. She bought two cappuccinos in a cardboard tray and carried them to Greville Street. It was evident, from the strong smell of paint emanating from the first-floor windows, that decorating was going on, and, taking advantage of a young man in overalls coming out of the main door, Melissa slipped inside and climbed the stairs.

The door to what would be the reception area for Peg's Project was wedged open with a sliver of timber. The walls beyond were newly, gleamingly, white. Stacey said that there were so many whites now on the market to choose from that she had opted just for plain old white in the end – brilliant white, eggshell finish. With a pale wooden floor and green sofas and plants. Lots of plants. And lamps. Overhead lighting in the dressing area but lamps in reception, didn't Melissa agree?

Melissa stepped inside. There were radios playing and draughts of clean, cold air blew in through the open windows. It felt exciting, full of possibility.

'Stacey?' Melissa called.

There was no answer. Melissa was about to call again,

more loudly, when someone emerged from the room that Stacey intended to use for interviews.

'Oh. Melissa,' Sarah Parker said.

—

Tom made a lasagne for supper. They had found a recipe online, a recipe that described the lasagne as being classic and authentic, but Tom, looking at the ingredients, said he didn't think he could face chicken livers. He didn't mind chicken meat but the thought of the chicken having guts and organs as well was a bit much. They went together to the huge American organic food store on Kensington High Street and bought ricotta and provolone cheese, and minced beef and pork sausage meat, and a bunch of parsley and a bag of spinach, and Melissa was very touched by Tom's seriousness over amounts and quality. Then she sat in the kitchen at one end of the table while he chopped at the other end.

While he was chopping and stirring, she had told him about coming across Sarah, by mistake really, in Greville Street, and how they had settled on the floor because there was nowhere to sit to drink the coffee she had brought, and how, although they would never exactly be friends, they weren't enemies any more. Melissa said that she was very regretful that she hadn't behaved better and in a more adult way, and she was sure that although the immediate future might look a bit difficult, Will and Sarah would be fine in the end, really fine.

Tom made no comment. He was impressively deft with knives and spoons, and he was doubtless concentrating and therefore unable to react to what she was saying. But she had the strong impression that at best, from his point of view, he was neutral. He was hearing her, he was even listening, but he wasn't going to give her the satisfaction of his absolution. He wasn't making a moral point by withholding it; he was simply keeping his own counsel.

When he did speak, what he said had no relevance to anything Melissa had been saying: 'Apparently,' he said, 'this sauce needs a bit of nutmeg. And we haven't got any. So it won't taste quite correct.'

'I won't mind,' Melissa said, stopping herself from adding, 'As you've cooked it, the first thing you have ever cooked for me, I won't care *what* it tastes like.'

He shut the oven door on the finished dish. He had a tea towel slung over his shoulder in a professional manner, and his hair was tousled. 'I think,' he said, 'that you should go and have a bath while it cooks.'

She got up, holding the glass of wine he had solemnly poured for her. 'Of course. I'd love that. Thank you, darling.'

He'd nodded, in a preoccupied way, as if he had other, more important things to think of. And as docilely as he had conspicuously failed to do when he was younger, she had gone up to the first floor and run a bath and thought how momentous her life was at the moment, with Tom cooking for her in the kitchen and Marcus Robshaw – single, manifestly interested and still hardly known, as yet – wanting to take her to her very first rugby game.

She stepped into the bathtub. The relationship with Marcus Robshaw would be another hurdle, of course. There would be Tom's headmaster to confront, naturally, never mind Tom himself. That is, if it lasted. And if it didn't? Melissa sank down into the water and lay back. If it didn't, she would not be in the position she had been in after Jack

Mallory or Connor Corbett or even Will Gibbs. She had made Hathaway after all, and she had made Tom. So if whatever it was with Marcus Robshaw didn't last, she was in a strong place – a stronger place – than ever before. She closed her eyes. Lasagne smells were floating richly up from the kitchen. Of course, it mightn't last. But then – it just might, too. Mightn't it?

CHAPTER NINETEEN

GABY

Modern curriculum vitae were, Gaby decided, pretty irritating. In the old days, a kind of British self-deprecation meant that you narrated your life, educationally and professionally, in a chronological and low-key way, culminating in your present achievements, described with a baldness that conveyed a certain modesty. Nowadays, a CV was quite the other way about. You started with an assertive blaze trumpeting your current glory, and then worked your way backwards to your invariably stunning performance at primary school. The six finalists, as it were, to be re-interviewed for Sarah Parker's job had all produced accounts of their working lives that seemed to indicate that they could run the free world with one hand tied behind their backs, so that a middle-management position in the investment arm of an international banking group was almost beneath their astounding qualifications.

There were four women and two men on Gaby's shortlist. She had mentally singled out the two most likely candidates already, and they were both women. She had nothing particular against the men, both of whom would be perfectly competent, but she wanted something that in her experience a woman could better supply: a rigorous attention to detail and a dedication to the work itself, rather than to the status it might imply. Martin had been one of those two men, and Gaby knew that he in turn knew that he wasn't going to be promoted.

'Not yet,' Gaby said to him, when they coincided in a lift one day. 'You're not quite there yet. You will be, but not till I've seen more evidence.'

He was smarting under that, she could see it. And, in consequence, would probably hand in his notice. Well, she couldn't help that, any more than she could help two of the female applicants for Sarah's job being head and shoulders above the others. Life wasn't fair, as she was constantly telling Taylor. It wasn't fair, but it was nearly always salvageable to some degree. You could make something of having red hair and big feet; you didn't have to regard them as some kind of unjust affliction.

'I will be sorry for you,' she said to Taylor, 'about the things that really are an unfair disadvantage. Suppose you had a stammer, or chronic juvenile arthritis. Or you were deaf. But I'm not going to manufacture sympathy for your personal dissatisfactions. It's up to you to come to terms with what you don't like about yourself, and *do* something about it.'

'Is that what *you* do?' Taylor said crossly.

And Gaby, taking her glasses off for emphasis, said seriously, 'All the time. And I am constantly failing. As Samuel Beckett said, Try, and fail. "Try again. Fail again. Fail better."'

She had decided to take the bull by the horns. She had asked Taylor outright what she meant by balling up an important letter from her and leaving it as if it was only fit to be thrown away.

Taylor had mumbled something.

'What?' Gaby said.

Taylor said, not looking at her, 'It wasn't you.'

'Explain.'

'I was – just fed up. With everything. With being me. It wasn't you. I just wanted to hit something. So I trashed your letter instead.'

'I see.'

'Are you cross?' Taylor said.

'No,' Gaby said. 'Not cross. But a bit hurt. Wouldn't you be hurt?'

Taylor shifted her feet.

'Wouldn't you?' Gaby said again, insisting.

Taylor nodded reluctantly.

Gaby said, 'It was a good letter.'

'I know.'

'And I meant it.'

Taylor looked at her, at last. 'I know,' she repeated.

Gaby folded her arms. 'What have you done with it now?'

'I've hidden it,' Taylor said, 'under my mattress. To keep it safe.'

Looking at the six CVs now, Gaby wondered if someone in her position would be looking at Taylor's CV in a few years' time. Taylor had been quite a different person the day Gaby had brought her into the office. An alert, interested, civilized person in a dress Gaby had never seen before, under a denim jacket.

'She's a bit of a hit,' Morag had said to Gaby admiringly, watching Taylor making a group of Gaby's staff laugh. 'Isn't she?'

Not someone I recognize, Gaby thought, flooded with sudden pride.

'Chip off the old block,' Morag went on.

'Oh, I don't know about that.'

'Gaby,' Morag said. 'Do you think I'd have stuck working for you all these years if it wasn't worth it? If you hadn't made it worth it, for me?'

Gaby had blinked. She never blubbed; it wasn't in her nature to cry. Even as a child she had only cried out of temper, her mother said – sheer, stamping temper. Taylor had cried from the moment Claudia was born; mainly, Gaby thought now, out of frustration, but looking at Taylor with new eyes, new and respectful eyes, made Gaby think that for all the bothers going on in the office after Sarah's resignation, and all the bothers going on at home at Quin's decision, there was light ahead, and from an unlooked-for quarter. And the thought brought a lump to her throat.

—

Quin was adamant. He wanted to sell the shop in London and the shop in Elgin. He didn't mind if they were sold as a joint business or as separate entities, but he was tired of running shops, even if he had managers in both, he was tired of what he sold, he was tired of people wanting to buy things he could no longer morally sanction their wanting to buy. He was, he told Gaby, tired of the whole idea of retail, and that was that.

Gaby pointed out that the Portobello Market was just about to celebrate a century and a half of its existence, and Quin said he didn't care. She said that he couldn't let down his father and grandfather in this way and simply sell off the business they had so painstakingly built up, and he said he didn't care about that either. She said, well, if he wasn't going to run the shops any more, what was he going to do, expecting him to say he had no idea, he would simply wait and see how he felt, and he said, 'Teach. Probably.'

'Teach?'

'Yes,' he said. 'There's a new Creative and Media Academy in Manchester. I'd like to start something similar in the south.'

'Start?'

'Yes,' Quin said. 'You're always telling women how it pays to be brave. So I'm being brave. I shall have to do teacher training, and I'll be the oldest person on the planet doing teacher training, but that's what I want to do.'

'Right.'

'No doubt it would be easier for you if I wanted to do something passive like be a Buddhist priest.'

'I wasn't thinking of me.'

'Weren't you? Isn't that what you always think about? You?'

Gaby looked at him. He was standing by the cooker making one of his famous fry-ups, surrounded by little bowls of leftovers.

She said as steadily as she could, 'Why are you angry with me?'

'I'm not.'

'Sounds like you are.'

Quin slid the frying pan sideways off the gas flame. He turned round. He said, 'I'm just rather envious of your focus.'

'I like work,' Gaby said. 'I like it. The money may be great – it *is* great – but it's the work I like, the people and the power and getting stuff done.'

'I know.'

'So don't take your feelings of being somehow thwarted out on me. It's exactly what Taylor does, but she's only fifteen.'

'I want,' Quin said, 'to believe in something.'

Gaby pushed her glasses up her nose. 'Go right ahead. I'm not stopping you.'

'My God,' Quin said. 'You don't give an inch, do you?'

'If I were a man, you'd admire that.'

'Shall we have a full-scale row, and chuck things?'

She shrugged. 'If you want to.'

He turned back to the frying pan. 'I just want to – to *dent* you,' he said. 'Somehow. Just a little.'

'I am dented.'

'Are you?'

'Can't you see?' Gaby said. 'Can't you?'

'Like how?'

'Like how I feel about the children? Like how I nurture people, especially women, in the office?'

'And me?'

'You can take care of yourself. You've done what you wanted. You're doing it now.'

Quin picked up a dish of cold potatoes and tipped them into his pan. 'I have always tried to be ordinary, to behave as if everything is normal, but I've had a knife in my chest all the time.'

'Is that me? The knife?'

'I think so,' Quin said.

Gaby took a step back. 'I think you should look again,' she said. 'I think you stuck the knife in all by yourself.'

—

Melissa said, 'I don't think I've ever seen you cry before.'

Gaby was sitting crouched on Melissa's sofa, where Claire had sat, sniffing into balled-up tissues.

'I don't cry. Ever.'

'I do,' Melissa said. 'All the time.'

'Nicely feminine, Quin would say.'

'Is he the problem?'

Gaby shook her head. 'Not really. He's just part of a whole lot of complicated things coming to a head, all at once, as they do.'

'Sarah leaving . . .'

Gaby raised her head. 'I spent four years training Sarah.'

'Yes.'

'I've been married to Quin for eighteen. I've worked for twenty-six.'

'Me too.'

'I can't imagine life without it,' Gaby whispered.

'Me neither. But you don't have to.'

'I said to Taylor, work'll see you through everything.'

'Yes,' Melissa said softly. 'You were right.'

'If Quin leaves . . .'

'Might he?'

'I don't know,' Gaby said. 'He could. He's very angry at the moment, and it's easier to tell me it's all my fault and that's the reason. So he might walk out in a temper and then not know how to come back.'

Melissa said, 'Do you love him?'

Gaby hesitated. Then she said, 'I think so. I'm very used to him. He makes me laugh. And I'm not easy. I'm headstrong and only interested in some things, few of which are domestic.'

'But he's domestic.'

'Very,' Gaby said. 'And I thought he liked it, that it satisfied him, cooking and taking Liam to rugby practice and throwing out Taylor's tights when they were more hole than tights. But it seems he has been boiling with resentment all along.'

Melissa held out the box of tissues. 'Do you believe him?'

Gaby blew her nose ferociously. 'I believe he feels what he feels right now. But I don't quite believe that he's felt it all along.'

'What are you going to do?'

Gaby blew again. Then she got up to drop the used tissues in the bin by Melissa's desk. She looked very small, standing there with her shoes off and her hair escaping from a loose ponytail. She said, 'Uncharacteristically, nothing. I'm going to appoint Sarah's successor – a very able woman from across the square who I've had my eye on all along – and promote Ellie who has thrived on flexitime, and as far as Quin is concerned, I'm doing nothing more. I thought it was working, the unspoken arrangement we had, but if he really thinks it isn't any longer, or even that it never has worked, really, then I can't stop him.'

'But the children?'

Gaby came back to the sofa. 'I'm their mother, I always will be. I also am who I am, and that's a given. I may have – I do have – many faults but I don't have a false self. I am truly me, through and through, and that means they get what they see. And they always will.'

Melissa said, 'I went to see them.'

'I know.'

'Did they tell you?'

'Taylor did,' Gaby said. 'Claudia seldom tells anyone anything.'

'I wanted to apologize to Claudia.'

'Taylor told me.'

'I was barking up the wrong tree,' Melissa said. 'Again.'

Gaby regarded her. 'You're a nice woman.'

'Oh.'

'Taylor said so. At least, she said you were cool. And I have to say, from my pink-eyed, red-nosed present perspective, you look amazing. Wonderful. Has something happened?'

There was a short silence. Melissa looked at the carpet, and then she looked at Gaby.

'Yes,' she said.

—

Alone in her office, Gaby Googled Melissa's Mr Robshaw. He looked perfectly unexceptionable to Gaby: a decent, rather outdoorsy youngish middle-aged man who cited Rilke and rugby as his two passions. Melissa said he was anything but unexceptionable. He was already suggesting that he should consider changing schools in order to make things easier for Tom, and Melissa said she had remonstrated with him, pointing out that they had only known each other for a month, and he had apparently simply looked at her and said, 'But I'm sure. Aren't you sure? I was sure after five minutes in your company,' in a tone that she said had no urgency about it.

She then said she felt safe with him, remarkably safe, and it made Gaby reflect that safety had never been something she needed in a relationship, or in life in general, for that matter. She wasn't a gambler by nature, but she could live with a measure of uncertainty, she knew she could. How else could she cope, just now, with living with Quin?

Claudia obviously felt much the same – as far, that is, as she could ever tell with Claudia – and Taylor, a wonderfully released and less distressing Taylor, was out far more than she used to be, if she wasn't holed up in her room with Flossie with the door shut. Only Liam seemed to be affected by the unquestioned perturbation in the air, and was constantly anxious to be next to her. He had also resumed carrying Heffalump around, not nonchalantly held by his trunk or a leg, but clasped against him for comfort, like a hot-water bottle. And when he was next to Gaby, or sitting on her, he wanted to talk.

'Are you going to New York?'

'Darling. I hardly ever go to New York. Maybe once a year. In fact I hardly ever travel. You know I don't. You know that when I took this job, one of my conditions was that I wouldn't have to travel all the time.'

Liam was fiddling with the pot of pens on Gaby's home desk. He was perched uncomfortably on her lap, with Heffalump held in one arm. He said, 'I don't want you to go to New York.'

'I told you. I told you I'm not going anywhere.'

'Ever, I mean.'

'Maybe you could come, if I did have to go. Like Taylor came to the office.'

'Taylor,' Liam said, 'is going to do psychology at uni.'

'Is she? How do you know?'

'She said to Flossie. Then she's going to do wellness in the banks.'

'What?'

'Wellness,' Liam said. 'Like not getting all stressy.'

'Oh.'

He selected a pen and sucked on it. Then he said, 'Banks are full of stressy people but we have to have banks to sort all the money.'

'I see,' Gaby said. 'And who told you this?'

'Taylor,' Liam said. 'She's made up her mind.'

'So I can see.'

'If you go to New York,' Liam said, 'how do I know you'll come back again?'

'Liam. What is all this about New York?'

He lay back against her, holding Heffalump in both arms. His hair, she noticed, needed washing.

He said, 'I don't want you to go there. I don't want you to go anywhere.'

'Please may I go to work?'

'OK.'

'And come back again. I'll always come back again.'

'From work?'

'Yes,' Gaby said. 'From work.'

Liam thought a moment. Then he said, 'If Dad doesn't have work to go to, what will happen?'

—

Gaby couldn't remember when she had last been in Shoreditch. It was wonderful on a Saturday with the markets in full swing, wonderful in the way that tourist guides would describe as 'vibrant'. It was energetic and various and colourful. By contrast, Wilkes Street, when she turned into it, was quiet and empty of people. Beth's front door looked closed in a strangely definite way.

Beth opened the door to her wearing a man's striped shirt over jeans. She had rubber flip-flops on her feet. She spread her arms wide and then gave Gaby a big hug. 'Honey.'

'I hope I didn't bleat on the phone,' Gaby said, into Beth's shoulder.

'Course not.'

'I thought I was fine. And then I found I felt a bit lost.'

'That,' Beth said, 'is what friends are for.'

Gaby released herself. She said, 'You look dressed for a purpose.'

'Sorting my study. It's a task and a half.'

'Sale going through?'

Beth held up both hands with her fingers crossed. 'Third viewing. It was a kind of miracle. They came, they saw, they almost made an offer standing in the kitchen.'

Gaby said, 'Are you sad?'

'A bit. Yes. More than a bit.'

'What you hoped would happen, and then what *has* happened?'

Beth began to lead the way to the kitchen. She said, over her shoulder, 'I still think about Claire.'

'Do you?'

'You don't stop thinking about someone just because they turn out to be awful.'

Gaby let a tiny pause fall and then she said to Beth's back, 'Quin isn't awful.'

Beth stopped walking and turned round. 'I know he isn't, honey.'

'I don't know how to help him,' Gaby said.

'Do you want to?'

'No,' Gaby said. 'No. I put it wrongly. I want him to be able to help himself.'

'That's better.'

'Is it?'

Beth went into the kitchen, making no attempt to shoo Bonus off the table. 'I always think there's a kind of imperialism in thinking that we, the great I, are obliged to sort everything for everyone else. We can't. We shouldn't.'

'Tell me about Lausanne.'

Beth made a face. 'Exciting. Terrifying. They've practically told me I can have whatever I want, I can design the course in fact.'

Gaby picked up the kettle. She said, 'Are they paying you well?'

'A hundred and twenty-five thousand dollars,' Beth said soberly.

Gaby gave a little whistle.

'I know,' Beth said. 'Just under 30 per cent female intake, and they want my new department up to forty in five years.'

Gaby crossed to the sink and began to run water into the kettle. 'A sort of dream ticket,' she said.

'In a way.'

'What way?'

'A work way,' Beth said.

Gaby put the kettle on the glass top of the electric hob. 'How do I turn this on?'

Beth carried on as if she hadn't spoken. 'It will be, potentially, the best job I've ever had. I'll be affiliated to all the best business schools in Europe, I'll be building exactly the academic structure I want, I'll be lecturing to the biggest plcs in Europe about management practices. It's incredible.' She paused and then she added, 'I keep asking myself if that is more important than a good personal life and if I could only have one of them, personal or professional, which would I choose. And, Gaby, I do not know the answer. If you'd asked me a year ago, I'd have opted for work. I thought I was so secure, I thought I was settled, *made*. Then look what happened. And it's thrown me.'

Gaby stood where she was, her hand on the kettle. 'Why does it have to be a choice? Why can't we have both?'

'We can,' Beth said, a little sadly. 'We just don't seem quite able to.'

'Maybe we haven't evolved enough.'

'Maybe.'

'I still think,' Gaby said, 'that work sustains us like nothing else.'

'But you have children.'

'I do.'

'Which means,' Beth said, 'that you don't really want Quin going anywhere.'

'No.'

'So – talk to him.'

'I can't,' Gaby said. 'Not any more.'

'Yes, you can.'

Gaby glanced at her. 'I thought you were on my side.'

Beth grinned. 'Whatever gave you that idea?'

'That's the way Claudia talks to me.'

'She's right,' Beth said, and then suddenly, switching topics, 'Does she like cats?'

Gaby looked a little startled. 'I think so. Liam wants a dog.'

'Would two cats do, do you think, instead of a dog?'

'What?'

'Gaby,' Beth said. 'Could you, as you kindly gave them to me in the first place, take Banker and Bonus when I go to Switzerland?'

—

Liam was lying on the kitchen sofa watching *Shrek* on the TV streaming service. Gaby sat down beside him and he immediately shifted so that his head was in her lap. 'Why are you watching this?'

'I love it,' Liam said.

'But you know it off by heart. We even have the DVD.'

'I like knowing it,' Liam said. 'I like knowing what they're going to say, *exactly*.'

'Can you turn the sound down?'

'But I can hardly hear it.'

'Liam,' said Gaby, 'if you don't turn down the volume, I can't tell you some very good news.'

Liam aimed the remote control at the screen without moving a millimetre from Gaby's lap. Then he said, 'What news?'

'You know how you've always wanted a dog . . .'

Liam half sat up. 'Are we getting one?'

'Well, we are getting two animals.'

'Two!'

'But they're cats, not dogs. *Boy* cats, I might add.'

Liam's eyes lit up like lamps. '*Two* cats!'

'Yes. Beth's cats. We gave them to her as kittens and now she's giving them back.'

'Oh, wow,' Liam said reverently.

'Pleased?'

He nodded vehemently. 'When?'

'Soon.'

'Tomorrow?'

'You can ring her and fix a date.'

Liam scrambled to his feet. 'Can I ring her now?'

'Yes. Where's Dad?'

Liam was halfway across the room. He didn't pause. 'Dunno,' he said.

Gaby went out of the kitchen. Quin wasn't in the room they fancifully called the study – nobody ever studied in there after all – nor up in the big sitting room. Gaby went up the stairs, quietly. Heffalump lay on the landing once more and the doors to the girls' bedrooms were open, revealing, in Taylor's case, uninhabited chaos. Gaby tiptoed into the bedroom she shared with Quin. He was in there, standing at the window with his hands in his pockets, staring out. She watched him for a while, the fuzzy halo of his hair outlined against the light. He was wearing a sweater with a hole worn in one elbow, and she could see the pale cotton of his shirt-sleeve through the hole. He was, she thought very nearly fondly, the least dandified of men.

'Quin?' she said.

He turned round – not hastily, but not reluctantly, either. 'Gaby.'

'Quin,' she said again, advancing into the room. 'Can we talk?'

CHAPTER TWENTY

BETH

'Dearest Trio,' Beth emailed from Switzerland.

> Here I am, in Lausanne, doing a bit of a recce. Someone – a nice woman who will be a colleague, and is responsible for career planning and development for post-graduate Masters in the Finance Programme here – has lent me her flat for a week. Or rather her late mother's flat, which is just off the Esplanade de Montbenon, and there's a view from the sitting room (just) of Lake Geneva. It is full of things in glass cabinets and I have to leave my shoes by the front door and shuffle about on the parquet in my slippers, but the hot water is boiling hot and my bed is so piled with pillows and duvets that the Princess and the Pea has nothing on me. There's a notice on the stairs that forbids anyone in the building to flush the loo or tramp up the communal staircase loudly between nine at night and six in the morning, and the recycling rules have to be seen to be believed . . .
>
> BUT. It is astonishingly beautiful. Mountains. Water. Air. And the school itself is a work of architectural art, glass and white plaster and fantastic structures.

I have been shown an office – if I like: if I like!! – with a view across trees to the mountains, and a huge space attached to it, also windowed to the floor, for Eileen – did I tell you that she is coming with me? They raised fewer than no objections when I asked if she might, and she reacted as if I'd proposed to her. (No, I didn't. I have no desire to propose to anyone.) I have also been offered a studio flat for a year, on campus, at a vastly subsidized rent, and of course I'll take it. Eileen says she'll commute from one of the suburbs, as the centre is inevitably expensive. She is behaving as if I've given her the key to the Promised Land, and it doesn't matter how often I say I could not contemplate this enormous task without her. Which I couldn't. Honest to God, as my father says – such an odd phrase for a man who doesn't believe there is any such thing – I couldn't.

I had no idea that selling Wilkes Street was going to be such a big deal. One of the biggest deals I have ever been through, I think, and if anyone else tells me what a comfort it must be to think of a proper family in Wilkes Street, I shan't be responsible for my reaction. It wasn't just that the house took so long to restore. It wasn't just that it was the first real house of my own that I'd ever had. It wasn't just that I believed Claire and I would live long and together there. It was all those things. All of them. Then the last year happened, and the brutality of my dreams becoming dust the way they did knocked the breath out of me. I'm not angry, I'm not even resentful, I am just abidingly horrified! At how much I didn't see in myself as well as in her. I look at myself in the mirror in the tiled and ferociously spotless old-fashioned Swiss bathroom here, and I say to myself, 'How could you be so obtuse? How could you be so blind?'

I feel, I suppose, that I am living with someone – me – that I don't really know. So I might as well get used to this stranger in a strange place, as anywhere. I know what I want to do academically, I can feel all the usual cogs whirring and clicking in a familiar way when I think about setting up this department, and the rest of Beth Mundy, as she has turned out to be, will, I hope, emerge and become comfortable enough to live with, as time goes on. And I will have time. I have signed up for five years.

Five years! In five years, Taylor and Tom will be twenty. My old dad – who has already discovered that he can fly direct from Aberdeen to Geneva for under two hundred quid – may not be around. The children in Wilkes Street will be making their A-level choices. I will be fifty-two. Who knows what will have happened by then, who I will have met, what opportunities I will have been offered . . . You must believe me, I'm not complaining, I'm – just saying. I don't often say, even to you three, but now I am. I'm typing this late at night, sitting on a hard sofa – the furniture in this flat, except for the beds, is somehow very reproving – with my laptop on my knee. I've had a glass of wine, but only one, so this isn't a sodden outpouring. It's just me. Now. Beginning again.

It's Sunday, of course. I don't believe in an orthodox faith any more than Dad does, but I ended up in a church today, just to the west of Lausanne. I went on the bus. It's called

Saint Sulpice and it's Romanesque and was once on the pilgrim route down into northern Spain, a Cluniac priory or something. I didn't pray, of course. I just sat there and thought about you all and wanted, most urgently and powerfully, for you to be happy and fulfilled, for things (Gaby and Quin, Melissa and Mr Robshaw, Peg's Project) to work out for all of you, to bring you at least enough resolution and satisfaction to be going on with. Which – the satisfaction especially – is all we really need or should hope for. Don't you think?

It's very quiet here. Very. I have yet to find the *quartier louche* of Lausanne. I have yet to find a lot of things. I know that I have to do most of that looking and finding on my own – Gaby would say 'Not before time' and Dad would think it – but I will need to see you regularly after September, when I start here in earnest.

Will you come? Often? All of you? Please. I'll be here from August.

Time to climb in under all those pillows on my bed. Time to lie in the silent Swiss darkness and switch off the whys in my head. And whatever I don't know (ah! So much!) I do know this – that we will, all four of us, leave our footprints in the sand.

Sleep tight, honeys.

Beth

CITY OF FRIENDS

READING GROUP GUIDE

1. What did you think of the depiction of female friendship in *City of Friends*? Did you find it authentic? Did you think they were *good* friends to one another?

2. Stacey feels a 'violent sense of injustice' over her firing. Were you shocked by the circumstances of her dismissal? Do you think the same thing would have happened if she were a man?

3. 'She loved her children, loved Quin, loved her friends, but she adored her work.' What did you think about Gaby's attitude to work, family and domestic life?

4. What do you think about Melissa's situation as a working single mother? Granted, she is not short of money, but what about the inevitable emotional pressure on her son?

5. Beth finishes her argument with Claire: 'what you did was one thing, but the reason you did it was quite another.' Did you think Beth was right to be so upset over Claire's actions?

6. Gaby contends in an interview that 'working women should be as commonplace and unremarkable as working men'. Do you think *City of Friends* agrees with Gaby's statement? Do you think the book represents

this as already being the case, or an attitude that still needs shifting?

7. Steve pressures Stacey to move her mum into a care home. Did you think this was fair? Who did you sympathize with most in the situation?
8. 'He's very angry at the moment, and it's easier to tell me it's all my fault'. Gaby doesn't see Quin's outburst coming. Did you? Do you think she could have done anything differently to curtail his resentments? Do you think she *should* have done anything differently?
9. 'Work and life aren't in opposition to each other, they enrich each other', Gaby proclaims in a seminar. What do you think *City of Friends* says about working women and work/life balance?
10. Do you think men and women work differently, and how does this affect how they are perceived and how they perceive themselves?
11. Are attitudes to the juggling of work and family life generational, cultural or economic?
12. What does feminism mean today?